YOU ONLY LIVE ONCE, DAVID BRAVO

Also by Mark Oshiro

The Insiders

YOU ONLY LIVE ONCE, DAVID BRAVO,

MARK OSHIRO

HARPER

An Imprint of HarperCollinsPublishers

Library of Congress Cataloging-in-Publication Data
Names: Oshiro, Mark, author.
Title: You only live once, David Bravo / Mark Oshiro.
Description: First edition. | New York : Harper, [2022] | Audience:
    Ages 8-12. | Audience: Grades 4-6. | Summary: "After eleven-
    year-old David Bravo wishes for a do-over of a disastrous
    day of middle school, he and a shapeshifting spirit guide try
    to right a wrong in his past"— Provided by publisher.
Identifiers: LCCN 2022007887 | ISBN 9780063008151 (hardcover)
Subjects: CYAC: Time travel—Fiction. | Adoption—Fiction.
    | Families—Fiction. | Gay people—Fiction. | Mexican
    Americans—Fiction. | Middle schools—Fiction. | Schools—
    Fiction. | California—Fiction. | LCGFT: Fiction. | Novels.
Classification: LCC PZ7.1.O844 Yo 2022 | DDC [Fic]—dc23
LC record available at https://lccn.loc.gov/2022007887

Typography by Jessie Gang
22 23 24 25 26   PC/LSCH   10 9 8 7 6 5 4 3 2 1
❖
First Edition

To all adopted kids everywhere: this one's for you

TUESDAY, SEPTEMBER 5
8:10 A.M.
The (first) first day of middle school

"What if we just *don't* go to school?"

I'm standing next to Antoine Harris, who's got his thumbs looped behind the straps of his backpack. His mom left the two of us here, staring at the steps that lead up to the entrance of Mira Monte Middle School. Other kids are rushing up them before the first bell rings, but the two of us? We're not moving at all.

"That's a really good idea, David," says Antoine. "But what are we going to do all day?"

I scratch at my chin. "We could walk to Target."

Antoine's raises an eyebrow at me. "Target?"

"I already came up with the perfect cover story," I say. "We were hired by LEGO to assemble the display models."

"Okay, but I get all the *Star Wars* ones."

I put my hands up. "They're all yours. I'll be busy assembling that huge fire station set they have."

"That's a good plan," says Antoine, smirking, but then he turns back to those daunting steps. He sighs. "It can't be *that* bad, can it?"

"We don't have any classes together!" I whine.

"And we have *classes*," Antoine says, frowning. "I don't get why we can't still have the same teacher all day."

"Whoever made up the idea of middle school is evil," I say. "We should turn around right now and head straight to the LEGOS."

Antoine hesitates, then scratches his scalp between two of the intricately braided cornrows he just got a few days ago. "I think my parents would be mad if I didn't show up to the first day of school."

"Well, of *course*," I say. "But think how excited they'll be to find out we've been hired by Target to put together all their LEGO sets."

He laughs at that. "How about this?" he says. "Let's regroup at lunch. At least then we don't have to become clichés and worry about where we're going to sit."

"Excellent plan," I say. "No after-school specials about us."

And then:

The Handshake.

We slap the back sides of our hands against each other's twice.

"Crisscross," we say in unison.

A dap, mine on top first, then his.

"Always floss."

(Because we both care about dental hygiene, okay?)

We grip each other's hands but only at the fingers.

"Always friends."

Then we pull our hands apart, so fast that it makes a little snapping sound.

"To the end."

Antoine bumps his shoulder against mine as the two of us ascend the stairs to Mira Monte Middle School. I don't know what our first day of seventh grade will hold, but at least my best friend is at my side.

And then, for the first time since we met in first grade when his family moved here from Virginia, Antoine veers off, waving, and heads to a different class than mine.

I have this urge to chase after him, but I don't. *No, David*, I tell myself, and I stop walking just short of the front gate. *You just have to make it to lunch.*

I can do that.

I think.

But maybe not. I don't like new things, like surprises or anything that interrupts my routines. Starting at this new school feels like a million surprises and interruptions all wrapped into one giant mess.

I breathe in. I breathe out. A part of me wants to give in to the sensation sneaking up on me and just *freeze*. I do that sometimes, especially when I'm overwhelmed.

There's also a bigger part of me that doesn't want to be

the weirdo standing outside the school when the first bell rings.

So I make myself keep going, past the iron front gate, and I join the stream of students at Mira Monte Middle School, walking into the uncertain and the unknown.

TUESDAY, SEPTEMBER 5
8:15 A.M.
First class (not the fancy seats in an airplane, unfortunately)

I reach into my pocket and pull out the folded piece of paper I stuffed in there earlier. I have all six of my classes marked in color-coded ink, but somehow, I forgot to include classroom numbers. So I know I have SOCIAL STUDIES first but absolutely no idea where it is.

Oh, this is going to be fun.

I move to the side as a river of more kids pours into campus. Mom and Dad brought me here a week ago for orientation, but they didn't give us a tour, and this place is like a never-ending maze. At least I'm not going to the other middle school—La Sierra Junior High—all the way on the other side of town. That has to be the ugliest campus I've ever seen.

I'm already sweating as I rush up to the closest building. It's always so warm here in California that our schools are made up of several buildings, spread out from one another. Antoine told me that his old school out in Virginia was a single building because it got snowy and cold during the winter. To be honest, the design of our schools here makes no sense to me. Who *wants* to be outside when it's super hot?

Like right now. The sign on the side of the building reads MATHEMATICS. A drop of sweat runs right into the side of my eye.

This is the worst.

I turn around and thankfully spot a sign that says HISTORY AND SOCIAL STUDIES on the building across the way. I unfortunately have to cut through a bunch of kids to get there, which earns me numerous dirty looks. Relief floods me when I see a paper tacked to an open door with the name of the teacher I'm looking for.

I walk into Mr. Bradshaw's class—room 213—and am immediately faced with another choice to make.

Where do I sit?

"Welcome, students," says Mr. Bradshaw, a tall white man with a shiny bald spot in the middle of his gray-and-white hair. "Please choose where you sit carefully. That will be your seat for the remainder of the year!"

More students shuffle in—tall, brown, Black, white, Asian, short, chubby, awkward, loud—and desks are disappearing quickly. I think about sitting next to the girl in the front row with the freckles and pigtails, but the empty desk beside her is claimed while I hesitate. Do I quickly make a decision before more desks are occupied? Oh, absolutely not. There are only two left by the time I dart over to the rear corner and sit next to an Asian girl who slams a notebook shut as soon as I turn to her.

"Hi," she says, a nervous edge to her voice. "Gracie. I wasn't doing anything."

I blink a few times at her. "Okay," I say. "I'm David."

She smiles but turns away.

Well . . . that happened. I put my backpack on the floor to my left, then pull out my own notebook and a pen. I don't actually know what I'm supposed to be doing. Antoine's older brother, Isaiah, told me when he visited over the summer that middle school was going to be a big change for me. "You'll have homework all the time," he explained. "And be prepared to have to take notes."

I'm not really sure what that actually means. What am I supposed to "note"? What the teacher is wearing? The things he says? *Everything* he says? Everything I'm thinking?

Wow. This is a lot already, and class hasn't even started.

The bell rings, and right as it does, the last two kids come tumbling into class. I don't need to be a middle school expert to know that I will *not* be friends with them. They're slugging each other in the shoulder repeatedly. The taller and browner of the two—who honestly looks like he's at least in high school—sneers at the other. "Man, you're *weak*," he says.

"Please take a seat, gentlemen," says Mr. Bradshaw, gesturing to the only two open seats . . . which are of course right in front of me.

"Where should we take our seats?" says the other kid, then grabs the back of an empty chair and lifts it up. "Should we take them outside?"

He's the paler one, and he's got this long, stringy blond hair that looks like what happens when the grass dries out in the fields behind my house. *Should I take notes on that?* I think.

"Yeah, let's go sit right outside the windows," says the tall kid.

Mr. Bradshaw's mouth curls up on one side. He doesn't exactly look happy. I glance over at Gracie, and she slams her notebook shut again and smiles.

O-okay.

As Mr. Bradshaw calls out our names and marks us down on his "map" of the classroom so he can do attendance more easily in the future, I learn that the almost-late kids are Tommy Rodriguez and Walter May. Tommy flashes two peace signs when Mr. Bradshaw calls out his name. "That's me," he says. "What are you gonna teach us, Teacher?"

Mr. Bradshaw frowns. "This is social studies, Mr. Rodriguez."

"Dope," says Tommy. "You gonna teach us about Twitter?"

Our teacher narrows his eyes at Tommy. "What?"

"You know," says Tommy. "Like . . . social media?"

This . . . this is going to be a long year.

There are so many other kids in the room. I don't catch all the names, but I know I'll remember Wunmi Onyebuchi because hers is so great. She's got this gorgeous dark skin and her hair is shaved down short all over. She even has on a *Julie and the Phantoms* shirt, so I'm pretty sure she's cooler than me. Gracie's last name is Lim, and Mr. Bradshaw smiles at her. "Good to have you here, Gracie," he says. "I've heard a lot about you."

Gracie goes red in the face. I have no idea what that means.

Finally, after Tommy and Walter interrupt about forty-five more times (I am guessing, because I didn't *actually* take notes), Mr. Bradshaw introduces his class to us. He tells us that we're going to learn a little bit of history about the world, but we're also going to spend time "expanding our horizons."

"It's my job to teach you about this wonderfully diverse and complicated world," he explains. "And I can't imagine a better way of doing that than assigning you homework."

I can't lie; like everyone else in class, I groan when Mr. Bradshaw says that.

"Homework *already*?" says Tommy.

"Yes, *already*," says Mr. Bradshaw. "But it's going to be an easy A. I believe everyone here can start the year off with a perfect score."

Gracie flips a few pages into her notebook to find a blank one, and I realize this must be it. It's time to take notes. I ready myself, my pen in my hand.

"Each of you is going to introduce us to the cultures of your home," says Mr. Bradshaw.

My heart leaps.

"You will give a short presentation—all oral, under two minutes—explaining what cultures make up your home and make you *you*."

Wait. *Wait.*

"Tell your fellow students about where you and your parents come from! Do you have interesting cultural practices or traditions in your home that you'd like to share?"

My throat tightens, and I try to gulp down all the spit in my mouth, but I have to choke back a cough.

Oh, no. No, I don't want to do this.

"I'll start," continues Mr. Bradshaw. "My family is originally from Boston, and I was born outside Cambridge, Massachusetts. But my grandparents are actually from a place called Rotterdam, which is in the Netherlands, just south of Amsterdam! Have any of you been to Amsterdam?"

There are a lot of head shakes, and a few kids softly mutter, "No." I want to blurt out that most of us haven't even left California before. The Netherlands?! I don't even know where that is on a map!

That's not why my skin feels like it's being shocked with electricity, though. As Mr. Bradshaw talks about having Dutch heritage and all the kinds of food he ate growing up, I realize just how hard this is going to be. I'm not like any of these people because . . . well, because I was adopted when I was an infant.

And I don't actually know what I am.

I've always known I was adopted. I mean . . . I would have figured it out if my parents hadn't told me. My mom is Japanese, born in Okinawa but raised in Hawai'i. So she's got a dark brown hue to her skin, and long black hair that's as straight as can be. Dad's parents are from Mexico and Brazil, and his skin tone is a lot like Mom's, though his hair is intensely curly.

Then there's me. I don't look like either of them. My skin is a lot lighter, though I tan super fast whenever I'm in the sun. My hair is black, but it's wavy rather than curly. I don't resemble my parents, either, so I usually get lots of weird looks when we're out in public.

Mom and Dad sat me down before I was ever in school to tell me that they loved me very much, which is why they *chose* to have me be a part of their family. They've been pretty open about it, too; Mom said I could always ask her questions about my adoption if I wanted to.

But what was there to ask about? The only question I had—all the way back in kindergarten, when Ms. Wells asked me if I knew anything about my birth parents—had already been answered. I was part of a "closed" adoption, meaning that no one but the adoption agency knew anything about where I came from. My parents were told that my birth parents were Latinx, but that's it. They knew exactly what I did.

Yet it didn't seem to matter when I told other people that. They *always* had questions, like Yasi in fourth grade, who wanted to know if I'd ever met my birth parents. Or

Ms. Gull, the substitute in fifth grade, who asked me what it was like knowing my past was a "mystery."

Oh, god, was I going to have to go through all of this again? I just don't like thinking about this stuff.

I haven't taken any notes or heard a single thing our teacher has been saying when I realize that my fellow classmates are staring down at textbooks. And there's somehow one on *my* desk. When did that show up?

I don't like this feeling, like there's an avalanche waiting around the corner and it's only a matter of time before it crashes down on me. I look to Gracie in panic, and she mouths "Page six" to me. I thank her silently and turn to it, desperate to catch up, but I still can't escape the growing panic inside me.

Why do I have to start my first year of middle school with this?

TUESDAY, SEPTEMBER 5
12:37 P.M.
Reunited with Antoine and then *cruelly* tortured by time

My reunion with Antoine at lunch is short-lived. When I enter the cafeteria, it's packed, and it takes me at least five minutes to get food, then another two minutes to find Antoine.

"What's good?" says Antoine, and we do The Handshake.

Crisscross. Always floss. Always friends. To the end.

A couple other kids stare at us when we do it, but it doesn't bother me. That always happened at Underhill, too. I sit across from Antoine, whose tray is already empty.

"Wow, you ate that fast," I say.

He shakes his head. "No, dude, I've been here waiting for you for almost half an hour."

That's how Antoine and I figure out we're on opposite lunch tracks. This school has this weird schedule where half the students have lunch from 12:00–12:45.(Lunch A) while the other half have lunch from 12:30–1:15 (Lunch B).

Guess which lunches we have?

"Well, this sucks," says Antoine. "But it's better than me thinking that you just ditched me completely."

I feign shock. "Me? Ditch *you*? Never, Antoine."

We catch up as best as we can in the remaining five minutes we have together. I run down my schedule, including the classes I've already had with Mr. López for visual arts, Mrs. Hall for science, and Mr. Marshall for English. Even telling Antoine about them again exhausts me. And we still have two more periods to go!

"Are your teachers boring and in love with assigning homework?" I ask Antoine.

"Basically," he says. "My science teacher, Mr. Peters, is so boring that he actually put *himself* to sleep while we were taking a pop quiz today."

"That's . . . that's really bad," I say, grimacing. "Why did you have a quiz on the first day?"

"Apparently, he wanted to know our 'scientific knowledge,'" says Antoine. "I don't think I got a single answer right. What about you? Any surprise tests?"

I shake my head. "But I *am* worried about this presentation I have to give next week."

"A presentation *already*?" Antoine rolls his eyes. "No, that should be illegal. School *just* started!"

"Exactly!" I say. "And it's for social studies."

"You got Mrs. Aden?"

I shake my head. "Mr. Bradshaw. And he wants us to

give a presentation about our parents and their cultures and like . . ."

"Ah," says Antoine, nodding after I don't finish my sentence. "And you're worried because people might not get your family."

I smile at him. "I knew you'd understand."

"You'll be fine," he says. "Just explain how dorky your dad is and how your mom is the best cook on the planet."

"But what am *I*?" I ask. "That's part of the assignment."

"You're . . . you're David Bravo," he says.

I make a face at him. "Yes, I know my *name*, but like . . . I don't know what I'm supposed to say if I don't know where I came from."

"Maybe that's what makes you so cool," he says, grinning. "No one else is like you."

My face goes warm at that. "Thanks," I say.

"At least we have cross-country together," says Antoine.

I smile and nod. I'm not really a good runner, but I wanted to stick with Antoine so that we'd have more time together.

A chime rings out, and Antoine frowns at me. "Back to class," he says.

"I've got something called 'pre-algebra' next," I say.

"I still don't know what that means," Antoine says. "Why can't we just do algebra? What comes before it?"

"Well, I'm about to find out."

We do our Handshake.

"Always friends," he says, grinning.

"To the end."

Then Antoine is gone. A bunch of other kids leave, and all of them—*literally* all of them—are strangers. I know that ten or so other kids from Underhill are supposed to be here, but I don't see a single recognizable face.

The food isn't bad, but I pick at it. I miss Antoine already. Even though I'm going to see him in an hour, it already feels like forever.

How am I going to make it through this whole school year?

TUESDAY, SEPTEMBER 5
6:38 P.M.
Homework is one of the great evils of the world.

It's been two hours, and while most of the homework I was assigned on my first day is done, *this* is my supervillain origin story. Antoine would love to hear about this, I'm sure, since he's into comics and fantasy books. What kind of villain would I be? I'll have to ask him.

There's a blank index card in front of me on the small desk in my bedroom. I've drawn a line down the middle, and on the left side, I wrote: DAD. Mom's column is on the right. I figured I would start here and list what I knew about my parents. That's easy, right?

I put down that Dad's parents are from two countries: his mom is from Chiapas, Mexico, and his dad is from Fortaleza in Brazil. I've never been to either place and Grandpa Felipe Bravo passed away long before I was born. That's not the case with Mom, whose parents are both originally from Okinawa, Japan, but moved to Hawai'i before Mom was born. We've traveled to Lalakoa in Lanai City multiple times, and I love visiting there! It's so pretty.

But . . . what did Mr. Bradshaw want? He wanted to know about things we did around the house. I could probably talk about how I've always taken my shoes off at the door, and it wasn't until I visited my grandparents in Hawai'i that I learned that other families did that. But what else? I could talk about food . . . maybe. But as I sit there, tapping the eraser end of the pencil on my desk, I'm not sure I *know* much else. What sort of stuff would Mr. Bradshaw want to hear about?

I'm thankful when Mom interrupts me to call me out for dinner, but she has her own barrage of questions for me.

"How many friends did you make on your first day, David?" she asks as I pull out a chair and sit in it.

"Jeez, Mom, it's been one day," I say. "Give me some time!"

"You're going to make friends, I *promise*," Mom says, plopping down next to me. "I know I sound like some terrible motivational poster in your counselor's office, but it's going to happen."

Dad sits down across from her and laughs. "Tsuruko, do they still *have* those posters anymore? We're old. They've probably withered away."

She swats at him and misses.

"But your mom is right," he continues. "You'll make friends, and I guarantee by the end of the year, you'll feel a lot different."

"Isn't Antoine there?" asks Mom.

"Yes, but only for cross-country. Plus, our lunch over-laps for barely fifteen minutes."

"Oof," says Dad. "That's rough. But I'm sure you'll meet someone this week who seems interesting."

There's a moment when I think that maybe I should ask them about the social studies project. I'm sure they'd want to help! But *how*? Is there anything they know that I don't?

Probably not. I guess I'm going to have to figure this out on my own.

TUESDAY, SEPTEMBER 12
8:40 A.M.
The moment of truth

After a week of more homework, getting lost on campus, running badly during practice, *and* missing Antoine even more than I expected, I spent all day Sunday thinking about my project for Mr. Bradshaw.

And I came to the conclusion that I've been overthinking this.

Which was an easy conclusion to come to because I overthink *everything*. It's not always a *bad* thing. It helps to consider all the angles, no matter how stressful that might be. But I realized—after spending most of Sunday pacing back and forth across my bedroom—that I could just *control* what I tell my classmates. I know what all the questions usually are, and I can simply answer them before they're ever asked!

Do you know who your birth parents are?

Nope.

Where are you from?

I was born in Los Angeles.

No, where are you from *from?*

Definitely born in LA!

Why did your parents adopt you?

Because they wanted to start a family!

So what does that make you?

It makes me David Bravo.

There! I mean . . . I was still a little shaky on that last one. Antoine was probably right, and I guess I could tell them that I consider myself Latinx, since that's the only fact I know about my birth parents. That would probably work out all right.

However, as I sit there in Mr. Bradshaw's class on Tuesday morning, a terrible fear creeps over my skin. It's the first day of presentations, and I'm supposed to go after Gracie Lim.

She just stood up.

My heart is in my throat. I look down at the white index card on my desk, and I'm reading over what I wrote down as Gracie starts talking. I don't really hear what she's saying; it's just background noise as panic takes over. What if this isn't good enough? Everyone else has such concrete things to say about themselves, like how Wunmi and her parents came here from Nigeria a few years ago and how hard it was to find other Nigerians in Riverside. Uli Sánchez talked about how he learned English from watching *SpongeBob SquarePants*. Brad Holland told a story about how his dad's family has a yearly reunion up in Big Bear, where they take over an entire campground for a weekend.

Man, nothing I'm going to say sounds that cool. Have I made a mistake?

I swallow down my fear and look up at Gracie, who has already finished and is looking at Mr. Bradshaw.

"Excellent work," he says to her. "And your older sister. She's your *real* sister?"

Gracie squints at him. "Um . . . yes?"

"Wow! I'd love to hear more about that someday," says Mr. Bradshaw, then nods at her to sit down. She rushes back to her seat, a scowl on her face. When she sits down, she's shaking her head. I don't blame her. What was *that* question supposed to mean?

"Up next, we've got David Bravo," says Mr. Bradshaw. He gestures to the front of the class.

I breathe in deep and stand up, which is also when Tommy decides to open his mouth.

"What kind of last name is Bravo?"

"Seriously," says Walter.

"Please, Mr. Rodriguez," says Mr. Bradshaw. "Let David present first, okay?"

I make my way up, ignoring Tommy and Walter, who are giggling at me. I stand at the small wooden podium Mr. Bradshaw teaches from and clear my throat.

This is a weird feeling, to have all the eyes in this room staring at me. It's hot up here. Like a thousand degrees. Like I'm going to burst into flames any second.

I look to Mr. Bradshaw, who nods at me.

"Hi," I say, and my voice comes out like I've spent the

whole day at Six Flags screaming my head off. I clear my throat again. "My name is David Bravo."

For a moment, I think everyone is going to say, "Good morning, David!" like we had to do in Mrs. Wentz's first-grade class. But no, this is middle school. Everyone just stares.

"I was born in Los Angeles, and I have a really different kind of home life," I continue, and then I don't look up. I know my hand is shaking because it's hard to read the words I wrote on the index card I'm holding, but I do my best to say it all. How my mom is Japanese but grew up on Hawai'i, how my dad's dad is Brazilian and his mom is Mexican, how I eat all kinds of food at home and sometimes, Mom and Dad combine what they know, like how one time Mom fried up Spam—which is *super* popular in Hawai'i—and used it to make tacos.

I get to the last bit—my big reveal that I'm adopted, followed by the answers to all the common questions I hear—and . . .

I swallow deep.

And I don't read it at all.

Maybe I should. Is my presentation too short without it?

"So, that's me," I say. "Thank you."

Mr. Bradshaw is actually *smiling*. "Wonderful, David," he says. "That's really interesting!"

"Thank you," I say again, lowering the index card and letting out a breath of relief.

"But what do you consider *yourself*?"

His question catches me off guard, much like the one he asked Gracie. "Huh?"

"Well, we know your parents' cultures, but what are *you*?"

"I'm . . . David Bravo?"

I'm not trying to be sarcastic, but Walter snickers anyway.

"Yes, but what would you say you are? Where do *you* come from?"

"You mean . . . like, where I was born?" I scratch at my head.

"Sure," says Mr. Bradshaw. "Is that what you consider your origin story?"

"Are you Mexican or not?" says Tommy. "'Cuz you look like some of my primos, dude."

"Well, I'm not really sure," I say, and the familiar irritation is back. I absolutely should have prepared the whole question-and-answer bit!

Instead, I sigh. "I'm actually adopted," I admit.

It's the truth, but I don't expect the reaction it gets. Mr. Bradshaw tilts his head to the side. I see Tommy and Walter look at each other. Gracie's eyes go *really* wide. Ugh, I should be used to this! This *always* happens! But I'm still as annoyed as ever that my classmates are judging me.

"Well, David Bravo, what are the odds of that?" says Mr. Bradshaw. "You should have included that in your presentation. So, where did you come from?"

"I don't know," I say, my voice shaking. "I've never known

anything about where I came from. I was . . . adopted. That's all I know, so I didn't see a point to adding it to my presentation."

Gracie is frozen, staring at me. Tommy whispers something to Walter, and this time, Mr. Bradshaw turns on them.

"Excuse me, gentlemen," he says sharply. "You're being rude. Do you have something you'd like to ask David?"

Tommy gives a sly glance to Walter, then turns back to me. The sides of his mouth are upturned in a malicious grin. "Did your parents give you up because they didn't want you anymore?"

I hear someone gasp. I think it's Wunmi. My mouth drops open.

"No," I say. Then: "Well, I don't know. I don't know anything about them."

"Maybe we shouldn't ask such invasive questions, Mr. Rodriguez," says Mr. Bradshaw.

My head is still spinning from Tommy's question when Mr. Bradshaw turns back to me. "So, what *do* you know about where you came from?"

It's the same thing all over again, and the heat rushes over my skin. I'm probably turning red at this point. A part of me wants to snap back at my teacher and tell him that I came from a hospital, just like him, but everyone is staring at me, their eyes locked on my face, and they're waiting for an answer.

What answer do I give them? I was adopted. The end. I

don't know anything. Mom and Dad don't know anything either, and that's . . . that's it.

But that's not a satisfying answer, is it?

It's like time has stretched out and slowed down. I gulp down spit, and my face is burning, and I can't decide. I can't decide whether to try to be funny or just repeat the truth, so instead, I bow.

Literally. I bow, and I say, "Thank you," and then I'm rushing back to my seat as people whisper around me.

"Okay, then," says Mr. Bradshaw. "Terry Jimenez, you're up next."

All I can hope is that everyone will forget this moment. But Gracie's still staring at me when I sit down, and I know that Tommy and Walter are saying *something* about me. They keep turning back and glancing my way.

Why couldn't I make a *decision*? Why do I always freeze up? Why am I *always* so afraid?

I tuck my head into my arm on my desk, wishing the world would disappear.

TUESDAY, SEPTEMBER 12
12:35 P.M.
One bad choice leads to an even *worse* choice!

I slide my tray down the counter in the cafeteria, and Norma Gutierrez—one of the cooks in our school—smiles at me. She's got the same skin tone as me, and a thought pops into my head: *Am I secretly related to her?*

I've thought this before. In fact, I've said it to Antoine when we've seen people in public who vaguely resemble me. It was always fun; Antoine had this theory that my birth parents were secret agents hiding from a shadowy cabal of monsters, and one day, I'd be revealed to be a mystical hunter.

But now, after what Tommy said . . .

This game isn't that fun anymore.

"Hola, mijo," she says. "How are you?"

I can't really explain it, but there's something about the way she calls me "mijo"—despite that I'm not her son—that makes me feel all warm inside. So I smile back at her, even though I'm not really in a smiling mood.

"I'm okay," I say. "I think I bombed an assignment today, though."

Norma frowns. "Lo siento. Let me make your day a little better." She puts two peanut butter cookies on my tray first. "My treat. What else would you like, David?"

I point at one of the chicken sandwiches, then a fruit cup. Today's the practice race that determines whether I am on varsity or junior varsity, though. I know I'm not going to make the top seven spots, but I decide I probably need something else that's supposed to be healthy. I gesture at the spinach. "That's supposed to give you energy, right?"

Norma makes a face, then shakes her head.

"No?" I say. "Bad idea?"

She looks around like she's going to share a secret with me. "I don't think this is our best batch," she says. "The spinach smelled a little weird this morning."

"Ugh," I groan. I should probably listen to her, but I don't want to bomb today's race either. Spinach has vitamins! Fiber! Popeye ate it! Okay, so I've never actually *seen* a Popeye cartoon before, but Dad talks about watching them all the time when he was little.

I take the spinach, despite Norma's warning.

"Ay, David," she says, "you're the only kid I know who willingly eats vegetables."

Well, at least I have that!

She waves as I leave, and I rush to find Antoine before the bell rings and he has to head to his fifth period. His tray is basically clean, so he probably ate the spinach! I'll be fine!

But after greeting Antoine, I manage only a few bites of the leafy greens before I push my tray away. "I think those are poisoned," I say.

"Poisoned?" He raises an eyebrow. "By who?" His eyes go wide. "It's the *cabal*."

"I don't think so," I say. "To be fair, I *was* warned they weren't very good."

"Can I have one of your cookies, then?" he asks. I nod and he grabs one, then eats it like he's never had a cookie in his life. Then I remember that he basically *hasn't*. Mr. Harris, Antoine's dad, was a track star himself until an injury in college put him on the sidelines. Now, when he isn't working for the mayor, he mostly coaches Antoine, and he's pretty intense about it, too. Antoine's meals are all planned, and he has a whole schedule of running outside of school hours. Sometimes, he has to run *before* breakfast.

Waking up before the sun comes up *and* working out? No, thank you.

I like sharing my cookies with Antoine, though. It's like we have a secret together. His eyes are warm as he takes a bite and chews on it slowly. "Thanks, David," he says. "I owe you one."

I pull the yellow lunch tray back toward me and take a few bites of my chicken sandwich, since I'm still starving, but something isn't sitting right in my stomach, so I don't finish it.

"How'd your presentation go?" Antoine asks as I push the tray away a second time.

I make a twisted face at him.

"That bad?" he asks.

"I think I threw it off a cliff at the end."

"Yikes," he says. "Well, I'm pretty sure I failed my first surprise quiz in pre-algebra."

"Mrs. Valdez?" I say.

He nods.

"Great, a surprise quiz!" I say. "It's like Mrs. Valdez expects us to know things she has *literally* not taught us."

Antoine throws his hands up in the air. "Right? Doesn't that defeat the whole purpose of being in school? I feel like I need a time machine just to make it through one of her classes."

"Middle school sucks," I say.

Right then, the chime sounds.

"Sometimes," says Antoine, gathering up his things. "But we got a race today! That should be fun."

My stomach rumbles in response. "I'm glad it's not a *real* race," I say. "I'd be too nervous for that."

Antoine claps me on the shoulder as he passes. "You're gonna be fine," he says. "Plus, you don't have to worry about placing on the varsity team."

"True," I say. "I will happily stay in the bottom seven today."

A warmth rushes through me as I watch him leave. It's

interrupted when a kid sits next to me and points at my tray.

"You eating that cookie?" he asks. It looks like he's gonna start drooling any second. He's got a mouth full of braces and brown skin, and his hair is as straight and dark as Mom's.

"No," I say. "Go ahead."

"Thanks," he says, grabbing it. "I'm Samrat, by the way."

"David," I say back, but then I fall into silence as lunch continues, without Antoine and without a calm stomach. I glance over at Samrat, and I wonder if I should talk to him more. Mom said I'd make friends eventually. But then I stare down at my tray, and I'm not sure what question to ask first. Should I ask him his last name? Oh, no, that's a terrible idea. I could ask him where he went to school before? But that seems boring. A few minutes later I stand up, take my tray and empty it in the trash, and head toward my next class.

Yeah, I don't know how to make friends. This is impossible.

Do I actually make it inside class, by the way? Oh, no, absolutely not. I get as far as the doorway to Mrs. Valdez's room when my stomach cramps and rumbles. *Seriously?* I think. *This can't be happening this fast! Is this a world record?*

It's clear that my body is completely rejecting everything I've eaten. I'm hunched over, clutching the frame with one hand and my stomach with the other, and then I make eye contact with Mrs. Valdez.

She gives me a look of pity, then waves me off. "Go, go!" she says.

I manage to sprint to the bathroom and make it to a toilet before it all comes up.

I slump down onto the cold tile and sit there for a moment. I'm the only person here, and it's like my own thoughts are echoing around in the bathroom. This day has been the worst. It's not just getting sick, it's not just the presentation, it's not just the frustration I feel all the time.

One thought in particular is louder than the others:

What if Tommy is right?

That can't be what really happened. Dad once told me that there are plenty of reasons parents put a kid up for adoption and that most people just want the best for the child. Which sometimes means giving them up so someone else can love them and support them! Plus, my parents *are* my parents. So what are the odds that Tommy Rodriguez—who cannot keep a single thought inside his brain for longer than sixty seconds—is actually right?

Of course . . . it could be something worse.

Oh, god, David, why did you think that? What could be worse?

This is new. I don't remember ever being bothered by not knowing, and yet, it's like . . . like there's a big hidden cave inside me that I didn't know was there. I don't know what's in it, and I can't *ever* know what's in it.

I wipe my mouth with the back of my hand and stand

up, then walk over to the sink to clean up. I splash water on my face, hoping to shock myself out of this new sensation I'm feeling. I go back to Mrs. Valdez's class and quietly take my seat, and I must look terrible, because she gives me a pitying glance. Then she plops a quiz on my desk.

I have no idea how I do on it. Things aren't so bad stomach-wise by the time sixth period rolls around. The locker room is loud and packed, since we're sharing it with the football *and* baseball teams. I quickly change into my running shorts and our team jersey, even though I'm not so sure I should be running today. It's just three miles, though. That's all I have to do, and I don't even have to do it *well*.

I find most of the cross-country team stretching in the middle of the track. Coach Williams—impossibly tall, impossibly skinny, impossibly made of nothing but legs—is doing these weird jump exercises nearby, and I don't know why. Is he going to try to race *with* us? He does stuff like that sometimes. I think he wants us to see him as one of us, but I'm not sure it's working.

When I find Antoine and drop down next to him, I'm already pouring sweat. It's pretty hot out, and the sun clearly does not agree that summer is over. As I go through my stretches on the ground, I almost feel like everything is swaying beneath me, despite being fully aware that I'm sitting.

"You okay?" Antoine asks. He stretches down and effortlessly grabs the bottoms of his toes. How does he *do* that?

"I'll be fine," I say. "Just nervous."

"Me, too," he says.

I'm not sure Antoine needs to worry about anything. He's always been not just the faster of the two of us but the fastest out of *everyone*. There's no one on the team who can beat him. Plus: still not a real race!

You can't really tell that to Mr. Harris, though. I watch him jog over to us, dressed exactly like you'd expect a coach to be. He has on a black visor, a pair of sunglasses, a sporty red polo shirt over black shorts, and some brand-new running shoes. He's even got a clipboard.

Do I need to remind you he's not *actually* our coach?

"You all stretched, son?" Mr. Harris asks Antoine, then nods at me. "Hey, David!"

Then he looks me up and down.

"You okay, buddy? You look a little gray."

"He's just nervous, Pop," Antoine says, then pats me on the arm. "He'll do great."

There's a burst of nerves in my stomach when he does that, and I turn away from him so that he can't see my reaction.

"Well, don't let it be infectious, Antoine," says Mr. Harris. "Keep your head in the race. Pace yourself. And remember—"

"'Every run is a race against yourself,'" Antoine finishes. "Yeah, I remember, Pop."

Mr. Harris helps him up. "You need any last-minute stretches?"

And then off they go, leaving me behind with the rest of the team. We are . . . a very strange bunch, from what I can tell from the last week of practices. There's Jorge Ramos, who walks every competition. I don't think it's for a health reason or anything. He just refuses to run, which is really weird for someone who joined a sport that is *only* running. I found out yesterday that Caitlin Queen recites the alphabet when she runs, which is unfortunate if she happens to be right behind you. I can't explain why, but it's *very* threatening to have the alphabet tiredly whispered at your back. I don't recommend it. Then there's Geoff, whose shoes come untied *every* time.

Yeah, we're not going to win a single race this year. Well, we might *frighten* the other team into losing, and I've made my peace with that.

I finally stand up and wobble from side-to-side before regaining my balance, but then the ground moves beneath my feet. Is this an earthquake? It would be my luck that there'd be an earthquake today. But I notice that no one else is reacting to a natural disaster, so . . .

Oh. It's just me.

Something is wrong. *Very* wrong. I close my eyes and hear Coach Williams's whistle nearby. "Everyone line up!" he calls out, and I open my eyes and twist around. The team jogs over to the starting line on the track. The plan is to head halfway around it, then veer off to head to the perimeter fence of the school. A loop around campus and back to the track is a mile, so we're supposed to make three laps before we're done.

I'm not going to last that long. I think that spinach is changing me like I'm in a superhero movie. Will my hair turn into leafy greens? Probably.

I stumble forward, and I think someone else on my team is calling out to me. My head is spinning. Coach Williams's whistle rings out again, and maybe that means the race has started. Ended? Both. Both are happening. Yes, of course! This race transcends all time and space!

Oh, I don't feel so good. I whirl around, but I don't see anyone running, and the sun has *never* felt hotter, like she's sitting on my shoulder. I need to make it to the locker room because I do *not* want to throw up out here where Antoine can see me.

Antoine.

Where is he?

My stomach churns.

I step onto the track, and when I look to my right, I can see that the runners have rounded the curve. Oh, no. Did the race start *without* me? Wow, I've messed up more times today than I can count.

"Bravo!" Coach Williams calls out. "What are you *doing*?"

I ignore him because I have bigger things to worry about. I think they're far enough away that I can make it to the other side, and then it's not that much farther to the bathroom. I can hear Coach's warning in my head that we don't cross the course when a race is in play, but this isn't *technically* a race, so I should be fine, yeah?

I am certain I'm sprinting to the other side of the track, but when I look up again—

Oh. Oh, I don't think I've moved at all.

And now all the runners are barreling down on me.

Go, go! I tell myself, but I'm frozen: frozen with indecision. Because I *could* turn back and everything would be fine, or I *could* move quicker across the track and everything would be fine, but what if I go the wrong way? What if I don't make it? What should I do?

All this happens in the span of a few seconds, and at the last moment—right as Antoine's eyes go wide and I see him dart to his right to go around me—I panic and push forward.

Right into Antoine.

When he collides with me, I briefly believe I now know what it feels like to fly, and it is *awesome*. It doesn't last long, because I hit the dirt track *hard*, the air rushing out of my lungs. I can hear someone groaning loudly near me, but it's soon drowned out by the yelling.

I can't make out whether it's Coach or Mr. Harris, but honestly, neither option is great. I gasp for air on the track, and then someone is blocking the hot sun out of my eyes.

Ah, it's Coach Williams.

"David Bravo!" he hisses.

I don't answer him at first because I don't have any air in my lungs, but I still push myself up on my elbows.

That's when I see Antoine clutching his right ankle, his face twisted up in pain. His ankle is already swollen, and it looks *nasty*. Mr. Harris is glaring at me, clearly furious, and the other teammates have gathered at the side of the track. Phuong looks horrified. Some of them are also very, very angry with me.

So, of course, my next immediate reaction is to throw up right where I'm sitting.

Like a cherry on top of the grossest sundae ever.

TUESDAY, SEPTEMBER 12
4:04 P.M.
Today was six hundred Davids.

For what it's worth, I actually feel fine after Phuong and Caitlin (not reciting the alphabet at the time) help me to my feet. I start apologizing to Antoine, but his dad and Coach Williams lift him from under his arms, and he limps off toward the locker room between the two of them.

I really, really messed up, didn't I?

Coach Williams only returns to tell me that I've got the rest of practice off. "Take care of yourself, Bravo," he says. "I don't want you infecting the other students."

With spinach? I think. But I don't say that; I nod and head straight for the locker rooms, avoiding the looks from my fellow teammates. None of them chase after me either, and I'm thankful for that. What exactly am I supposed to say?

I stand under the shower for a long time, letting the hot water fall over me. Eventually, I realize I *have* to get dressed and go wait for Mom to pick me up. All I hope for is Antoine to come through the door, his ankle totally fine, and maybe we'll hug and joke with each other, and I won't have hurt him (and possibly ruined his season) at all.

But that doesn't happen.

When Mom's small black car pulls up, I get inside and immediately thump my forehead against the window after closing the door. She knows that means I'm not really up for conversation, so it's quiet on the way home. In fact, she doesn't say anything to me until I'm facedown on the cold tile just inside the front door of our house.

"David," she says, reaching down to pick up my backpack, which I let fall to the floor as soon as I got inside. "Please get up, honey."

"No," I mutter into the tile. "This is where I live now."

"David."

"I *am* the floor now."

"David, honey."

"Sorry, I can't hear you. Floors don't have ears, Mom."

"If you don't have ears, how can you respond to me?"

I clench my eyes shut. I don't like it when Mom uses logic. That seems deeply unfair.

After a few seconds, she sits next to me on the tile, then grabs my hand and rubs it with her other one. This is her secret weapon; it's her way of calming me down when I'm upset. Even though I try to resist, I'm soon relaxing under her touch.

"You had a bad day, didn't you?" she says.

"It was the worst, Mom," I say.

"The worst? Like, the absolute worst?"

I finally lift my head and gaze at her. "They will measure all bad days based on this one."

"Really?" She cocks her head and brushes her long black hair out of her face. "That bad?"

I roll over and stare at the ceiling. "We learned about measurement systems yesterday in Mrs. Hall's class," I say. "Like meters and grams and pounds, that sorta stuff. And I think next year, the David will be used to measure human misery."

When I glance over at Mom, it's clear she's trying to hold back a laugh. "You mean like, 'Hey, Barbara, did you feel seven Davids today?'"

I nod at her. "Exactly. And today was six *hundred* Davids."

She smiles. "So. You wanna tell me about it?"

"Not really," I say softly.

"Are you sure about that?" she says. "I promise to listen to whatever you have to say."

"I'm sure," I say. "Just bury me here."

"David."

"I'm sure you could pay someone to come build a little bridge over my body."

"David."

"It'll look really neat. You can even name it after me."

She sighs loudly. "I'm sorry you had a bad day, David.

Maybe you can go over to Antoine's, see if he can—"

I don't even let her finish before I let out the loudest groan that's ever come out of my body. She actually flinches.

"David! Don't be rude!"

"The bad day involves Antoine," I whine. "I don't know if he'll want to see me ever again."

She is quiet for a moment, enough so that I hear the car pull up into the driveway. "Papi is here," she says, but she doesn't stand up. "Do you maybe want to get up so that he doesn't trip over you?"

"Nah," I say, still staring at the ceiling. "He needs to get used to me being here. You know, since I'm never moving again."

Before Mom can say anything, the front door opens, and I see the shadow of my dad over the ceiling. He stops. I am sure he is looking down at his son and wondering a million things, but I remain silent.

"Hi, David," he says, then steps forward so he can close the door behind him. He raises his bushy eyebrows at me, and I notice that there's paint on his army-green overalls. He works in construction, mainly building homes, so he is always covered in whatever project he is working on.

Dad smiles. "Having a good time down there?"

"The worst," I say. "Would you like to join me?"

He casts a glance at Mom, then he shrugs.

Soon, Dad is on the other side of me. We don't talk for a

while, and the silence becomes really uncomfortable.

"I think I'm cursed," I say.

"Cursed," says Dad. "Like . . . a pirate who found haunted treasure?"

"It's like you can read my mind," I say. "But no, not that awesome."

"Why do you think you're cursed, David?" Mom asks.

I can feel the indecision mounting in me, so I blurt it all out before I'm unable to say anything: I tell them about the presentation. About being unsure of what or who I am. About the spinach and the upset stomach and the collision and Antoine. The one thing I leave out is Tommy's question. That doesn't feel like something I am ready to share.

Once I'm done, I realize how ridiculous the story sounds, but it's *real*. It actually happened. Mom and Dad are silent, but not for long. Dad rubs my scalp with his fingers.

"You know, David, that sounds like a really hard day," he says.

"Now I know why you said it was The Worst," adds Mom.

"It was a full David of a day," I say.

"So how's this feeling?" Mom asks, placing her hand on my stomach.

"Ugh!" I groan and sit up. "*Now* it feels perfectly fine. Of course!"

"Maybe you got it all out of your system," she says. "Bodies can be very efficient like that." When I frown at her, she raises a finger. "I know the timing was terrible, David, but I don't think you're cursed."

"Well, Antoine probably hates me, and I'm sure the rest of the team does, too."

"David," says Dad, a warning in his tone. "What have we told you about saying negative things like that about yourself?"

"You've both said a lot of things," I mutter.

"Please, honey," says Mom.

I sigh. "It's okay to be frustrated or disappointed, but I don't have to take everything out on myself."

Mom nods, and it's times like these that it's impossible to forget that she's a therapist. She's *really* good at this kind of stuff.

"Most of this was just bad luck and coincidence," says Dad. "And those things don't make you a bad person."

"Well, I could have listened to Norma, and then I wouldn't have hurt Antoine."

"Then you learned an important lesson," says Mom as she stands up. Dad follows after her, and then he sticks his hand out to me.

"No, sorry, I can't," I say.

"Up, David," Dad says.

"This is my new home," I explain. "You weren't here for that part. Better call your construction buddies to build a bridge over me."

Dad thinks for a bit. "Will it have running water underneath it?" he asks.

"Uh, *duh*. Absolutely. Maybe we can build a whole pond like those ones we saw in Waimea when we visited Auntie Kai. Fill it with koi and everything."

"Fernando, don't humor him," says Mom from the kitchen.

"Sue, think of all the money we could make!" he calls out. "We could charge admission. 'Come see the boy at the bottom of the koi pond!' People pay for stuff like that."

"I suppose you're right," she says, coming back to us. "You think we could get ten dollars a pop?"

"Easily," says Dad. "You and I could go visit your family again after just a week of business."

I know they're joking, but it's like a spike in my chest when Dad says that. *Without me?* I think. Suddenly, this joke doesn't feel so funny.

I stand up quickly. "Hey, I can hear you, you know!"

They both look at me, and Mom smiles. "Oh, so you *do* have ears," she says.

Mom and her logic! She is too good at this! I grimace. "Yes, I do."

"Good," she says. "So you can definitely take the garbage out, since you're fine."

"What? That's not fair! You cheated."

"I don't think that's cheating," says Dad, grinning from ear to ear.

There's no winning with them. Mom's got a little smirk on her face, and I want to joke back with her because that's what I always do, but Dad's comment about the two of

them leaving to visit family still stings a little. I mean . . .
they wouldn't *actually* leave me behind, would they?

Like my birth parents did.

I wipe at my face once that thought fills my head. No,
no, David, stop thinking these things! It's just Tommy getting under your skin again.

The thing is, the more you tell yourself to *not* think
something?

The more you do.

As I burst out the back door with the trash bag, I release
a breath of air, then shut my eyes tight. "I wish I could do
this day over again," I say.

Like that ever happens.

TUESDAY, SEPTEMBER 12
4:31 P.M.
I meet the creepiest dog of all time.

When I open my eyes, there, sitting at the bottom of the steps, is a dog.

At least, I *think* it's a dog. It's got black . . . skin? I don't know how to describe it. It has no fur at *all*, except for a small tuft on the top of its head. It's got a black collar on, and there's a small tag hanging from it, which looks like . . . like the number eight?

Weird.

"Hi," I say.

It's a dog, so it doesn't say anything back. It just sits there, staring at me. I don't get a sense that it's dangerous, so I take a few slow steps toward it.

The dog does not move.

At the bottom of the steps, I put the trash bag on the ground, then crouch so I'm on the dog's level. I reach out, careful not to make any sudden moves, and pet the top of its head.

The little tuft of fur there is soft. It's kind of an ugly-looking dog, but at least it's nice.

It doesn't move until I scratch it under the ears.

"Oh, that's the *spot*," a voice says.

In my head.

I jerk away so fast I nearly trip over the bottom step behind me.

No. No, that didn't just happen.

The dog is definitely not talking, because dogs don't talk.

I pick up the trash bag and make a beeline for the bins, and just as I'm pitching it toward the brown one for garbage, I hear the voice again.

"Well, *that's* rude. Are you going to keep ignoring me?"

I'm so shocked by this that the bag doesn't make it all the way into the bin, meaning a bunch of garbage spills over the side and onto the ground.

"I'm flattered, really," says the voice, which sounds like an older woman. "But I don't eat garbage."

It's in my *head*! I don't get it! It's like my own thoughts, but someone *else's* voice is in there.

I turn, slowly, to the right.

The weird dog is standing there at the end of the little alley next to my house.

"No," I say.

"Yes," it says.

"No, this is not happening."

"You can keep saying that, but it's definitely happening."

The dog saunters up to me, and I yelp. I kick an old bag of carrots in their direction. They dodge it easily because I'm not exactly a good shot. I don't play soccer. I'm barely any good at track.

"Carrots? Really?"

"Is that you in my head?"

"Is there anyone else around here?"

I actually look around, and . . . no, we're alone in the alley.

"So, can we move past this point, David?" The dog scratches at the ground. "We got a lotta work to do. The sooner we start, the better."

"Wait, you know my name?" I ask, my jaw practically hitting the ground.

"Excellent, we're now past the point where you realize that you're talking to a dog," the dog says. "And yes, I know your name, David Bravo."

"Hold on, I'm not past *any* point," I say. Then I put my palm to my forehead. "What am I doing? Why am I talking to a dog?"

"Because I started talking to you first?" The dog licks their paw. "That's generally how conversation works."

I'm talking to a dog who is *also* a jerk. Great. Today is *fantastic*.

I do my best to pick up the trash on the ground, but it's gross and slimy. This day truly can't get worse.

"Stop ignoring me, David."

I ignore them.

"I can literally do this forever," the dog says, and when I glance at them, I discover they've come a *lot* closer to me.

"How are you in my head? How is that possible?"

"It just is," they say. "Accept it, and let's get going. We need to figure out where your timeline diverted down the wrong path so I can retroactively grant you the agency needed to repair your stream."

"Those *sound* like words, and yet I understand none of them," I say as I walk over to the bag of soggy carrots and pick them up. I toss them in the bin and slam the lid shut. "Also, none of this is happening."

"Is this where I should sigh dramatically, David?" the dog says, coming up to me. "Will that convince you to get over this?"

"Why are you like this?" I say. "Is this how you talk to *everyone*?" I hesitate for a moment. "Wait, *do* you talk to other people?" I hesitate again. "No, no, I can't do this."

I run for the back door of the house, but before I make it there, the voice rings out *real* loud in my head.

"David Bravo, don't take another step."

I don't take another step. I spin around, and the dog is right there again, staring at me.

"Just stop and listen to me," they say.

"You're a weird-looking dog," I say, crossing my arms over my chest.

"You're a weird-looking boy."

"Whatever, fea."

"Fea?" The dog sits down and lifts their head. "That's all

you can come up with? I am a gorgeous and *grown* woman, thank you very much."

"You look like a dog," I say. "Not in a mean way! Like . . . you look like an *actual* dog."

"Right now, sure," she says. "I can change if it'll make this easier for you."

"Kind of an ugly dog, actually."

"Yes, I figured that out when you gave me a name that literally means 'ugly' in Spanish."

"Tell me what you are," I say. "I've never seen a dog like you."

"A xoloitzcuintli," she says.

I frown deeply. "That's . . . that's not a word."

Fea starts panting in exasperation. "I just said it."

"You can say a lot of things. Doesn't make 'em real."

"You're going to be a difficult one, aren't you?" she says. "Are you ready to go yet?"

"No," I say. "Give it to me again."

She sighs. *(In my head!)* "In English, we're called Mexican hairless dogs. But one of our original names is xoloitzcuintli, and it was my favorite breed of dog."

"That's a mouthful."

"Sho."

"What?"

"Say it after me," she says. "Sho."

"Sho," I repeat.

"Lo."

"Lo."

"Eats."

"Eats."

"Queent."

I grimace. "Queent?"

"Lee."

"Lee."

"Now say it real fast," Fea says. "I believe in you, David!"

I practice it a few times, and my tongue trips up near the end a bunch before I can pull it off. But as I say it with a growing smile—"Xoloitzcuintli! Xoloitzcuintli!"—reality comes crashing down on me.

"What am I doing?" I back away from her, right up against the door to the house. "This isn't happening. It's a joke, right?"

Fea twists her head to the side. "It's not a very funny joke. Where's the punch line?"

"Because dogs don't talk, so this isn't real," I say for what feels like the millionth time.

"Honey, who are you talking to out there?" Mom calls out from in the kitchen.

I glare at Fea. "Absolutely *no one*," I say, directing the words at her.

"I'm here to fix your life," says Fea. "And I won't leave you alone *until* it's fixed. So you can try to ignore me, but pretty soon, you won't be able to."

"Dogs don't talk," I whisper, giving her a sarcastic smile. "You aren't here."

"Fine," she says. "If this isn't happening, then you won't

mind if I pay a little visit to your wonderful, neatly organized home."

And before I can do anything, Fea darts between my legs, up the steps, and into my house.

Seconds later, there's a crash.

"David?!" Mom's voice calls out in alarm from somewhere in the house. "David, what's going on?"

Oh, *no*.

This actually *is* happening.

I rush into the kitchen through the back door, and Mom isn't anywhere in sight. Then I run into the living room, where one of my mom's vases—the one that was holding some gorgeous tulips—is now shattered on the floor.

"David, what happened?"

I spin around to see Mom and Dad. I can already tell Mom is upset.

"Mom, it wasn't me!"

"There's no one else here, David," she says sadly. "Oh, I just got that vase from your grandma!"

"I was out back throwing the trash away when I heard the crash!" I say.

And then *she* appears.

Fea, behind my mom. I can see her between Mom's legs.

I promise you: she *winks*.

Then she darts off farther into the house, and although a large part of me still refuses to believe this is happening,

I run after her, pushing past my parents, who shout out in protest as I bolt toward the back of the house. Fea stops, looks back at me for maybe one whole second, and then darts into my parents' bedroom.

"NO!" I shout, ignoring Mom and Dad yelling at me to stop being so loud.

I stop in the doorway and spot Fea: she's right in the middle of their bed.

"All you need to do is accept that I'm here," she says, rolling over onto her back, "and everything will be fine. I promise."

"Go away!" I shout.

"You're not talking to *me* like that, are you?"

I whirl around. Mom's staring at me, and she doesn't look sad over the broken vase anymore. She looks *furious*.

"No, Mom, I was—"

"Because I know you've had a tough day," she continues, "but that's no excuse for being rude, okay?"

"Apologize to your mother," Dad says, his hands on his hips. "Now."

I don't even know how to deal with what's happening, but I don't want my parents to be angry with me. I take a deep breath so I can say I'm sorry, but then I feel a cold, wet nose on the back of my leg.

I nearly jump out of my skin. I look down and sure enough, there's Fea, looking up at me with her dark eyes.

Mom and Dad . . . they aren't looking at Fea.

Meaning they definitely can't see a Mexican hairless dog standing behind me.

"Accept that I'm here," Fea commands. "That's all you have to do."

"No," I say.

"David!" Dad says sternly. "Yes, you will!"

"No, I'm not talking to you!" I say, and when confusion passes over my parents' faces, I grimace. "I was talking to . . . myself."

They don't look any less confused.

"Like I do sometimes," I add quickly.

"Okay," says Mom, dragging the word out and scrunching up her eyebrows. I think Dad's head is going to explode at any second.

"I'm sorry," I say. "I just wish I could start today over."

"I could help with that," says Fea. "Honestly. If only you'd listen to me, David."

I glare down at Fea, but otherwise ignore her.

So she farts.

Extremely, extremely loudly.

It sounds like someone letting air out of a balloon. If she wasn't an invisible dog who was trying to have a telepathic conversation with me, I would assume she was really, really sick and needed to be taken to the vet.

But she's not here.

Farting.

No. She's *still* farting!

"Oh, my *god*, David," says Dad, and I watch in horror as he covers his mouth with one hand. "Is that because of the spinach you ate?"

"What?!" I say. "What are you talking about?"

Mom groans. "Wow, David, you really *must* be feeling sick," she says. "That's a stinker."

I can't believe it. This isn't happening. How can they *smell* Fea but not see her?

"I'm sorry," I say, and even though I'm not looking at her, I hope Fea knows I'm talking to her. "I promise I'll listen to you."

"Thank you," says Mom. "Let me go get you some Pepto Bismol for your stomach," she says, and heads to the kitchen, where she keeps most of our medicine.

"You okay, David?" Dad asks.

I really need him to leave. As soon as possible. "Yeah," I say. "Just feeling weird, that's all."

"Fernando, where's the Pepto Bismol?" Mom calls out from the kitchen. "I bought a pair of them last week when they were on sale. Where did you put them?"

"Above the fridge!" he calls out, then looks back to me. "Be right back, bud, okay?"

When he's gone, I glance down. Fea isn't there anymore, so I turn around and find her splayed out on the bed. Like it's hers. *Again.*

"Okay," I say. "You win. You're here. You're real. That good enough for you?"

"I knew you *actually* believed I was there in the alley," she says. "You wouldn't have kicked a bag of carrots at me if you thought I was fake."

"Are you *serious*?" I say with clenched teeth. "Then why did you do all this?"

She curls her lip at me like she's going to snarl. "Because it was fun? Look, David, when you do this job for as long as I have, you have to find ways to entertain yourself."

"I'm sorry, do *what* job? What are you talking about?"

"I help people."

"I don't really believe that."

She rolls over on her back. "You don't really have a say in that matter. I told you, if you just believe what I have to tell you, this will work a lot better for the both of us."

"Fine," I say, and I put my hands on my hips. "Tell me, then. What is your job, Fea?"

"First of all, my name is—"

She stops, then rolls over so she's standing on all fours.

"Never mind, not important," she says. "I'm your guide."

"Guide to what?"

"To you. To your life."

"Pretty sure I know my own life."

"You do," she says. "But I'm here to help you *fix* it."

"It's not broken."

"Did I or did I not hear you tell your parents like fifteen minutes ago that you were *cursed*?"

My mouth drops open. "You heard that?"

Fea nods her doggy head. "Yep," she says. "The universe

is listening to you, David Bravo. I've been tasked with helping people whose timelines have gone wrong."

"Whose *what?*"

"Do you interrupt *everyone* when they're trying to explain themselves?"

I sigh. "Sorry. This is all just . . . it's all a little weird."

"Get used to weird, David Bravo, because it's only going to get weirder." She trots across the bed until she's right at the edge of it, then looks up at me. "Accept that I can talk in your head, and accept that I can appear wherever and *when*ever I want. And however I want, too!"

"You mean you *chose* to look like this?" I say, gesturing down at her. "Wow, so you woke up this morning and chose *violence.*"

"First of all, I don't 'wake up' quite like that," she says, exasperated. "I'm not a person anymore."

"Anymore?" I tilt my head at her like she did out in the alley. "What does *that*—?"

She cuts me off. "Keep up, David. At some point in your life, you made the wrong choice. You got sent down the wrong path, and *that* is why you feel like this. It has nothing to do with spinach or track meets or anything like that. Or maybe it does, tangentially, but we can talk about that later. My job is to take you back through your own life, find the point where you went wrong, and then allow *you* to correct it."

"Wow," I say.

"Pretty cool, right?" she says, and I swear, it looks like she's *proud* of herself.

"No, I meant that everything you just said is impossible, unless you're in one of those books Antoine reads."

"You really need to change your understanding of impossible," she says, and leaps off the bed.

"David!"

As predicted, Mom calls out to me from the kitchen. Fea smugly walks over to the doorway, bouncing as she does so.

"You'll see me again soon, David," she says. "Think about your life. I'm sure you can think of something you've always wanted to do over again. We'll start once you do."

"Where are you going?" I ask her.

"I'm a busy guide," she says. "I have other people to help. You just came up on my list, so I thought I'd introduce myself."

She rips another terrible, awful fart.

"See ya, David Bravo."

And then she's just . . . gone.

Like . . . she just *vanishes*.

Mom walks in from the kitchen. "David, did you hear me—?"

She freezes, then wrinkles her nose. "Ooof, David," she says, "come take something. And *soon*. You're a smelly boy today."

I follow her down the hallway in a daze. *I don't care what Fea says. This is* totally *impossible.*

TUESDAY, SEPTEMBER 12
5:17 P.M.

I'm sure she didn't intend it, but Fea provided me with the perfect reasoning for the current disaster: I was clearly still sick. That's how I explained the garbage left outside the trash can and the broken vase: I was "sick." I mean, I didn't feel great, and the excuse was too perfect not to use.

Still, I didn't want my parents to be mad at me, so I told Dad it was only fair if I finished picking up the garbage. So that's where I am when I hear Antoine's voice next door.

"Dad, I promise I'm okay," he says, and the Harrises' back door shuts.

I take a deep breath. I really, really hope Antoine still wants to be my friend.

"That you, Antoine?" I call out.

"David?" His voice sounds higher than usual. "You okay over there?"

"I should be asking *you* that," I say as I throw the last of the trash in the bin. Then I head over to my mom's planter, where she's growing some veggies and petunias. I hop up onto the side of it, and then I can see over the fence into Antoine's yard.

He's in a chair on the small patio, and his foot is elevated in front of him, an ice pack resting on his ankle. There's a pair of crutches leaning against the chair, too.

"It's not so bad," he says, gesturing to his leg, but as he leans forward, he winces. It sends a jolt of guilt through me.

"I'm really sorry," I say.

"It's fine." Antoine shakes his head. "Just . . . annoying. Mom gave me some ibuprofen, so it doesn't really hurt. Especially when I don't move it."

"I don't know what came over me."

He raises a hand to stop me. "Bruh, it's *fine*. Seriously!"

But when he says it, his words come out sharp, and I look away from him for a moment, unable to keep eye contact. The guilt comes right back. He wouldn't even be in this position if I hadn't hurt him.

I glance back at Antoine, and he swings his leg down off the chair across from him. He sets it gently on the floor, then looks up at me peering over the fence.

"I'll be okay in a week or so," he says softly. He smirks. "You, on the other hand, I'm not so sure about. I don't think I've ever seen someone throw up that much in my whole *life*. So congrats on setting that world record."

At least that makes me laugh. "Still, I feel terrible. If you need anything, let me know. I'll carry your books all day if you want."

He laughs. "I'll let you know."

"Is your dad angry with me?" I ask.

The smile leaves Antoine's face. "You know Pop," he says. "He takes this track stuff so seriously. But he'll be okay. It's not like I haven't sprained my ankle before. He's mostly mad that Coach Williams won't put me on varsity until I complete a timed run."

"Ah, that sucks," I say.

"You kinda did me a favor," Antoine mumbles, looking at the ground.

"Huh? What do you mean?"

His eyes snap up to me. "Never mind. I'll be back on my foot within a week, so it's all good."

Antoine goes quiet. I want to ask him what he meant by a "favor," but the moment has passed. It would just be too awkward. Besides, I could ask him and he could tell me that I'm being nosy, and then he would try to hobble back inside and he would trip and break his leg and then his family would move away and I would lose my very best friend.

Yeah, better not to say anything at all.

As Antoine uses the crutches to bring himself upright, I sense that something is still wrong between us. I don't like it. I've never had to deal with hurting him before, and it makes me feel like the torn bag of garbage from earlier today.

"Well, I've got some homework to do," I say, breaking the silence. "See you at school tomorrow?"

"Yeah, man, of course," he says, nodding at me. "See you tomorrow."

I wave goodbye and quickly dart back into my house, my face flush with guilt.

Mom's in the kitchen. "Antoine doing okay?"

I close the back door. "Yeah. He's icing his ankle."

"He mad at you?" she asks.

"A little bit, I think," I say. "I don't know."

"He knows it was an accident." She pushes a mug of steaming tea my way. "Drink that. It'll help your stomach, too."

I sit at the kitchen island and pull the hot mug close. "I kinda expected him not to want to talk to me."

Mom frowns. "You don't *want* him to be mad, do you?"

"No."

"Then don't worry about it."

"What if he gets angrier later?"

"Well, that's his choice," she says, blowing on her mug of tea. "And you can cross that bridge when it arrives."

"But it *could* happen, Mom," I protest, then sip at my tea.

"Maybe. But for now, I think you should take Antoine at his word."

She calls out to Dad, and I focus on my tea. It's this mix Mom makes; it smells pretty bad and doesn't taste all that great, but it works for an upset stomach. When Dad comes into the kitchen, they start doing that thing where I can tell they have something to say to me, but neither of them wants to be the first one.

"What is it?" I ask, setting my mug down on the counter.

"We don't want to put too much pressure on you," Dad says, "but your mom and I were talking and . . . David, do you *really* feel like you don't know who you are?"

I gulp down the immediate stone in my throat. "Uh . . . what?"

"I get why you probably wanted to do the presentation on your own," Dad continues. "But if you were struggling, you also could have asked us."

"Just because you were adopted doesn't mean your life has to feel like a big secret or something," says Mom.

"I know that," I say, but I'm not too confident when I do, so it comes out hesitantly.

Dad tips his head to the side and gives me a sad look. "We know it's probably a challenge at times to not know anything about your adoption."

"Maybe," I say.

Mom frowns. "Do you know if there's something we can do to help you? We had an idea, but I think it's best to hear from you first."

I shrug. "I mean . . . there's not much you can do, right? None of us know."

"Well, we can always do more to help you understand *our* families," Dad says, gesturing to himself and Mom.

"And we say this while acknowledging that most of

our families don't live here on the mainland," adds Mom quickly. "What with my family being mostly in Hawai'i, and your father's spread through Mexico and Brazil, I'm sure that's got to make things feel a little less real, right?"

I raise an eyebrow at her. "Actually . . . yeah. It kinda does feel like that sometimes."

"So, like I said, your father and I had an idea," says Mom. "But we don't want to force this on you. We'd rather come to a decision as a family."

"Okay," I say, another burst of nerves shooting through me.

"We were thinking of starting something called Project David," Mom continues. "Just a little thing we can do to show you a bit more of where your father and I came from so that it *doesn't* feel like a guessing game."

"Project David?" I take another sip of the hot tea. "This isn't going to be like . . . more homework, is it?"

Mom laughs. "No, it's not homework. If anyone has work to do, it'll be me and Dad, since we're the ones who need some time to come up with some fun outings to help show you a bit more about who we are."

"I don't need time," says Dad, grinning. "I already know what we're doing."

Mom rolls her eyes. "It isn't a race, Fernando."

He kisses her on the temple. "But I bet David likes my activity more."

I don't love that they're talking *about* me, not *to* me, but maybe this will be a good thing. "Well . . . okay," I say. "I'm down."

Mom claps her hands together in victory. "Wonderful!" she says. "I promise, you're going to love it. But look, honey, you're only eleven. You have your *whole* life to figure out who you are, so we don't want you feeling like you need to know immediately."

"Exactly," says Dad. "Consider this a first step. We want to make sure you feel supported, okay?"

I nod at them and finish off my tea. After excusing myself, I wander off to my room to lie down before dinner. I do like the idea of Project David, but am I now the type of kid who's a *project*?

I think about Fea. A talking dog. A talking dog who might not be a dog, and who is convinced she can help me fix my life. That should be magical and wonderful, right? It's like every Disney movie come to life!

But doesn't Fea's very presence mean that my life *is* broken?

I bury my head in my pillow and groan. This is way too much for one human brain to think about.

WEDNESDAY, SEPTEMBER 13
8:15 A.M.
Do I even have a normal anymore?

Usually, Antoine and I walk to school together, but today his mom drove him there before she went to work. So I walked there all by myself. It wasn't very far, but summer still hadn't left, and I was sweating by the time I walked up the steps at Mira Monte. *Six classes*, I told myself. *You just have to make it through six classes and you'll be fine.*

But will I? Oh, man, how awkward is practice going to be today?

Once I get to Mr. Bradshaw's, I sit down next to Gracie, and she once again slams her notebook shut when I get close.

"Hi, David," she says.

"Hi," I say back. "What's in your notebook?"

Unfortunately, I don't really hear Gracie's answer (if she even gives one), because I am immediately distracted by something else. There is a high-pitched tweeting sound in Mr. Bradshaw's classroom, and it seems *close*. At first, I assume the birds are going wild in the trees outside, but when Mr. Bradshaw closes the door after the bell rings, it's still just as loud.

Chirp, chirp! Chirp, chirp!

I look around the classroom but don't see a bird.

Until my eyes fall to my desk. There, on the left-hand corner, perches a small brown sparrow with gray flecks.

Who chirps at me.

I glance around at my classmates, but none of them are looking my way. Do they not *see* this magical occurrence? There is a *bird* on my *desk*!

"Focus, David," says Fea's voice.

In my head.

No. No *way*.

"I did tell you I would visit you again," she says.

Who isn't a sort-of-ugly dog anymore. She is a *bird*. She's still got that black collar around her neck with the weird tag, but all of it is smaller.

"Let's go talk," she says.

"So, who's up first today?" says Mr. Bradshaw. He checks his notepad on his desk. "It's day two for presentations, and that means—"

"Daaaaviiiiiiddd," sings Fea, drowning out Mr. Bradshaw. "I'm not just gonna go away."

Fea takes off from my desk and lands on my right shoulder. Panic rips through my body. What is she doing?!

"Okay, David," says Fea, jumping up and down on my shoulder. "If you won't talk to me, I'll have to resort to drastic measures."

I glare at her, then pull a notebook from my backpack. I flip to a blank page and write in block letters:

STOP IT, FEA. I CAN'T TALK TO YOU HERE.

Fea flies back to my desk and hops over to the notebook, looks down at it, then looks back up at me.

"I'm a bird, David," she says. "I can't read."

Does it make me a bad person if I want to squish her with my social studies book? I scoff at Fea, but I do it too loudly because then the other kids in the class are looking at me, as is Mr. Bradshaw. I cover it up with a cough.

"Sorry," I say.

One of the other kids, whose name I don't know, is giving their presentation, but it's impossible to pay attention because of this *bird*.

"David, look at me."

I don't.

"Come on, David. I know you want to."

I really don't.

"Tweet, tweet, tweet, tweet—David, I could actually do this for way longer than you think I possibly could— tweet, tweet, tweet—that's what birds sound like, right?"

I want to yell a million things at her, but I can't. Not right now.

She keeps saying bird sounds as words.

Literally.

"Tweet, tweet, chirp, chirp, warble, warble."

I wait for my opportunity. As everyone claps at the end

of a presentation, I lean down and whisper, "Shut up, Fea."

"Never!" she says. Her voice sounds overjoyed in my head. Fea flies away and lands on Tommy's desk, and she poops on it. Like . . . little poop pellets. Right on his desk.

I stifle a laugh, and when Mr. Bradshaw looks at me, I raise my hand quickly.

"Sorry," I say. "Can I be excused to go to the restroom?"

"No," he says without missing a beat.

"I have to go *really* badly."

Mr. Bradshaw frowns at me. "Class *just* started, David. Why didn't you go before you got here?"

Which is when I see that Tommy has noticed the pellets on his desk.

To my great surprise and horror, he picks one up and then *puts it in his mouth.*

Yeah, I can't be in this class anymore. I'm both grossed out and ready to bust up laughing. "Mr. Bradshaw, I think I will *actually* wet myself if I stay here."

Tommy groans. Is that a response to me or the fact that he just ate bird poop?

(And how was that poop *real*?)

(Also: who just picks up random things on their desk and eats them?)

(Also: what is happening?!)

Mr. Bradshaw finally waves me toward the hall pass. I rush out of my seat.

"Tommy, you're up next," Mr. Bradshaw says.

Tommy is coughing. I can't look at him or I might *actually* pee my pants from laughing, so I run out of class as fast as I can.

Fea—still a sparrow—flies out the door with me. It's even warmer than it was when I walked to school, and the sweat from that journey hasn't even dried yet. I make a beeline to the boys' room while letting loose the laugh I was holding in.

"About time," she says. "Pooping on his desk was the only plan I had, so it's a good thing you actually responded to that one."

I keep walking, though I've got a huge smile on my face. "Okay, you're *really* annoying, Fea," I say, "but that was the funniest thing I've ever seen."

"Finally, he recognizes my humor!" She lands on my shoulder. "Honestly, no one appreciated my jokes when I was alive."

I stop. "Alive?"

"Not important right now," she says.

"I disagree!" I say. "You're *dead*?"

She flies around my head like those birds do whenever someone gets hit really hard in the old cartoons Dad watches. "An inconsequential detail, David. Are you ready for an adventure?"

I slow down as I near the bathroom. "Is this about that whole thing you said about taking me back through my life?" I ask. Then I frown. "Are you going to make me miss school?"

"David, you've got to think bigger," she says, then lands on my shoulder. "I'm sure you have questions, and I can *definitely* answer them all." She pauses. "Okay, maybe half of them. Or a third. Or like . . . four questions total."

I push my way into the bathroom and check that it's empty before hiding in one of the stalls. "Fine," I say. "I'm listening. But you have to make it quick so I can get back to class."

"That doesn't matter, David Bravo," she says, "because I am here to change your life."

WEDNESDAY, SEPTEMBER 13
8:30 A.M.
Fea finally tells me (almost) everything.

"Yeah, I don't know what that means," I say. "What exactly *are* you?"

"Oh, so you're ready to *finally* listen to me?" She flutters off my shoulder and sits on the roll of toilet paper.

"You really are this annoying all the time, aren't you?"

As much as she can while a bird, Fea bows. "And proud of it."

"By the way, I can't start talking to something no one else can see. Why do you always show up at the worst times?"

"I told you, I'm busy hassling other people," she says.

She *did* mention that before. "You're helping other people, too?" I ask.

"Yep. Humans are, as a whole, very prone to making mistakes. Which is where I come in! The technical term is 'non-corporeal timeline guide.' I can take you to any point in your life where *you* made the wrong decision, then put you back in your body for a moment so you can make a different choice. Your life continues on that new timeline, you forget I was ever here, and that's that!"

I stare at her, my mouth open.

"Are you okay, David? You waiting for a bug to land in your mouth for a snack? I can feed you if you want. Fea the Momma Bird to the rescue!"

I close my mouth and make an annoyed face at her. "I'm going to ignore that," I say. "But . . . it's a lot to take in. And I still have questions. Like . . . how can you change what you look like?"

She twists her bird head to the side. "Will you be fine with me just saying that it's all magic?"

"How come no one else can see you?"

"Also magic."

"How can you travel anywhere in an instant?"

"Magic."

"And . . . you being able to take me back in time?"

"M-A-G-I-C," she says. "Honestly, I can't give much of an explanation. The Powers That Be don't really tell us much."

"I'm sorry, the *who?*"

Fea moves her little bird feet quickly, sending the roll of toilet paper spinning beneath her so that it begins bunching up on the floor. "You know, the mysterious beings who run everything. Life, death, everything in between and after. Don't they teach you this stuff?"

"No, I don't know anything about any Power . . . of . . . the Bees?" I say. "This is all new to me!"

"It's the Powers *That* Be."

"What does that *mean?*"

"They're like . . . invisible forces in the world. They just . . . be? They exist, they've always existed, that sort of thing."

"So, these Power of the Bees people—"

"No, David Bravo," says Fea, exasperated. "It's—"

"I know what they're called now, thank you," I say. "But I'm gonna call them the Power of the Bees because . . . well, bees are powerful, you know. Have you had honey before?"

Fea ignores this. "All you need to know is that this is my job in the afterlife, and I've been assigned to you." Then she adds, with a whole lot of sass: "By the Power of the Bees."

I'm going to have to interrogate her on the whole being-dead thing, but I have a bigger question right now. "So . . . what am I supposed to *do?*"

"Don't worry, David Bravo!" Fea says. "You're going to be an easy one."

"How do you know that?"

"Because I've never been assigned a kid to assist before! I'm expecting this to be a cinch."

I am not sure what to say to that. Why does it feel so insulting?

I frown at Fea. "Why are you so certain?" I ask.

"You're eleven," she says. "How many mistakes can you have possibly made in only eleven years?"

"That sounds like a challenge," I say smugly.

"You're going to be difficult, aren't you?" Fea says, and she pecks at my leg.

"Look who's talking!" I shout, and it echoes in the bathroom. "You *literally* broke my mom's favorite vase because I wouldn't pay attention to you!"

"We're not talking about yesterday, David Bravo!" she says in a singsong voice. "Unless we *are*." She flaps her wings and hops on her feet. "Oh, this is my favorite part. Tell me, David. What's your biggest regret? What do you think went wrong in your life that sent you down the wrong path?"

"I don't know," I say. "Everything?"

"Come *on*, David! Think. What's something that happened that you really wish hadn't happened?"

I don't actually have to think back very far. I scrunch up my face as the image of Antoine colliding with me replays in my head.

"Ah-ha!" exclaims Fea. "I recognize that look. You thought of something."

"And it *did* happen yesterday," I say. "I got sick and because of that, I ended up hurting my best friend, Antoine. He didn't make varsity, and I think it might have ruined our friendship."

"And you care about this Antoine."

"He's my best friend in the whole world."

"Hmmm," she says. "It's not common for a mistake to be so recent in an assignment's life. But you know what? *You're* not common, David Bravo."

"Why do you always say my whole name like that?"

"Sounds wonderful, doesn't it?" She chirps at me again. "David Bravo, David Bravo, let's go visit this terrible moment in your life. You ready?"

"Ready?" I shake my head. "Fea, I have to go back to class soon. It's the middle of first period!"

"I told you, don't worry about that," she says. "Time is an illusion."

She lands on my left shoulder.

"What are you doing?"

"I must be in physical contact with an assignment to be able to travel back through their timeline with them," she explains. "Never forget this, David Bravo. It's very important."

Then, without any warning, she screams, "Here we go!"

Something . . . happens. There's this weird feeling, deep in my stomach, like someone is pulling on me from inside it. It kind of tickles, to be honest.

Then it's like my whole body is yanked into the toilet I'm sitting on. Lights rush by me, and I can't make out what they are because I think I've been folded in a thousand different places. I'm screaming—I'm sure of that—while Fea is letting out a long peal of joy.

"Wheeeeeeeeeeeee!"

And right as I think I can't take this any longer, I hit something—hard. But I'm standing upright and it's bright out and—

Wait.

Wait.

I'm on the field in the middle of the track. There are a bunch of other kids around, stretching and warming up and—

I gasp.

"Welcome, David Bravo," says Fea. "We are now in your past!"

TUESDAY, SEPTEMBER 12 (AGAIN!!!)
2:41 P.M.

Something is fluttering in front of my face. I swat at it instinctively, and Fea cries out.

"Hey! Watch it!"

A monarch butterfly—bright orange and black—lands on my hand.

She's . . . she's a butterfly now.

I'm distracted by the sight of Fea's new form, but only until I hear something familiar.

Antoine's voice.

"You okay?"

Just to my left, sitting about ten feet from me, is Antoine. Sitting across from *me*.

"I'll be fine," Past Me says. "Just nervous."

Past Me doesn't look nervous. Past Me looks *sick*.

"How?" I say to Fea. "How are we here, Fea? Is that *me*? Is this the past?"

"Catch up, David Bravo," she says, and she launches off

my hand, and it even *tickles* a little. "Because you're about to make a new choice."

I am not exaggerating when I say that everything freezes. I don't mean like that feeling I get when I can't make a decision. The entire world around me is frozen: Past Me and Past Antoine are locked in conversation. Phuong is stretching forward, unmoving. Jorge is actually stuck in midair while jumping up and down to warm up his legs. I approach myself and . . . This is weird. *Too* weird.

"Fea," I say hesitantly, "did *you* do this?"

"Yep. This is me. I can manipulate time in service of my mission. So I've frozen things here so you can choose differently."

"Choose differently?" I whirl to face her. "What does that mean?"

"Once you're ready, David, I will put you back into your body." She flutters past me and lands on Past Me, who still looks like he's about to throw up everywhere. Which he is—I mean *I* am—going to do. Could I choose *not* to puke?

"So, I would like to not walk out onto the track and trip Antoine," I say to her. "That way, he won't get hurt, and we'll definitely still be friends."

"Perfect logic," she says. "Then choose differently, David Bravo, because you only live once!"

That tugging feeling happens again, but this time, I'm being pulled toward Past Me, and then there's a POP! sound and then I'm . . . sitting. In front of Antoine.

"Me too," he says.

Oh.

Fea wasn't lying. I'm now in my own body . . . but in the past.

This is actually happening!

I turn in anticipation of what I know comes next: Mr. Harris jogs over to the team, complete with his coach's outfit and clipboard. This is so weird! I know everything that's going to happen!

"You all stretched, son?" asks Mr. Harris, then he nods at me. "Hey, David!"

Like he did before, he looks me up and down. "You okay, buddy? You look a little gray."

"He's just nervous, Pop," says Antoine, patting me on the arm. "He'll do great."

But I am *not*. And I *won't*. This is it: I can do something different! I just . . . won't leave this spot, and then I won't hurt my best friend.

"Well, don't let it be infectious, Antoine," says Mr. Harris.

I don't move. But as everything else unfolds exactly as it did before, there's a new, growing terror inside me. I can't mess this up again. Antoine leaves with his dad to go do some last-minute stretches, and I sit there, the ground swaying, my stomach bucking like that bull I saw at the rodeo Dad took me to a few years ago. I just have to . . . make a new choice. That's easy, right?

But what if it's the wrong choice?

What if I hurt him again?

What if by staying here, I make something *else* happen?

Oh, no. Something is wrong. *Very* wrong. Despite the fact that I know not to move from this spot, I am standing up, wobbling from side-to-side, then putting one foot in front of the other. Why does it feel like someone or something else is controlling my body? I'm stumbling, ignoring whoever calls out my name, and I still can't stop. I can't seem to choose differently. What's happening to me?

I step onto the track, knowing full well what's about to happen.

Go back! I tell myself. *Stop this!*

But I don't, and moments later, it all repeats just as it did before: Antoine's eyes go wide, he tries to pass around me right as I do the same, and then we're both on the ground, Antoine is groaning in pain, and I can feel the spinach coming up and—

The tugging sensation rips me away from my body and I cough as I double over, a few feet away from Past Me and Past Antoine.

"David Bravo," says Fea, landing on the grass in front of me. "You were supposed to do something different."

I look at Past Me and see that Fea froze me about one whole second before I puke everywhere. Wow, I look awful.

"I couldn't decide," I say. "I thought I was going to make another wrong choice!"

"Another one?" says Fea. "David, you have to try *something.*"

"Okay, okay," I say. "Maybe I'm overthinking it. I should

just tell Antoine not to run that race or something."

"I'm not convinced this is your big Wrong Moment," says Fea. "Just humor me and do something different here, David Bravo. *Any* choice at this point will be better than nothing at all."

She flutters up and over to Past Me bent at the waist and ready to hurl.

"Better than this," she says. "You ready?"

I nod at her.

"Off you go!"

And then I'm being pulled and folded back through time, until I'm sitting across from Antoine. "You okay?" he asks.

Oh, my god, it's happening *again*.

TUESDAY, SEPTEMBER 12, FOR THE THIRD (AND FOURTH) (AND FIFTH) TIME
2:42 P.M.

"No!" I blurt out. "No, I'm not okay. I still feel sick."

"I'm sorry," says Antoine, and he reaches over and pats my shoulder. "Don't run, then. It isn't necessary."

When his dad comes over, he comments about me looking gray, and this time, I agree with him. I say that I'm not going to run.

"Well," he says. "Let's go stretch, Antoine. Hope you feel better, David."

They both leave and . . .

That's it.

I did it! I made a choice!

I still feel queasy as I sit there on the ground, and I clutch my stomach. *Okay, Fea,* I think. *Snap me back to my body! I really don't want to relive getting sick again.*

"Uh, Fea, you can get me now," I say out loud.

"Who are you talking to?" asks Geoff, slipping his running shoes on. (He ties them, but I'm not sure what the point is. They'll come untied anyway.)

I raise my eyebrows at him. "Um . . . just . . . no one?"

He frowns.

"Myself?"

Geoff nods at that. "Cool."

I shake my head, anticipating the tugging in my abdomen any second now.

I wait. The rest of the team gathers at the starting line on the track. Coach Williams blows his whistle, and a short burst of nerves flares in me. But I'm sitting down! Everything's going to be fine.

Antoine rounds the track, leading the group.

"Come on, Fea," I mutter. "What gives?"

Raymond, one of the other varsity boys, briefly pulls ahead of Antoine, and then—

"No!" I cry out.

Antoine clips the back of Raymond's left foot, and then he tumbles down, rolling over a couple of times, already clutching his ankle, his head thrown back in pain.

"How is that possible?" I scream.

The tug hits me, and everything on the track finally freezes. Suddenly, there's a small black dog with a tuft of fur on her head in front of me.

Fea.

"Yeah, I don't think this is going to work," she says, licking her paw. "I'm pretty sure that this *isn't* what the Powers That Be meant for you to change."

"How could it stay the same?" I say sharply. "I chose

differently! Let me try again."

Fea twists her head to the side. "Wow, I didn't expect that kind of go-get-'em attitude from Mr. Indecisive."

"I can change this," I say. "I promise!"

"Be my guest," says Fea, and she yawns loudly.

I'm pulled back in time again, away from Fea and into my own past, and I'm breathless when I arrive at the exact moment that Antoine asks if I'm okay.

I totally am, by the way. I got this!

. . .

I find out the hard way that I really, really don't got this.

The first time, I try to convince Antoine not to run at all by telling him that I've heard someone on the team is going to trip him. He thinks I'm committed to some sort of comedy routine, so he leaves me there on the field, laughing as he does.

He trips on Raymond again.

The second time, I attempt a different technique. "Maybe you should let someone else win," I say. "Fake them out. Give them confidence they can beat you, and then *destroy* them during the actual race."

Antoine twists his face up at that. "But . . . they're my teammates. I want them to do better, too."

"Right, but—"

Once again, he trips on Raymond and sprains his ankle.

The third time, as Antoine jogs away from me to stretch with his dad, I chase after him and tackle him. "No, you *can't* run!" I yell as we tumble to the ground.

Antoine lets out a pained yelp and clutches at his ankle while I fall to the side.

"Are you *serious*?" I say. "Fea!"

She appears as the xolo dog, freezing the scene as she does. "You rang?"

"Okay, I get it. I can't change this."

"Your powers of deduction are *astounding*," she says.

"And your powers of *annoyance* are, too."

"David, need I remind you that this is all about *your* choices. I get why you tried to change Antoine's mind, but this isn't about him. It's about *you*. You have to change one of *your* choices, okay?"

"I guess," I say. "This just seems really hard."

"It can be," says Fea. "But that's why you've got a non-corporeal timeline guide. Ready for one last bit of travel today?"

"Uh, not really," I say.

Clearly, I don't get a say, because a second later, I feel the tugging inside, and then I'm folding over, yanked away through time, with Fea traveling alongside me. *Whistling.*

I really, really hate her.

WEDNESDAY, SEPTEMBER 13
8:40 A.M.
A "smooth" landing in the present

A moment later, my butt slams into the hard seat of the toilet in the boys' room.

"Fea!" I say. "Seriously, couldn't you put me down somewhere more comfortable?"

"Isn't this where we left from?" she says. I don't see her at first. Then I spot her—back in the sparrow form—on the roll of toilet paper. "And you'll be happy to know that it's only been a few minutes since we left."

"Huh?" I pull out my cell phone and power it on—we're supposed to have them off all day unless there's an emergency—and sure enough, she's right. It's September 13, and I've been gone maybe ten minutes.

"That's . . . wow," I say. "I can't believe it."

"Well, believe it, David Bravo," says Fea. "You just traveled through time."

"So, you can travel anywhere in time?" I ask.

"Well," she says. "Not exactly. The Powers That Be allow me to transport myself and my assignment to any point in *their* past. But I can't just time travel all willy-nilly! It's for a purpose. And I've never been allowed to travel to the future." Her voice drops in volume. "The future is unwritten, David Bravo. That's *always* up to you."

I squint at Fea. "What's that thing around your neck?"

Fea twitches her tiny bird head. "This necklace, you mean?"

I nod, then peer closer at it, noticing that there's a charm attached to it. Most of it is green, but one part is red. "Why is it a sideways eight?"

"That's not an eight!" She takes flight again. "Hold out your hand."

I do as I'm told, and she lands on it.

"It's the infinity symbol. Do you know what infinity is?"

"Something like . . . forever?"

"Yes. And also no. It's everything."

"Everything."

"All time past and present and future, all possible numbers, all possible timelines."

She practically sings the last word. I still don't really get it.

"So, why is it red and green like that?" I say.

"Progress, David Bravo."

"Progress?"

"Mine, to be exact," Fea explains. "When this little thing fills all the way up with green, I'll be done being a non-corporeal timeline guide."

"And then what happens?"

"Your guess is as good as mine," she answers. "All I know is I'm *mostly* done now. So, again: I need you to think about your life, David Bravo. When did things go offtrack for you? What do you suspect is the pivotal moment when you could choose differently?"

"I told you, I—"

"Nope," she says, and jumps off my hand. "Not the race. Go back to class. Really *think* on it. That might be hard for you, what with your being eleven and all. But fear not! I believe in you!"

I'm not so sure about that. She doesn't know a thing about me aside from what she's overheard or seen in the last day. How can she believe in me already?

"When will—?" I begin, but . . . she's gone. She popped out of existence!

I leave the stall and wash my hands out of habit, then head back to Mr. Bradshaw's, my head spinning. I pass Samrat in the hallway, and he waves at me, but before I can wave back, he darts for the bathroom like he's going to pee his pants any second. Mr. Bradshaw doesn't say anything as I take my seat. Gracie glances at me, but this time, she doesn't close her notebook. I manage a quick look, and it seems like she's been doodling in the margins of her notes.

As I try to think of what else I could possibly change in my past, I find myself staring at Tommy. He's moving his tongue around his mouth, and he's got a disgusted expression on his face.

I can't help but smile at that.

WEDNESDAY, SEPTEMBER 13
3:49 P.M.

Cross-country practice is pretty awful that afternoon, but I guess it could be worse? Antoine seemed excited to see me, and I asked Coach Williams if I could sit with Antoine to keep him company.

"Are you feeling sick again, David?" he asked.

"Well . . . no."

"Then you run."

Antoine gives me a look that's somewhere between supportive and sad. "It's okay," he says. "I'll watch from the stands."

We have speed work that day, which means that instead of having us run longer distances, Coach Williams makes us do repetitive sets of sprints. I am *not* good at sprinting, which is weird because you'd think that if I wasn't that great at long-distance running, I'd somehow be better at drastically shorter distances. But no! I'm somehow worse! My lungs feel like they're about to explode by the time I finish my fourth 400-meter sprint. Sprinting the length of a *whole* lap? Who allowed such a thing?

After practice, I rush out of the locker room to see how Antoine is getting home, but I'm too late. Mr. Harris's truck is already pulling away from the parking lot, so I start my walk home. It's not far, but by the time I make it through my front door, I'm covered in sweat. You know what's a scam? Showering and then being covered in sweat again ten minutes later. I plop on the cold tile in the entryway, breathing heavily.

"Nope, not today," says Mom, standing over me. "Get up, David. We're not doing this again."

"Doing what?" I say.

"There will be no footbridges built over your body. Sorry to disappoint you."

I push myself up. "I'm actually just hot," I say. "This floor is like a glacier."

She laughs and walks toward the kitchen. "Follow me. I'll turn the AC on and get you some ice cream."

That gets my attention. "Ice cream? But it's not even dinnertime!"

"You've earned it!" Mom calls out.

One delicious ice cream sandwich later, I've finally stopped sweating, and Mom's doing that thing where she's pacing back and forth in the kitchen. I twist to face her from the dining room table.

"Okay, what is it?" I say. "You want to say something, don't you?"

Mom stops and sighs. "Sometimes I forget how perceptive

you are," she says. "Well, your father has graciously decided that he wants to go first, so he's got somewhere to take you this Friday after you're out of school."

"Where?" I ask, my heart pattering in my chest.

"He won't actually tell me," she says, frowning. "He's taking this Project David thing very seriously."

"That sounds like Dad. I just hope it's fun."

"I'm sure he'll do his best." She pauses, then looks me in the eye. "He really cares about this, David. So maybe go in with an open mind, okay?"

"Sure," I say. "I'll do my best."

"And you promise to give whatever he has planned a try?"

"Um, why would I *not*?"

"I don't know," she says. "Sometimes, you freeze up a little bit when you're in new situations. I just want to make sure you're comfortable."

"It'll be fun," I say, but then I can't help but think of how I froze up this morning when Fea first took me back in time. What if that happens again?

What am I supposed to choose, anyway? I don't feel like anything went that badly before this year. I mean . . . maybe I could revisit that moment when Ms. Gull, the substitute, asked me about being a mystery. But . . . is that really my Wrong Moment, as Fea called it? Is there something I've forgotten?

I go to my room to do some of my homework, but I don't really have the motivation. This doesn't make sense.

I couldn't even stop Antoine from getting hurt. And now I'm supposed to put my whole life back on track? Is it even *on* the wrong track?

I'm full of doubt. None of this feels right.

After struggling through my homework, I wander into my backyard before Dad gets home and starts making dinner. I peek over the fence, and sure enough, Antoine is out with his injured leg propped up in a chair.

"Feel any better?" I call out.

He looks up at me. "A little," he says. "Mom says I might be able to use it by the weekend."

"That's good," I say.

"It's kinda nice to have a break, though. You know, from running and stuff."

I think about the face he made at practice, and I'm pretty sure he *misses* it. "Yeah, but you *love* running, Antoine."

He smiles, but it doesn't fill his whole face like it usually does. "Yeah, I do," he says quietly. "But it's okay. I have more time to read some of the books I've been ignoring."

I quickly change the subject once the guilt starts gnawing at me again. "Well, if you're not practicing this weekend, do you want to hang out? We could go to the park. Or I could come over and we can play Xbox or something."

"What about Friday?"

"My dad is taking me somewhere," I say.

"Fancy," he says. "You leaving right after school?"

I nod. "Apparently. Supposed to be some sort of adventure."

"Unfair," he says. "You're leaving me here all injured while you go on an adventure? What kind of friend *are* you, David?"

He's practically laughing when he says this, but there's still a sharp, sinking sensation in my chest.

"Sorry," I say. "I really didn't mean to hurt you."

Antoine dismisses me with a wave and swings his leg off the chair it was resting on. "I promise you, it's okay," he says. "I was just joking! Where are you going with your dad?"

I tell Antoine about the whole Project David thing while he slowly limps over to the fence with his crutches. By the time he gets to me, he's sweating.

"I wish I could go with you," he says. "I bet it's going to be fun!"

"Yeah, probably."

I say it softly, because it's dawning on me: It *would* be fun to have Antoine there. But he couldn't come even if I convinced mine *and* his parents. He's hurt.

And it was my fault.

Antoine tells me he's taking a break from icing his ankle to go help his mom with dinner, and my chest still aches as

I watch him hobble away from me. I did that. All because I ate that horrible spinach!

Wait.

That was a decision I made. One I made despite a warning from Norma!

Ha! Fea is wrong. There is something I can change about that day!

I head back into the house with my mind made up. All I have to do is tell Fea, and this whole disaster will be fixed!

WEDNESDAY, SEPTEMBER 13
7:15 P.M.

After this epiphany, I discover something.

I can't really *summon* Fea.

After Dad comes home, I help him prepare dinner. He's tired from work, but he insists on making his rolled tacos, which always come out perfectly crispy. He stuffs them with shredded chicken—which *I* shredded, thank you very much—and then tops them with lettuce, crema, guacamole, and this amazing red-hot sauce he keeps in a plastic container in the back of the fridge.

The whole time, I'm trying to get Fea to show up.

I mostly stick to nonverbal requests. If she can communicate with me telepathically, maybe that's how I reach her! So when I pass Dad the bowl of shredded chicken, I think:

Now would be a great time for you to show up, Fea! I'm not busy, and I could sneak off and talk to her.

She doesn't show.

I then worry all through dinner that she'll appear and ruin things, but it's silent on that front. Dinner is fine, even though I'm distracted. Mom keeps trying to get Dad to tell her what it is we're doing Friday afternoon. "It's for research purposes," she says.

"You mean you want to know if *your* day is going to be better," Dad shoots back.

"Oh, I *know* David and I are going to have the best time," Mom says confidently. "I believe David will appreciate my interpretation of the assignment."

"Now who's the competitive one?" Dad asks. Mom sticks her tongue out at him.

"You know this means that *I* get to be the winner," I say, pointing a half-eaten rolled taco at Dad. "No matter what happens."

"Cheater," Dad says to me, then winks.

Later, after brushing my teeth and washing my face, I sit on my bed and try the spoken approach. I ask Fea to show up as soon as she can. "You can make fun of me for five whole minutes!" I offer. "About anything. I don't care."

But the rest of the night is silent and uneventful. And somehow, that's now a *bad* thing.

. . .

The next morning, when Fea doesn't interrupt a single one of my classes, I start to wonder if I've imagined everything. Maybe I've just been talking to the air! Or my life is one of those plot twists where it's all been a dream! Because it certainly feels that way.

That's what I'm thinking about when I cross under the sycamore tree in the middle of campus and something drops right in front of my face.

I make a sound when it happens. It's something close to the cry a dying animal would make. I am, *of course*, not alone, because this is a fully functional school, something that seems lost on Fea. Other students stop to watch as I scream at absolutely nothing, because none of them can see what I can:

A giant sloth hanging from one of the low tree branches.

"David Bravo, it's been ages since I last saw you," says Fea.

I turn around in a panic and make direct eye contact with Gracie, who had been walking behind me.

"Hi, David," she says, a single eyebrow raised in concern. "You okay?"

I glance over at the low-hanging branch on the syca-more. The sloth is still there. Correction: Fea *as* a sloth is still there.

I quickly run a hand over my face.

"Spiderweb!" I explain. "I walked right into one."

Gracie nods. "That's the worst."

I know I should say something else, but I can *hear* Fea breathing.

"Well . . . I'll see you in the cafeteria?" Gracie says.

"Yes!" I say, too quickly. "Yes, in the food . . . place."

I can see Fea moving out of the corner of my eye. Why is she doing this to me?

"The . . . food place," says Gracie. "Uh . . . sure."

"Why don't you sit with my friend Antoine?" I say, guiding her toward the cafeteria. "He's usually in the back corner."

"Aren't you coming?" she asks.

My eyes go wide, and Fea yawns loudly behind me.

Oh, no, she's preparing to ruin everything, isn't she?

"I am," I say. "I just . . . have to use the bathroom first."

"Okay," she says, and she stares at me with a confused look on her face.

She finally turns and leaves. Once she's out of earshot, I turn back to the sloth, only to discover that Fea has now dropped to the ground and is slowly turning her head up to look at me.

"I don't like you," I tell her quietly. "Not even a little bit."

"I'm absolutely your favorite," she says. "Who else entertains you like I do?"

I kneel and pretend to tie my shoe. "You think this is *entertaining*? I'm not exactly popular here, Fea. You popping out of trees and making me freak out isn't going to help me."

"Well, if only you weren't taking *forever* to come up with an idea so that I can actually help you, maybe I wouldn't have to do this."

"Forever?"

"That's why I'm a sloth today," she says. "Because you're so slooooooowwwwwww."

I angrily retie the shoe I just untied. "Fea, it's been *one day* since I last saw you."

"Has it?"

"Yes!" I say. "Didn't you hear me calling out for you yesterday?"

"Calling out? To *me*?"

"Ugh, why are you like this? Yes, Fea. I know what I need to change, and I was trying to get your attention all night!"

"I can't believe it," she says.

She then slowly—oh, my god, she is SO SLOW—raises her left arm, and I figure out she's pretending to look at a watch. Which she doesn't have!

"I experience time differently than you do, David," she says. "Since I last saw you, I have helped approximately . . . one hundred and eight other humans."

My mouth drops open. "That's a lot. How?"

"I can travel the timestream to any point in the past. So sometimes, I'm actually in a hundred and eight places at once."

"Still don't get it," I say. "But can you possibly change into something faster? I can't stand around here talking to empty air."

Fea leans back into a sitting position—slower than a snail—and starts to raise both her arms.

"What—what are you doing?" I ask her.

She keeps raising her sloth arms.

"Am I supposed to pick you up? Is that what that means?"

She starts moving her arms closer together.

"Oh. Okay. No? No picking up?"

Closer.

"Are you ignoring me because it's funny?"

Her sloth paws come together, and that's when I realize what she's doing.

Thankfully, there's no one else around when I groan loudly. "Are you *clapping*?"

"Congrats, David," she says. "You figured out what you want to change! I'm just celebrating that!"

"I'm done," I say, and I start walking away.

A small brown lizard darts in front of me, its skinny tail curved up behind it.

"All right, all right," says Fea. "Fine. Walk and talk with me, David Bravo."

So I head toward the cafeteria as I tell Fea my theory. It's pretty simple: everything went wrong when I chose to eat the spinach. *That* is what set me on my path to ruin!

"All you have to do is take me back to lunch on that specific day," I say. My heart is racing with excitement. "It'll work. I promise."

Fea—still in lizard form—crawls up my leg, which tickles. I yelp again just as I'm about to open the cafeteria doors.

"Always so dramatic, David," she says, and then she settles on my shoulder.

"Why can't you just be *normal*?"

"What's normal to someone like me?" Fea asks.

I hesitate at the cafeteria door. "That's a good point."

"Anyway, my answer is no," she says.

I go to yank the door open, then freeze. "I'm sorry, *what?*"

"Yeah, I'm not doing that."

I try to turn and look at Fea, but . . . Well, you try to dramatically turn on someone when they're sitting on your shoulder! I must look like I'm just spinning in place, and Fea laughs at me.

"You are *special,*" she says. "But I'm serious. You really have to think bigger, David! You're still focusing on someone else, not yourself. What can David change about *his* life?"

"That's what I'm trying to do!" I snap.

Fea huffs loudly on my shoulder. "David, earlier today, I helped a woman who hadn't spoken to her mother in twenty years over a petty argument," she says. "I've helped people who dropped out of school. Who quit jobs. Who never confronted people who hurt them. *That* is the kind of regret I'm talking about when I ask you to think bigger."

Fea jumps off my shoulder and turns into a sparrow. "I just need you to take this seriously, okay?"

I frown. "I am taking this seriously, Fea. Things have been odd between me and Antoine ever since that day. It *has* to be the Wrong Moment."

"Maybe, but I think there's something else in your life that's . . . bigger."

She flutters around my head a few times. "This is your

only life, David Bravo," she says in a singsong voice. "You only live it once. So think big, bigger, biggest!"

Fea flies off toward the sycamore tree, disappearing before she reaches it, and that's when the bell rings and kids come pouring out the door in front of me. Great! I'll probably barely catch Antoine as he's leaving. I rush inside, pushing past the other students trying to get out.

But when I get to our table in the back, only Gracie is there. She's sketching something in her notebook, and half the food on her tray is eaten. She looks up at me.

"Hey, there you are," says Gracie. "Where were you?"

I ignore her question. "Where's Antoine?"

One side of her mouth curls. "He already left. He told me to tell you hi."

I want to scream. Once again, Fea just made things worse. Why couldn't she at least let me *try* changing my past?

"Ah, okay," I say. "I'm gonna go get some food."

"Sure," Gracie says, then focuses on her notebook again.

I head to the now-empty line for food, but the truth is that I've completely lost my appetite.

FRIDAY, SEPTEMBER 15
3:48 P.M.

At least on Friday I have something to look forward to. Dad reminds me in the morning that he'll be leaving the jobsite early so he can pick me up after cross-country practice.

"Make sure you shower," he says. "Because where we're going . . . it's *fancy*."

"How fancy?" I ask, crinkling up my eyebrows.

He gently hits my shoulder with the side of his fist. "I'm just playing with you," he says. "Though I will have something special you'll need to wear."

I'm completely perplexed. Where on earth is he going to take me?

I let this distract me all day because—if I'm being totally honest with you—I need it. It becomes dangerously hard to pay attention in my classes because I can't stop thinking about Fea, timelines, and Antoine. Fea's given me a lot to ponder. The other people she's helped had such big problems and regrets. But do I have anything to compare to that kinda stuff? It makes me feel a lot smaller and younger than

I am because . . . well, I'm *eleven*. What is so bad in my life that these Power of the Bees (or whatever they're called) felt they had to send Fea to me to repair everything?

There has to be something. I think about the kid who bullied me for maybe a week in fourth grade—his name was Robert. He thought my haircut was "stupid" and kept asking if I did it myself. It was a simple fade like every other kid at school had, and after I told him that his face looked like a pothole, he left me alone.

So that can't be it.

Trying to figure this out makes my head hurt.

Practice is remarkably easy that afternoon, and I can tell that Coach Williams doesn't really have his heart in it. I keep seeing him glance over at the stands, where Antoine is sitting with his leg propped up while he reads.

Coach is still upset about Antoine being hurt, isn't he?

Even though Coach Williams probably has no idea I noticed what he was doing, it stings a little. So I'm thankful when he dismisses us after just three miles, telling us to go stretch and shower. "Our first real meet is coming up next week, so no slacking after this weekend!" he calls out.

I run off with a quick wave to Antoine and take what must be the quickest shower *ever*. I don't want to make Dad wait, plus I start realizing how hungry I am about halfway through my shower. After putting on a clean change of clothes, my phone buzzes in my locker.

Ah, Dad's here!

Okay, maybe I'm a little *too* excited about this. I don't

even know where he's taking me.

Breathe, I tell myself as I exit the locker room. *You'll find out soon enough. No need to get yourself all worked up.*

When I climb into Dad's pickup truck, the cargo bed is actually empty for once. Dad usually fills it with his enormous red toolbox and whatever else he needs on his jobs, but today, it's totally cleaned out. "Wow," I say as I climb in. "The back of your truck is basically naked."

"Ha, ha," he says, then pulls me over and kisses the top of my head.

"So, where are we going?" I ask, and the truck lurches to life. "Or are you keeping it a secret the whole time?"

Dad keeps his hands on the steering wheel and his eyes focused on the turn out of the parking lot.

"Dad?"

"Hmmm?" he says, snapping out of a daydream or something.

"Did you hear what I said?"

"I don't know," he says. "I thought I heard a small voice asking me to spoil the surprise I worked on all week, but . . . you know, I'm just not sure."

I roll my eyes. "You are being *very* dramatic."

"This is worth the drama," he says. "I wanted to do something that might help you deal with this question of who you are."

"Like what?"

"You'll see," he says, smirking like he's about to pull a prank on me.

We drive for nearly twenty minutes before Dad pulls into a long strip mall, the kind where all the single-story shops stretch over a single block. I think we've been over here before, and I recognize the panaderia that we get breakfast at some Saturday mornings when Dad isn't working.

"Getting pan dulce, are we?" I ask. "I'm okay with this. Fill me up on sugar and pan, please."

He laughs. "No, David, we're not."

We pull up in front of a brightly lit building, one I've seen from the road but have never been inside.

INLAND EMPIRE BOWL.

I make a face at the sign. "Dad, is this where *bowls* are made? I don't know if I'm any good at that."

He looks at me with utter delight. "I love that that isn't even a joke," he says.

"I'm confused."

"David, your father has had a secret all these years, and I'm going to show you what I do in my free time."

"You make bowls?" I say. "Like the ones we have at home?"

"Bless your heart, David." He gets out of the truck, and I follow suit, but then he reaches into the back seat to pull out a dark blue shirt with a black collar, which he puts on over his white tee. He buttons it up, then grabs a leather bag I've never seen before. "Let's head inside!"

He locks the truck and comes over to me and grabs my hand. Truthfully, it makes me a little nervous. I have no idea what is about to happen, and I really don't like not knowing what's in my future. Dad seems so certain I'm going to like whatever is beyond the doors of this place, but . . . it's bowls, right? Does he seriously think I like making *bowls*?

I do feel pretty silly once we head inside the noisy building and I realize what "bowl" meant on the sign.

Bowling.

It's a *bowling* alley.

I've never been to one before, but as I look up at my dad, it's clear he's in the greatest place in the world. His eyes are wide open, and there's a huge smile on his face. It's almost like I'm not even there next to him.

"Welcome to heaven," says Dad. "This is *my* happy place."

He walks me over to a counter, where a teenage boy asks me what size shoe I wear. He gives me these leather shoes that look super old and worn, and the bottom of them is perfectly smooth, almost like dress shoes. "Why do I need these?" I ask. "I already have shoes on."

"Well, the floor here is made of a specific material for bowling," says Dad, "and we don't want to damage it. So you can't wear normal shoes when you're bowling."

"I don't know how to bowl, Dad," I say, but it doesn't faze him. He takes me over to a lane at the far end of the building, and I watch as bowling balls are flung down the shiny lanes at the white pins. Aren't bowling balls heavy? How are these people *doing* that?

Dad helps me pick a ball that's right for my size, and

I end up with a sparkly red one. Yet after I get my shoes on and get comfortable standing in them—they're a little slippery on the tile—how pretty the ball is doesn't matter because oh, my *god*, it's so heavy! I have to hold it in two hands, and my fingers barely reach to fit in the three holes.

"This is where I come to blow off some steam when I'm stressed out," he tells me while stretching his arms and shoulders. "I'll rent a lane for a couple hours and just bowl over and over, and it honestly calms me down."

"I don't get it, though," I say. "Why *bowling*? What does this have to do with Project David?"

Dad stretches his arms as he looks at me. "Your identity is part choice and part heritage. My heritage *is* important because it informs who I am. But at the same time, your heritage can be a little hard to define."

"Meaning what?"

"Well, take our last name, for example," says Dad. "We're Bravos. But while we've inherited *my* father's name, he wasn't in my life when I was a kid. I grew up in Texas. My mom was Mexican, all the kids around me were Mexican or Guatemalan, and I considered myself Mexican. Technically, though, I'm Brazilian, too. But I've always felt weird about calling myself that because it wasn't really part of my life, you know?"

I nod at him. "Yeah, that does seem confusing."

"This part, however?" He gestures to the loud, shiny lanes. "This is the part that's about choice. I love what bowling has done for me and my life, and I get to *choose* for this to be a huge element of who I am. Because at the end of the day, I still get a say in who I can be."

He grins widely. "But no more theorizing! Let's get you bowling."

"Okay," I say, still nervous about this. I watch as Dad bowls a few frames, and he flings the ball so smoothly down the lane! He only misses hitting all ten pins *once*. It's just one strike after another. (I do know one thing about bowling.) Numbers appear on a small TV screen above our heads and the math makes no sense, but Dad says not to worry about that yet.

"I'll teach you the rules eventually, but right now, I just want to focus on getting you comfortable."

Oh, I'm not comfortable at *all*. Dad has me stand at the end of the lane, and I've got the bowling ball clutched to my chest like it'll break if I let it touch anything else.

"You've got to relax, David."

"Dad, I'm basically carrying a giant rock," I say. "I don't want to drop it."

"You're not going to drop it, David."

"What if my hands get sweaty and it slips out?"

His eyes light up. "Actually, there's something here to help with that!" He holds his hands out, and I quickly give him the ball. Then he guides me to the end of the automatic ball return that sits between the lanes. "These all have a little vent so you can dry your hands," he says.

Dad has me come back to the end of the lane after I do so. I take the ball back, and it's still just as heavy, but not as slippery. Dad tells me that I can crouch and roll the ball with two hands to start with.

Well, that's easy!

Because of that, I get a *little* too confident the next round. I decide to hold the ball in *one* hand.

I look over at the lane next to us, where a Black woman is holding her ball in front of her. She takes a couple steps forward while swinging the ball back in her right hand, and then she sends it flying down the lane. Tens pins go down, and I think I can do that.

I mimic her as she bowls again, holding the ball in front of me like she does.

"Eyes on your own lane, David," says Dad. "You don't want to be distracted by anyone else. Just focus on your own bowl."

I stare ahead.

I take one step.

Two.

My left foot goes forward as I swing the ball back, and that's when I make my mistake. Because I cross my foot *over* my body, and when I throw the ball, it smashes right into my left ankle.

I don't even really experience the fall because it happens so fast. One moment, I'm upright, and the next, I'm looking at the ceiling, and my foot hurts, and this is the worst thing that's ever happened.

A face appears above me. It's Dad.

"David, are you okay?"

His mouth is open in shock. I can't blame him. Like . . . who bowls into their own leg?

"I'm okay," I say. "I think."

"Come on, David," he says, dropping his hand and reaching toward me.

"No, the floor is much better. I can't ever show my face here again."

"I don't even think anyone saw you."

I push myself up, and I'm actually surprised to see that the woman in the next lane really *isn't* looking at me. No one is.

Dad helps me up and rubs my foot to see if it's hurt. It's not that bad; I don't think I actually injured myself.

"How about this?" Dad says, crouched in front of me. "I'll bowl some more frames to show you the correct form so you don't make that mistake again."

"Sure, Dad," I say, but my heart isn't in it anymore. I give it a few more attempts when Dad pushes me to. I never hit more than four pins. It's true that I don't bowl into my own leg again, but I don't think I'm ever going to be a professional bowler. Dad seems completely pleased as he drives us home for dinner, but . . . I don't know that this helped. I can choose who to be, but I have no idea *what* to choose.

It feels like that's what everyone's waiting for: me to decide *something*.

I just wish someone would come and give me the answer.

MONDAY, SEPTEMBER 18
8:59 A.M.

By the time Monday morning rolled around, it was like I'd slept in a bog all night. I've never *been* to a bog, but I imagine they make your skin feel sticky and gross, and it's gotta be hard to sleep in one because . . . well, it's a *bog*.

I didn't get to hang out with Antoine once. I certainly tried, but his ankle started to feel better. Which is great! But that also meant that his dad started to give him modified workouts. He *really* wants Antoine to get his timed run in to qualify for varsity as soon as possible. So on Saturday morning, they did a twenty-mile bike ride. Sunday, Antoine was across town at the Poly High School track, which was one of those fancy all-weather ones that makes it feel like you're bouncing as you run.

I should be happy for my best friend. But I also miss him. I know he's been busy with practice, but what if he *also* doesn't want to see me? Things are still weird between us, so it's possible, right?

I do my best to pay attention in Mr. Bradshaw's class,

but it's hard to when Tommy and Walter keep turning around and looking at me. I can't hear what they're whispering, which only makes it worse. Mr. Bradshaw's trying to tell us what citizenship laws are, but none of the words are sticking in my brain.

Suddenly, Tommy's hand shoots up. "Is David even a citizen, Mr. Bradshaw?"

Mr. Bradshaw frowns at him. "Please don't be rude, Tommy."

"I'm *just* asking a question," he says. "Can I not ask a question?"

Of course, we all know that's not what he's doing. I see Wunmi roll her eyes, and Gracie fake vomits when I look at her.

"Questions are always welcome in this class, Tommy," says Mr. Bradshaw, "but not when they're clearly designed to antagonize other students."

Walter narrows his eyes and leans closer to Tommy. "What does 'antagonize' mean?" he asks quietly.

I want to say something back to him, but it's like there's a rock in my throat. The words simply won't come out.

Instead, it's *Gracie* who speaks up. "It means you make someone else angry on purpose," she says. When I look at her with a raised eyebrow, she adds, "My older sister taught it to me."

"You have an older sister?" I say.

Her mouth drops open a little and she scowls at me. "Um . . . yeah?"

"Even *I* knew that," says Tommy. "Didn't you pay attention to her presentation last week? You weirdos are the same."

I don't even have a sibling, I think.

Mr. Bradshaw sighs. "Can we please get on with the lesson *without* interruptions?"

The class falls silent. I've lost my chance to say something funny back to Tommy, or *anything* that might get him to stop asking all his little "questions" about me.

So I do nothing to stand up for myself. Nothing at all.

Just like I did the first time.

When first period ends, I find myself slowly trudging to my next class. I don't feel like Tommy is bullying me or anything; he's just *annoying*. Why can't I stick up for myself in the moment, though? *Now* I can think of at least five comebacks, but it's too late. I wish I could just go back and—

Oh. Wait a second.

"Ribbit."

I freeze in place, annoyed that this sound has interrupted my new epiphany. For the record, it's not a frog making a sound. This is someone *pronouncing* the word "ribbit." And I know only one being in the whole world who does that.

I sigh. "Hi, Fea," I say. "Where are you?"

"Ribbit, ribbit," I hear in my head.

I slowly turn to my left, and there, stuck against the window, is a bright blue frog.

"Well, you're actually quite pretty today," I say.

"Thank you!" she says. "Ribbit."

I walk away from her because I will not be caught talking to a window. "You can drop the act," I tell her. "What do you want?"

"Slow down!" she cries out, and I glance behind me to see her hopping along the concrete. "Wow, I really did not think this through. Frog transportation is hard!"

"If you're here to annoy me, you've succeeded."

"I've never annoyed you!" she says innocently.

Instead of taking the bait, I decide to run my theory by her. "Fea, have you ever thought of a really great comeback, but like . . . an hour after it would have been perfect?"

Right then, the world freezes around me. I almost run into the back of Gracie. "Whoa, what are you doing?" I ask Fea.

"Sounds like we need to talk," she says. "This probably makes that easier, and . . . Yes, David. I know exactly what you're talking about."

"Well, you got me thinking," I say. "I know I have a lot of trouble making big decisions."

"I might have noticed," says Fea.

"So there are times I *could* do something, but I just . . . don't."

"You are trapped in your own indecision," she says knowledgeably. "It's actually very common."

"Really?" I say. "Because I feel like everyone else is so

sure of themselves. They always know what to do."

"That's what *you* think," she says. "But it's actually not the case."

"So . . . you could take me back to the start of class on the day I give my presentation, right?"

"I could."

"Because . . . well, something happened that day."

Even though she overheard part of my conversation with my parents while I tried to become the floor, I fill her in on *everything*. That includes what Tommy said and how Walter joined in, too.

"I think it's going to get worse, first of all," I say. "Like, if I don't stand up to them from the beginning, Tommy and Walter are just going to get more and more annoying."

"But not like me," says Fea, and she *ribbits* very loudly.

I laugh at that one. "Yes, not like you. But it's also . . . I really hate what Tommy said to me. About my birth parents."

"I'm sorry you had to hear that," says Fea, and she actually doesn't crack a joke at me. "It's really not fair. It's not like you *chose* to be adopted, and it sounds like he struck a nerve you didn't even know was there."

"Exactly!" I say. "I had this whole plan for my presentation, and then I got too nervous, and it was like . . . Tommy took control of *my* story!"

"Ribbit!" says Fea, and then she jumps onto my leg. "So you really think this is it?"

I take a deep breath. "I do."

"Then let's fix it, David Bravo."

"Wait—"

But she doesn't wait.

I am folded into a human pretzel and the last two weeks of my life begin to flash rapidly before my eyes. I twist and turn in the chaos of my timeline, and then my feet slam into the ground, and I swear, it feels like my knees nearly explode.

I'm breathless and disoriented, but I reach out and balance myself against the nearest surface, which turns out to be a doorframe.

"All right, David Bravo," says Fea. "You ready to make a different choice?"

I can't see where she is. All I *can* see is Mr. Bradshaw's classroom in front of me.

Gracie sits down at her desk and next to her, there's *me*. I look like I'm going to crush the index card in my hand.

"This is so weird," I say to her.

She cackles. "This never gets old," she says. "Time to change your timeline!"

A moment later, after another brief burst of twisting and turning, I am staring up at Mr. Bradshaw, who clears his throat.

"David Bravo?" he says. "It's your turn. Are you ready?"

Oh, I really hope so.

TUESDAY, SEPTEMBER 12
8:40 A.M.
The moment of truth (again!)

I breathe in deep and stand up. I know what Tommy is going to say, but it's still weird to hear the words coming out of his mouth.

"What kind of last name is Bravo?"

My heart thumps wildly in my chest. This is the first thing Tommy ever said to me, and I have to say *something* to let him know that he shouldn't mess with me.

So here goes my comeback.

"It's *my* last name," I say, "and you'll find out more about it if you actually pay attention."

There are a few snickers around the classroom, and it gives me a boost as I approach the podium.

"Yes, let's keep the commentary to ourselves, Mr. Rodriguez," says Mr. Bradshaw, then he turns to me. "Go ahead, David."

Dad told me that I get to *choose* who I am. Last time, I faltered and didn't tell anyone I was adopted, and Tommy and Mr. Bradshaw got to control my story. Well, not this time! I'm going to do what I should have done before!

I toss my index cards to the side; I know exactly what I'm going to say. Wunmi gasps, and Mr. Bradshaw raises an eyebrow.

"I had a whole presentation prepared for you today," I begin, and suddenly, I'm sure that this is *exactly* what I should have said all along. "But I think I need to start somewhere else. It's true that I have an odd last name, and it's also true that my upbringing is different from most people's because I was adopted."

Eyebrows rise all over the classroom. Even Gracie looks like she's about to explode. Ah, this is perfect!

"But that doesn't make me interesting. I'm not special *because* I'm adopted!"

Gracie's face falls while Tommy turns to whisper something at Walter, and I decide to go for it.

"In fact, I'm just as much Latinx as Tommy is," I say, and he whips his head in my direction. "And I know what you're going to say, Tommy. 'But what about your original parents?'"

The look on Tommy's face is *priceless*. It's like he's seen a ghost!

"How did you know I was going to ask that?" says Tommy.

Without any hesitation, I quip, "Oh, I'm a mind reader, Tommy. And you don't have many thoughts in your head at any given time, so it's pretty easy."

Tommy is *offended*, his mouth curling down, but Walter

cackles. "He got you good, bro," says Walter.

"Hush, boys," says Mr. Bradshaw, then: "Please stick to your presentation, David."

I nod at Mr. Bradshaw. "The truth is that I don't know who my birth parents were, and I don't know why I was put up for adoption. But who cares about that? It doesn't affect me now, and I think it's ridiculous that anyone thinks this sort of stuff is important. I get to *choose* who to be now."

Because that's what Dad said, right? And it feels good saying it now.

I know I absolutely crush my presentation. I tell them about my parents and how my home is like a collision of cultures. I even slip in another little dig at Tommy when he tries to interrupt again.

"Wait, are you related to me?" I say.

"Huh?" He scowls at me.

"Oh, just wondering, since you keep trying to talk during my presentation about *my* family."

Some of the kids laugh, and Mr. Bradshaw frowns at me. "No need to be snappy, Mr. Bravo," he says.

"Sorry," I say, throwing a mischievous smile at Tommy. "I'm all done!"

This time, there's applause when I finish.

This time, Mr. Bradshaw doesn't ask the questions that upset me last time.

This time, Tommy is silent when I sit down.

So is Gracie, though. I smile at her once I'm back at

my desk, but she turns away from me. I look up and see Wunmi glaring at me.

What did I do?

"Bravo, David . . . Bravo," says Fea. "Wow, I never realized how weird that must be."

I look down at the blue frog on my desk, then roll my eyes. "Just take me back," I whisper at her as Mr. Bradshaw calls up the next student to present.

"As you wish," she says, and hops onto my hand.

Seconds later: Twisting. Turning. It *still* feels uncomfortable, but at least this time around, I feel like I've done something to *really* change my life.

MONDAY, SEPTEMBER 18
12:44 P.M.
I have definitely fixed everything!

I am clutching my side outside . . . the cafeteria? Wait, why am I *here*?

"Fea, what's going on?" I say. "This is the wrong place!"

"You ask a lot of questions, David Bravo," says Fea, who is back to being a frog. "And unfortunately, there's no time, as the bell for the end of first lunch is about to ring."

"What?" I say. "Fea, that's like . . . four hours. You brought me back *four hours late.*"

"I realize that," she says. "It . . . hasn't happened before. I'm always on time!"

"What am I supposed to do, then?"

"Figure out how your life has changed," she says. "You're now in a new timeline!"

I look back to the cafeteria door as my heart races. So . . . on the other side of that is my new life. Wow. That's hard to wrap my mind around. Have I really changed *everything*?

"Thank you," I say. "For helping me."

"It's what I do," she says, then catches a fly with her

tongue. "And I feel I must remind you once again that you only live once, David Bravo. Remember that. And please stay being such an excellent weirdo."

"Whatever. As long as you're not around to ruin my life anymore."

She sticks out her frog tongue. "You'll miss me. Well . . . not *actually*. Since you won't be able to remember any of this."

"Wait, *really?*" I say.

"Yep. It's a safety measure. The Powers That Be don't want a bunch of humans running around with knowledge of magical powers and time travel. So don't worry, in a few minutes you'll forget how annoying I was."

I give her a sarcastic smile. "Good riddance, then, Fea," I say. "Go troll someone else."

"I absolutely will!" she says, her voice thick with joy.

She pops out of existence, and immediately after that, the bell rings, just as she said it would. I pull the door open, desperate to catch Antoine before he leaves. Because if this worked? I just fixed my life with *time travel*. Part of me wishes I could tell Antoine, since this is exactly the kind of thing he likes reading about. But I guess it will all be gone in few minutes anyway.

I make my way through some of the students who are leaving, and I spot Antoine at the end of our normal table. My heart thumps at the sight of him. Is this it?

But a few steps away from the table, I freeze.

No.

I have to be imagining this.

Antoine waves to Gracie, and then turns, repositions his crutches, and limps away.

What?

How is that possible? Antoine was getting *better* when I last left him! He'd gone on a bike ride and trained with his dad. Why is he still on crutches?

Oh, god, did something *worse* happen in this timeline?

I rush over to the table and call out his name. "Antoine!"

He turns and gives me a strange look. "David?"

I run up to him. "Hey, how are you?" I say.

"I'm okay, I guess," he says.

"Um . . . how's your ankle?"

He looks down at it. "It's getting a little better, I guess. Still hurts, so I'm stuck with the crutches for now."

"Cool," I say, then immediately regret that. "I mean, it's not *actually* cool; it was just . . . nevermind."

Antoine frowns. "Well, I've got to head to class," he says, and without another word, he hobbles out of the cafeteria.

No. No way! How is this even *more* awkward than before?

I sit down across from Gracie. "Is he doing okay?" I ask her.

Gracie has frozen midbite. She puts her noodles back in the container on the table. "You mean Antoine?" she says.

"Yeah. I didn't realize his ankle was that bad."

Gracie actually flinches when I say that. "Okay," she says. "Well, I think he's doing his best."

She resumes eating, but she's no longer looking at me. It's almost as if I'm not even sitting here.

What is going *on*?

I don't get an answer to that because I hear my name called out from across the cafeteria. Gracie quickly stuffs a bunch of her food in her mouth, snaps the lid onto the container, then puts it in her backpack. "I'll see you tomorrow," she says quickly.

And then *she's* gone. Before I can process that, Tommy and Walter come slinking up, their lunch trays held out in front of them. "What's good?" Tommy says.

"Ugh," I say. "No, don't try whatever it is you're going to try. It's not gonna work."

Tommy puts his tray down on the table. "We just came to have lunch with you. Is that a *crime*?"

"It feels like one!" I shoot back. "Why would you want to have lunch with *me*?"

Tommy gives Walter a confused look. "You told us to."

"When?"

"Uh, this morning, dude," says Walter.

I rub my eyes with my right hand. "I . . . I don't remember that."

I can't remember something that would *never* happen, can I?

Except then it hits me: I'm on a new timeline. Which *Fea* made possible. That means I'm now seeing what became of my life since I stood up for myself.

Does Tommy want to be *friends* with me?

This is too weird. I tell Tommy and Walter I'm not feeling well. They both look completely confused, but they don't say anything else as I walk away.

I pass a different table, and Wunmi flinches when I do.

I thought this was supposed to be fixed! What's going on?

But then a worse thought appears in my head:

Why can I still remember Fea?

She said I would forget her in a few minutes.

But . . . nope, I can definitely remember her—and how she messed up my life!

MONDAY, SEPTEMBER 18
4:01 P.M.
A warning

Antoine isn't at cross-country practice, which makes the brutal five-mile workout all the more awful. We were tasked with running off campus and down to the park a couple miles away, which was bad enough by itself! But once we showed up at the park, Coach Williams had us do a mile's worth of sprints. It isn't until we have to somehow run two miles *back* to school that I figure out how he beat us to the park.

I watch him cut over to the parking lot and climb into his pickup truck.

"He's a *cheater*," I hiss to Bea as she hums alongside me. "Why does he get to drive when we have to run?"

Bea doesn't respond. She gives me the side-eye, then speeds off ahead of me.

Why are people acting like this around me? I thought—

Oh. Great. I can still remember Fea. It's been *hours*.

When I hop in Mom's car after practice, she scrunches up her nose. "David, you're a smelly boy this afternoon," she says. "Did you not shower?"

"I didn't have time," I say, slipping on my seat belt. "We basically ran a million miles."

Mom pulls out of the parking lot. "Well, I'm glad you decided to stick with cross-country. Sounds like you're really committing to it."

"Yeah, I guess," I say, fiddling with the hem of my shorts.

"It's just I thought you'd give it up after Antoine's accident."

It's like a sharp knife just plunged in my chest. My heart skips. "Yeah. Well, I'm trying."

"Good," she says. "I know you've had some trouble this past week, so it makes your father and me happy to know you're trying."

My eyes go wide. *Okay, what does that mean? What kind of trouble?* But I can't ask her about that!

I don't like this. There's a nervous energy creeping all over my skin. I think long and hard, hoping that memories of this new timeline will suddenly appear, but they don't. And how could they? I didn't even *live* the past two weeks. They just . . . happened without me.

"You're quiet," says Mom, turning into our neighborhood.

"A little tired," I say.

"Anything else on your mind?"

"I don't know. Maybe schoolwork and stuff."

"Are you still hanging out with those two boys from your social studies class?"

I turn to her slowly. "What? Who are you talking about?"

She narrows her eyes, deep in thought for a moment. "Tommy, I think? I only met him that one time in the park down the street. His friend is named Wally?"

"Walter," I say softly, uncertain how I'm supposed to believe what she's saying. There's no *way* I've willingly been hanging out with Tommy and Walter.

Except . . . I have. This is what Fea was talking about, wasn't it? I'm experiencing my new life right now.

"That's right!" she says, snapping with her right hand. "I know you're getting to the age where you have to start making your own decisions, but those two really gave me a bad feeling."

"No, I'm not hanging out with them," I mutter.

"Good," she says. "Oh, and remember that I'm checking you out early this Friday, okay?"

"For what?"

"It's our turn!" she says, the offense rising in her voice. "You know, Project David?"

That's still a thing?!

I don't blurt that out, though I want to. Instead, I nod at Mom. "Right," I say. "And you're not going to give me a hint of what we're going to do, right?"

Mom pulls into the driveway of our house. "Oh, absolutely not. Where's the fun in that?"

She's delighted with herself, but I can't escape the fear creeping through me. There's no doubt that my life has changed in huge ways, but . . .

I don't like a single one of the changes.

I try to summon Fea—who I can still remember with perfect clarity—but there's nothing. Apparently, I have to get through all of this *alone*.

TUESDAY, SEPTEMBER 19
8:15 A.M
Everything gets worse!!!

The next day is not better in any measurable way. It is one thousand Davids.

When I sit down at my desk in Mr. Bradshaw's class, Gracie physically turns her body away from me. She doesn't even have her notebook open, so it's not like she's trying to hide what she's drawing like she's done before. I don't understand. Something must have happened during the missing time to make her react this way to me, but I nearly burst into tears just trying to think of it.

How can someone treat me like this over something I don't even remember?

In my visual arts class next period, Mr. López greets me with, "Can we expect more of your outbursts today, Mr. Bravo?"

I come to a full stop in front of his desk. "Huh?"

Mr. López twists his mouth up, making his pencil-thin mustache look all squiggly. "No need to act all innocent,

Mr. Bravo," he says. "Just keep your extraneous thoughts to yourself today, okay?"

"Sure," I say, because what else *should* I say? I have no idea what he's talking about!

This continues throughout the day. In Mrs. Hall's class, third period science, no one wants to sit next to me, so I have a three-person table to myself in the back. Mr. Marshall asks me if I'm actually going to read in class or crack jokes. I end up leaving English at the same time as Gracie, and I say, "What's up?" to her. She frowns at me.

"Hi," she says softly.

"Is everything okay?"

She actually stops dead in the hallway. "Are you serious?"

I wince. "Yeah, I am."

"David, how could you say all that stuff about me?"

Oh, no, I think. What did I *do* in this timeline?!

I know this might make it worse, but I have to figure out what happened. "What stuff?" I say.

Gracie's whole face crumples. "Your presentation," she says.

Wait. What? I narrow my eyes at her. "What are you talking about? I didn't say anything about you in my presentation!"

"Yes, you did! All that stuff about how it isn't special to be adopted and that it doesn't matter."

"That was about *me*!"

"But I'm adopted, David!" she says, her voice rising.

"And you went right after me! What was I supposed to think?"

My stomach drops to the floor. Probably literally.

I said I didn't get why anyone would care about me being adopted. Right *after* Gracie gave a presentation about being adopted!

More memories—of my original timeline!—pour in. Her sister, the weird questions Mr. Bradshaw asked after her report, the way she's been avoiding me since yesterday.

"Oh, no," I say. "Gracie, I'm sorry. I didn't mean to sound like I was talking about you. I didn't even hear your presentation!"

"How? You were right there!"

I groan. She's right—technically. "I'm sorry," I say again. "I was so nervous about what I wanted to say that I just zoned out. I honestly didn't hear what you said."

"Oh," she says, her gaze falling downward. "Well . . . okay." Then she snaps her head back up. "But it still hurt."

"I'm sorry," I say immediately. "So sorry. I shouldn't have said any of that. I was just trying to shut up Tommy and Walter, and it . . . backfired."

"Okay," says Gracie. She lingers for a moment, then says, "I'll see you around."

She leaves me behind, and I'll be real: I feel absolutely awful.

TUESDAY, SEPTEMBER 19
12:37 P.M.
Antoine tells me the truth.

I set down my tray across from Antoine. He's got one of his science fiction books planted right in front of his face, but I don't get to see what he's reading before he puts it down to look up at me.

"You sure you want to sit with me?" he says softly.

I sit down on the opposite bench, my face scrunched up. I still haven't even remotely recovered from the truth about Gracie and how badly I've hurt her. But I *have* to try to repair things with Antoine. "Of course, dude. Why wouldn't I? You're my best friend!"

"Okay," he says, then cracks open the book again.

"What are you reading today?" I ask. "You always find all the interesting books in the library."

I'm giving him a full, toothy smile when he looks over at me. "What's with the good mood?" says Antoine, then he moves his injured leg out to the side. I notice he's got a pretty intense brace on his ankle. Great. How bad is *this* injury? It doesn't look like a sprained ankle!

I frown at him. "What do you mean?"

"Well, you know," he says. "You can be a little harsh sometimes."

"Harsh?"

"I don't know," he says. "Ever since we got to this school, you're always joking at people, you know? Do you *always* have to be like that?"

What he's saying doesn't make sense. That *isn't* what I'm like. Sure, I like making fun of things, but usually it's myself, not other people.

That anxiety returns, climbing up from my stomach and gripping my heart. "And you think I've been like this since the first day of school?"

He tilts his head to the side, thinking. "Well, no, not the first day," he says. "It was like a week later. After that presentation you were worried about." Antoine grunts. "You've changed, bruh."

"I'm sorry," I say softly, because even if I don't recall any of this, it's obvious that I've hurt my friend in more ways than one. "I just . . . got caught up in everything after Tommy tried to make fun of *me*."

"I get that," he says. "I really do. Some of the guys on the cross-country team . . . I heard them talking about me in the locker room. Saying they're glad you accidentally tripped me, because it means *they* can start winning now."

"Oh. I'm so sorry, Antoine," I say. "I really am."

"I know you are," he says. "Really. I promise I'm not mad at you. It's been kinda nice to take a break from all the practicing, but mostly, I just miss being your friend. And some days, it's like someone else slipped into your body and *changed* you."

That one hits the hardest. My eyes well with tears, and I have to turn my face away from Antoine for a moment.

I hurt Gracie. I hurt Antoine.

In *two* timelines.

"I'll be better," I blurt out, turning back to him. "I promise."

Antoine offers me a curt smile. "It's all good," he says, then, using the crutches lying beside him on the bench, he pushes himself upright.

"Where are you going?"

"I need a head start to get to class," he says. "I'll see you at practice?"

"Of course," I say.

"I'll cheer you on from the stands," Antoine adds. "If that helps."

I don't even know what to say to that. I watch as Antoine limps off toward the exit.

I'm left alone at the table. No one—not even Tommy and Walter, who apparently think I want to be friends with them—is sitting here. I'm by myself. And if what Antoine told me is just the tip of the iceberg, how can I blame anyone? I'm *awful* in this timeline.

How did this go so wrong?

As if on cue, there's a loud *thump!* in front of me. Lukewarm pasta sauce splashes across my arms.

Fea—in the form of a *raccoon*—has fallen directly onto my lunch.

"David Bravo," she says, huffing and puffing.

"Fea!" I whisper harshly. "I didn't even get to eat a bite of that!"

"We can worry about your hunger later," she says. "We have a problem."

"Yes, we do!" I exclaim. "What's going on with my life? What did you do? What did I do?"

She rears up on her hindquarters and rubs her tiny raccoon hands together.

"David, you definitely did not make the right choice," she announces.

TUESDAY, SEPTEMBER 19
12:46 P.M.
Eat your veggies.

"I'm well aware of that." I seethe at her, ignoring the fact that some of the kids at the table to my right are looking my way. At this point, I've already trashed my reputation at Mira Monte Middle School—but I'm going to make Fea change it.

In a low voice I tell Fea everything that's happened since I last saw her. "So, look, obviously that was the wrong decision to change," I say. "Just undo it, and I can start from scratch."

Fea starts shaking her raccoon head rapidly. "No, nope, not happening," she says. "David, it's impossible."

"I thought you said I should change my idea of what impossible means!" I cry. "Just use your magic!"

"I literally can't," she says, wringing her tiny paws together. "Once I do my thing, that's it. Your new decision is set in stone."

"So . . . what happened? How did you even know what was wrong?"

Fea reaches up and touches her infinity charm. "This

contains all my assignments. Like I said, the green portion shows my completed ones. But whenever I touch it, it tells me who I'm supposed to visit next. Sort of like what I imagine it's like to hear me talking in your head."

"Okay," I say. "Then what's the problem?

She reaches down to grab some of the baby carrots on my tray and starts munching on them. "Something has happened that's literally *never* happened while I've been a timeline guide."

I groan. "And what would that be?"

"You're still on my assignment list."

I actually have to sit there in that eerie silence for a few moments to take in what she's said.

"Still?" I finally say.

"Still," she confirms.

"Wonderful," I say. "I'm so cursed, I mess up *literal magic.*"

"Maybe not cursed," says Fea, and she doesn't make a joke at my expense. "I've helped so many people, David, and no one is ever *cursed.* Maybe they have problems or they made mistakes, but they're never impossible to fix."

"But you've never dealt with someone like me," I say. "You just said that! Plus, aren't I the first kid you've ever been assigned?"

Fea rolls over onto her back like she's a dog in a mud pile, except the "mud" in this case is my now-cold pasta. "I can't *undo* the choice you made," she says. "But if the thing we need to repair is at an earlier point than your presentation, then I guess whatever we do next should replace all this. . . ."

She gestures with the end of her baby carrot. "So just embrace the chaos until then!"

"Until *when*?" I say sharply. "You're not leaving me, are you?"

"I got others to help," she says, "and I'm going to pay a visit to the Powers That Be to see if they've got any guidance for me."

"Do you normally have to do that?"

She grabs another baby carrot. "Actually . . . nope. Never. I rarely see them."

"You aren't making me feel great about this."

She crawls off my lunch tray. "Eat your veggies," she says, and then . . .

Poof. She's gone. The kids at the table on my right turn away quickly when I glance at them.

I stare down at my food, which looks like it's been hit by a localized hurricane. I get up and dump it in the trash, while everyone at the nearby tables watches me. Are they expecting me to keep talking to myself? Or maybe they're worried I'll make fun of them.

My stomach twists up. It isn't just hunger but something else.

If Mr. Bradshaw's presentation wasn't the key to my life being on the right track, what *is*?

FRIDAY, SEPTEMBER 22
12:48 P.M.
Project David (Mom edition)

Fea doesn't show up for *three days*.

I'm not sure if things are better with Antoine. We haven't had all that many chances to hang out, but at least we're still friendly with one another when I see him. I can't seem to crack Gracie, though, and the more she avoids me, the more I hope Fea will hurry up. I don't think there *is* a solution in this timeline. I messed up. I shouldn't have said what I did. It's going to take Fea to fix that.

But by the time Friday rolls around and Mom checks me out of school early, I still don't have any idea when Fea will show up, nor can I think of a single moment from my past that would require the aid of a timeline guide. Elementary school was pretty great! It was probably *better* than middle school, since I was with Antoine all day, every day.

Even though he lives next door, I miss my best friend.

I don't talk on the long drive out to Los Angeles. There's lots to look at as the landscape changes from the brown, rolling hills of the Inland Empire to the densely packed cities of LA County. There are so many cars on the freeway, zooming along with us. As the towering skyscrapers of downtown Los Angeles come into view, there's a tingle over my skin. I can't really explain it, but I always feel at home here. It is where I was born, and even though I don't remember my time in foster care before Mom and Dad adopted me, it still feels like I'm coming back. Like maybe this is where I am supposed to be.

My stomach is growling as we pull into a parking garage, and it's so loud that Mom actually stares at me when she comes to a stop in a spot.

"I'm sorry that I made you starve," says Mom as she gets out of the car. "But I promise you, in about fifteen minutes, you're going to be so happy that you came on an empty stomach."

"I hope you're right," I say. "It's cruel to make me suffer so much."

Mom laughs at that, and we exit the parking garage into the bright afternoon sun of Little Tokyo. I twist around to see the downtown skyline behind me in the distance. There's an enormous hotel across the street that seems to have a garden spilling out of the second story. It looks really cool—I want to stay there someday. Mom holds my hand as we trot across the crosswalk. The shops here look a lot different from the ones we have out in the Inland Empire. We pass one with huge windows and lots of colorful clothing and shoes on display. It's next to a fancy skateboard shop, which is next to another store that sells colorful kettles, mugs, and tiny plates.

"What is all this stuff?" I ask, pointing at the shop as we pass it.

"Tea sets!" Mom says. "There are a lot of shops here in Little Tokyo that bring things in from Japan. I mean, some of it isn't authentic, but I always come down here to get my nice teakettles."

"Cool," I say, and we round a corner. Moments later, we reach the entrance to an outdoor shopping mall, but Mom takes us up to a restaurant on the corner instead with a big sign that says, "KURA."

"Is this food? It better be."

Mom holds the door open. "It is indeed food, and it's time for us to eat as much as we can."

The place is brightly lit, and it looks like nothing I've ever seen. There are a lot of tables spread around the restaurant, but all of them are next to a tall shelf that—

Wait, no. That's not a shelf. I notice that there are little plates of food *moving along* this structure.

"What is *that*?" I say, my eyes wide.

"There are places like this all over Japan but especially in the big cities," she says. "Here, we call them revolving sushi bars, but I knew them as kaiten sushi."

"Sushi?" I scrunch up my face. "Isn't that all raw fish?"

She nods, then flags down a waiter, who immediately

seats us at an empty table. "Some of it is," she says, "but not everything."

"What if I don't like it?" I say, watching the plates on the conveyor belt as they move past. I can see tiny rolls, cut into pieces, on brightly colored dishes.

"They have plenty of other things you like, but don't worry. The portions here are *very* small. It's designed so you can try new things without having to commit to a huge plate!"

A woman comes by and asks us for drink orders, and Mom orders green tea and water for the both of us. The waitress then briefly explains how it works, showing me that once I finish, I can put the plate in a slot at the end of the table, which will keep track of how much we've eaten.

Mom excitedly pulls a couple plates down off the belt and puts them in front of us. "Feel free to use your hands or your chopsticks," she says. "You can dip the fish side in some soy sauce if you'd like a little extra salty flavor, but some of these are good as they are."

She pushes a plate with two pieces of sushi on it toward me. "That's a salmon nigiri," she says. "Nigiri sushi is basically a piece of fish on top of a little bit of rice. If you see sushi *without* rice, that's sashimi."

"Okay," I say, and I gently pick up one piece of nigiri with my chopsticks. I'm glad Mom taught me how to use them years ago, because now all I have to worry about is whether or not I'll actually enjoy this.

I dip the piece in a tiny little plate of soy sauce, then bite half of it. The saltiness of the soy sauce hits my tongue first, and then I'm tasting the salmon. It's also pretty savory, and the texture is kind of . . . nice. It's not all that different from cooked fish. Maybe a little gummier?

"Not bad," I say, then try the other half. It's . . . good! Like *really* good.

I can tell Mom's almost as anxious as me. She's staring at me in anticipation, her eyes wide. "Is it okay?" she asks.

"Yeah," I say. "That was pretty delicious."

"Okay, well, salmon is pretty mild," she says. "I won't make you try sea urchin or conch just yet."

My mouth drops open. "Did you say *sea urchin*? Those weird spiny things we saw in Waimea Bay?"

She nods. "They're a delicacy. I *love* them."

"You're weird," I say. "How can you eat it with all those spines?"

Mom laughs *really* hard, throwing her head back. "Oh, David, you don't eat the whole thing. It's just the insides."

I'm still not convinced. But soon, Mom is handing me plates with tuna and seared salmon, which isn't raw. Then ebi, which is the name for shrimp, and then she gets me to try saba nigiri. It's from a fish called a mackerel, and even though it's *super* salty, I think it's my favorite. I don't understand how this is *raw* fish and so tasty at the same time! She also teaches me that there's a plate with slices of ginger on it that's meant to "cleanse my palate" in between pieces. "Think of it as a way to clear out your mouth so you can taste each new piece as much as possible," she explains.

Seems fancy, but you know what? After a few times of doing it, I think it's working.

And it's not long before I understand why Mom didn't stop to get lunch before we left. I feel like I can eat a million pieces! Even better: *it just keeps coming.* Who's making it? Is it just descending from the heavens?

"I feel you've been a bad parent for not taking me here sooner," I say after what's probably my tenth or eleventh plate. "The absolute worst."

Mom chuckles. "To be honest, I was scared to take you here. I was so worried you wouldn't like this part of my culture."

"Why?"

"There are a lot of people who think raw fish is gross and unsanitary," she says. "You know, one of the hardest things to deal with when I first moved to the mainland was when people made fun of all the things I grew up with."

"Like all the tea you make," I say. "And I guess I never really noticed your fancy teapots, either, but you have a lot of them."

She nods. "It's more than just food or plates. Living on the island was completely different, and it was a huge adjustment."

I put a piece of something called a California roll in my mouth and chew for a bit. "So did you come here a lot? Like, to Little Tokyo?"

She nods. "When your father and I got married and

decided to move to the mainland, I told him I needed to be on the West Coast. We lived here in LA for a while before you were born, and I was *always* hanging out in Little Tokyo. You'll see more of it after lunch. It's not exactly like Hawai'i, but this place felt familiar to me."

Mom looks away from the table. I'm not sure what she's staring at. But when she turns back, her eyes are red.

"Sometimes, you need that reminder," she says softly. "Of where you came from, of who loves you, of the things that give you comfort. The food in this part of the city does that for me. So do the old ladies up at the ramen shop over on First Street, as well as the man who sells me kettles around the corner."

"Does it remind you more of Hawai'i or Japan?" I ask her, confused. Because she said this place reminded her of *both*.

Mom doesn't answer at first. She sits there, thinking, then reaches over and grabs another plate of sushi. We each take a piece; it's a square of crispy fried rice topped with fresh crab. (It's also *delicious*.) Then she rests her chin on one of her hands.

"That's hard to answer," she says, and she swats at a small fly that tries to land on her half-eaten sushi. "I know that presentation of yours confused you, but sometimes, identity *is* really confusing."

I must have had a talk with Mom and Dad in this timeline about the presentation, but how did we end up here again? Why is Project David still a thing?

It is yet another mystery in my life. I'm a pile of mysteries now, aren't I?

"Well, *that* doesn't help," I grumble at Mom, wishing she hadn't been so vague.

Mom smiles sadly. "I know. But life isn't so easily categorizable. I say I'm Japanese because that's where I was born, and most of my parents' traditions come from Japan. At the same time, I feel really comfortable in Hawai'i and the culture there. But despite the fact that there *are* native Hawai'ians in our family, and it's where I lived almost all of my childhood, I don't always feel it's my place to identify as Hawai'ian. There's a very complicated history there, since most of my family aren't original inhabitants of the islands."

"But it's also your home, isn't it?"

"Sure," she says, nodding. "I couldn't choose where my parents raised me, and I do love Hawai'i a great deal. But language can be a powerful tool, so one thing I am conscious of is how I choose to identify myself."

I drop the empty plate in the slot. "So, what am I?" I ask.

"That's a journey you're going to have to take over the course of your life," she says. "How you choose to identify now may be completely different than ten years from now. But all these experiences you're having? They'll help you decide."

When I start to frown at her, Mom raises a finger. "I

know this is frustrating, and I don't know if this whole Project David thing is actually working. I'm just asking you to give us a chance, you know? We're trying."

"Okay," I say.

"Dad told me about your bowling adventure," she says. "Do you think it answered any questions?"

"Maybe," I say. "He said something about . . . like, maybe it doesn't matter where we come from. That we get to choose who we are."

Mom raises an eyebrow. "Hmmm. I think I see what your dad was trying to say, but . . . I don't think I agree with him."

I'm not sure I do either, especially not after changing my presentation like I did. I thought that not caring about where I came from would feel better, but it's clearly made things more complicated.

"Why do you say that?" I ask her.

"I think where we come from helps place us in the world. It gives you a space to occupy that's all yours. And sometimes, it's really wonderful to find other people in that same space. I love that I've met other people born in Japan but raised in the US. It's even more meaningful to meet those who grew up in Hawai'i."

Mom reaches across the table and grabs my hands. "Baby, it could be that you just need to find someone else who lives in the same space as you. It isn't always easy, but maybe that's what's missing from your life and making this so hard for you."

"Maybe," I say. "But what if I already found them?"

Mom tilts her head to the side. "Who?"

I tell her about Gracie, but not *everything*. I can't explain the double timelines or the do-over that Fea granted me. "But I'm not sure she actually wants to be friends with me," I say. "I said some things I shouldn't have."

"Well, just like I told you with Antoine," she says, her gaze soft, "you have to give people space to feel what they feel when you've hurt them."

I swallow hard as a lump forms in my throat, then look down at the table and start picking at the edge of it.

"Baby, what is it?" Mom says.

I look back at her. "I'm worried," I say. "I don't know what to do about Antoine."

"Because you tripped him?"

"We're definitely not how we used to be," I say. "I'm worried we might stop being friends. And it really hurts when I think about that." I hesitate. "Actually, it's like I can't stop thinking about it. And him. Why is that happening?"

Mom's eyes twinkle. "You have a lot of strong feelings for Antoine. You two have basically been joined at the hip since he moved in next door. And now, things are changing. It's a scary thing to have happen, especially since he's been such a constant in your everyday life."

"Is there something wrong with me?" I ask.

"No," Mom says without any hesitation, and she swats

at the fly again, which buzzes off to another table. "You're allowed to feel however you want to feel about Antoine. You can miss him, too, even if he hasn't gone anywhere."

"But what am I supposed to *do*?"

"Talk to him when you can," she says. "I know I'm slipping into therapy mode, but honestly, honey, you'd be surprised how often I'm just telling my clients to communicate with the people they love."

"Love?" I grimace. "He's my best friend, Mom."

"And there are many types of love, David," she shoots back. "Platonic love between friends. Romantic love between couples. There's love in between that, too. But it doesn't make it any *less* of a type of love, and it's clear that Antoine means the world to you. So, find some time to see how *he's* feeling. Maybe he's been distant because there's something going on in his world that you don't even know about."

I nod. "Okay," I say. "Thanks, Mom."

"Anyway, no more heavy talk," she says, and she flags down our waitress. "We have more places to visit."

"Is there something you can push me around in? Like maybe a wheelbarrow or a shopping cart? I can't move a muscle 'cuz I'm so full."

"I'm disappointed, honey," Mom says, frowning.

"What? Why?"

She gives me a mischievous grin. "Because we're still going to get dessert."

I groan. "Mom, there is literally no space left in my stomach." I slap a hand on it. "I could not fit a single grain of rice in me if I tried."

"That's too bad," she says, then glances down at the lone plate left on the table, sitting close to the little slot where you drop the empty plates. There's one last piece of the crispy rice and crab sushi.

And I try. I really do.

But my willpower fails.

And it's *delicious*.

FRIDAY, SEPTEMBER 22
8:26 P.M.
A new theory

It's been hours since my sushi lunch with Mom, but I feel like I ate twenty minutes ago. I'm laid out on my bed, my feet sore from walking around Little Tokyo, and I really wish I could fall asleep.

Except I can't.

Because there's a *fly* in my room.

I can hear it buzzing around. The only thing worse would be a mosquito invading my room, but this is barely better! I must defeat this great evil!

However, I barely make it off my bed—standing up is so hard when 50 percent of your body is now sushi—before the fly lands on my nose.

I raise my hand to swat at it, willing to hurt myself in confusion in order to destroy the fly, when her voice rings out in my head.

"I swear, David Bravo, you better not kill me before I'm done with my assignments."

I groan. "Fea?!"

She buzzes off my nose and lands on my left shoulder, which seems to be the one she favors. "Yeah, this form is terrible."

"Wait," I say.

The fly at the sushi restaurant!

"Was that *you* earlier, buzzing around my face?"

"Uh, *duh*," she says. "How else was I going to eavesdrop on your conversation?"

I don't say anything at first because I'm so annoyed.

"I could squish you right now."

"You *wouldn't*."

"In like a whole second."

"You'd be a murderer."

"And every jury would say I'm not guilty! They would all agree that you should be put out of your misery for being so irritating."

Moments later, there's a xolo on my bedroom floor.

"'Sup, David Bravo." Fea rolls over on her back, like she wants me to pet her stomach.

I will not fall for such tricks. "What is the reason for your visit now?"

She sits up. "I think I might know what's going on."

I breath out in relief. "Okay, then! Tell me. Because this timeline is *garbage*. Basura. Would you like me to learn that word in another language? 'Cuz I will."

"It's not *that* bad," she says.

"It's pretty awful!" I cry out. "Gracie probably hates me, and I still tripped Antoine. He's hurt even worse than he was the first time, and things still feel weird between us."

"I believe you are confirming my theory at this very moment," says Fea.

My eyes go wide. "How?"

"I have some questions first."

"Shoot."

"They're actually *about* Antoine."

My mouth drops open a bit. "Antoine? But *why*? Didn't you say this was about *my* timeline, not his?"

"Well, yes, but—"

"I don't know what I'm supposed to change, Fea. It's obvious there's no way to change Antoine getting hurt, so is this about something else?"

"I'm trying to—"

"Do I have to go back to elementary school? Did I do something there that put me on the wrong track?"

"David, please, I—"

"You told me I had to come up with another idea! Well, what else is there?"

"David Bravo!" Fea shouts, and then stands on her back legs. "Do you *like* Antoine?"

I stare down at her. "What?"

"Like . . . do you *like* him?"

"Well, he's my best friend—"

"No, silly," she says, sitting back down. "Do you *like* him?"

I groan. "You just asked me that."

"Do you like it when he smiles at you?"

"Yeah. I do."

"Does it make you feel good to hang out with him?"

"Always," I say.

"Do you find yourself looking forward to seeing him again, so much so that you *join sports teams you don't actually want to be on*?"

I suddenly don't like where this questioning is heading. "I mean . . ." I turn away from Fea as heat rushes to my face.

"What's happening right now," she says, racing around me and then hopping up on my bed, "does that happen sometimes when you think about Antoine?"

Oh, my god. It happened at lunch, didn't it? That same familiar rumble in my stomach hits me, just like it has when I think about Antoine's smile or his face or when he gets all excited talking about a book.

"*Do* I *like* Antoine?" I ask, slumping down on my bed.

"That's up to you, David," she says, wagging her tail. "But I noticed that you kept talking about him, and you were obsessed with stopping his injury. And based on your conversation with your mother earlier today, I think that—"

"Which is really weird, by the way," I interrupt. "Do you spy on all your assignments?"

"I *have* to," she says. "The Powers don't give us any info on the humans we help. We have to figure it all out through observation and communication. And what I'm observing is: I think you like him a *lot*. And maybe he feels the same way about you."

"But I've never liked someone that way."

"Well, there's no wrong time to start," says Fea, leaping up toward me. "You don't want to—"

She goes completely still on my bed and her ears point up.

"Oh, my stars, I think I figured it out!" Fea takes off from the bed, launching herself onto the carpet. She zooms to the opposite corner of the room and then hops back up on the bed. "David, I was thinking of this all wrong!"

"Okay, okay!" I say. "What is it?"

Fea races back to me. "David Bravo, what if your past isn't broken?" she says.

I frown. "Okay?"

Fea looks like she's going to explode from excitement.

"David, what if I was sent here so you don't make a mistake in the *future*?"

FRIDAY, SEPTEMBER 22
8:37 P.M.
Fea explains it all.

"I . . . don't get it," I say.

Fea howls in glee. "Oh, David Bravo, it's so obvious to me now. This must be why this has been so hard for the both of us. The Power of the Bees wanted to give me a *real* challenge before I finished!"

"I thought it was the Powers *That* Be."

"Your name for them is a million times funnier, so I'm running with it," she says.

"So, explain what you mean, then!" I sit back down on my bed. My confusion is rapidly turning into frustration. "I don't understand."

Fea sits obediently at my feet. "I've maybe mentioned a few times that I was once alive."

"Yeah," I say. "You've been very vague about it."

"That is by design," she says. "I never reveal details of my own life to my assignments. But I was once like you, and I believe that's the whole reason I'm here."

"Like me? *How?*" My eyes bulge. "Oh, god, am I as annoying as you are?"

"No, *David*," she says, but she definitely sounds annoyed. "But I was just a regular person once, and I was in love with my best friend."

Silence falls in my bedroom. I stare at Fea as her words bounce around in my head. I can't even deal with her telling me that she was a person before this because that *other* thing is way, way bigger.

"I'm not *in love* with anyone," I say softly, but then I think about what Mom told me earlier today about love and all the different forms it comes in. Is it possible I *am*?

"I don't know about that," she says. "When I was your age, I had this big terrible crush on another girl in my school."

I practically fall off the bed. "Wait, you went to school?"

"Yes, silly!" says Fea.

"When?" I say. "Like, are you *ancient*? Did you go to school back when there were covered wagons?"

She groans. "No!"

"I bet you're a thousand years old. That would explain a lot."

Fea curls up next to me. "Look, I don't really know when I died *exactly*. The final moment is fuzzy in my memory. But I was your age in the 1950s."

"So you *are* a thousand years old."

"I'm ignoring your clear inability to do basic math," she

says. "It wasn't *that* long ago. And you're distracting me from my point! I was building to something!"

"I will use this against you in the future," I say, "but okay. Sorry. What are you trying to say?"

"I've been trying to figure out why I've been given an assignment like *you*. Everything about you is different and unorthodox."

"Th-thanks?"

"That's a good thing, David. I've never been assigned a kid. I've never been assigned someone who didn't immediately know their greatest regret. I've never had a choice be immediately rejected by the Powers!"

"Well, now I feel awful," I say. "I've been trying!"

"But at the *wrong thing*," she says, and she stands up and wags her tail frantically. "David, the reason I was made a guide in the first place was because I died with a great regret in my life. And now, I don't think it's a coincidence that they've assigned me to you!"

She pushes her head into my leg and whines. "I believe I have the unique chance to do something no other timeline guide has ever done: change the future."

"I don't know," I say. "Why now? Is there some reason I have to think about this when I'm *eleven*? This is way too much."

"You don't need to make a choice now," says Fea, and she hops off the bed. "I'll give you a few days to think things over, but the next few times you see Antoine, I want you to pay attention to what you're feeling!"

"Okay," I say. "Like what?"

"Like, when he talks to you or asks to spend time with you."

"Just that stuff?"

"Not *just* that. Think about what happens when he smiles at you."

I immediately frown. I kinda already know the answer to that. "Okay."

"Think about what you feel if he happens to touch you."

"Sure," I say. That sounds weird!

"And think about how you feel when he *leaves*."

I'm still making a scrunched-up face at Fea. "I guess," I say. "I don't know if that's going to help."

"Trust me," she says. "We are closer than ever to cracking this mystery!"

And with that, Fea disappears, leaving me to sit there in this new chaos left behind in her wake. I didn't even time travel, but it's like my whole life has been put in a blender.

Again.

MONDAY, SEPTEMBER 25
7:43 A.M.
To Antoine's house I go!

My homework from Fea goes unfinished until Monday morning, unfortunately. Just like during the previous weekend—from a different timeline, of course—Antoine's ankle started feeling better, so Mr. Harris had him doing some workouts so he could test onto the varsity team. On Friday, they went to the nice track over at Poly. And on Saturday, the two of them headed to Mount Rubidoux, which still terrifies me even though I've only run up it once. It's this massive mountain beyond downtown Riverside that Coach Williams calls a "hill."

It's not a hill. It's a mountain. I refuse to let him lie to me.

So I'm surprised when I get a text from Antoine on Monday morning. "Come over!" it reads. "Doctor gave me the go-ahead. We're walking to school."

I show it to Mom, and she gives me the okay. "Be safe!" she says, then kisses the top of my head. "Let me or your dad know if you need to be picked up today."

"Okay!" I call out, already heading for the front door. My heart is racing as fast as I am on the way over to Antoine's, but before I reach his place, I pause in the driveway.

Wow. I'm *really* excited. And I've got that butterflies-in-the-stomach thing going on, too.

Hmmm. Fea told me to pay attention to this kinda stuff. Okay. So I am. But what does it mean? I think I'm mostly just happy that Antoine wants to hang out with me again! That doesn't have anything to do with love or crushes.

I approach his door and knock on it, and Antoine opens it almost immediately. He doesn't have his crutches with him, and his ankle is brace free.

His face erupts into an enormous smile, one that stretches wide and makes me . . .

Oh. It's like that feeling when you're on a roller coaster and you plunge down the first big drop.

What does *that* mean?

"I'm glad you could make it!" Antoine says, and then he steps out onto the stoop and wraps his arms around me.

He holds me tight for a few seconds, and I stretch my arms around him, too, and there's a rush inside me of . . . something. Warmth, I think. And as he holds me, I'm also *relieved*.

If Antoine didn't really want to be my friend anymore, he wouldn't do something like this.

"Come on in!" Antoine says.

The first things you see in the Harris household are the photos. There's a framed one directly across from the front door of Mr. Harris, back when he was still competing. It's honestly very impressive. He's got his arms raised up as he crosses the finish line on a track far ahead of the next runner. There are medals hanging near the photo and a few trophies on the mantel in the living room. I know one of them is Antoine's, because he won first place in a fun run our elementary school held. But everything else here . . . it's the legacy of Mr. Harris.

I wonder if it makes Antoine nervous. Those seem like some big shoes he has to fill.

Mrs. Harris greets me with a hug, then moves her long locks behind her. "Good to see you, David! Thanks for walking Antoine to school today."

"Of course," I say. "I'm just happy he's back on his feet again."

She heads toward the kitchen. "You already get breakfast back home?" she calls out.

"Yes!" I say.

"Gimme a second," Antoine says. "Lemme go get my bag."

He darts upstairs to his bedroom, passing Mr. Harris on the way. Antoine's dad glances at me and gives me a smirk. "Good morning, David."

"Good morning, Mr. Harris," I say.

"No more injuring my son in practice, okay?" he says.

My face must turn as red as a fire engine. I'm sure of it. "I promise," I say.

I can't actually tell how serious Mr. Harris is being until

Mrs. Harris comes over to kiss him on the cheek. "Leave the boy alone, Jamal," she says. "It was an accident. They happen."

This time, his smile seems a little more genuine when he looks at me. "I know. You up for some morning practices with Antoine this week?"

"Ugh, Dad," groans Antoine, coming back down the stairs. "Don't force him to do them, too."

"Well, I've been going over your sessions and results, and I really think you'll benefit from a few early-morning runs. *Before* breakfast, that is. Those fasted runs will teach your body to use your stored energy."

"Sure, Pop," Antoine says, but then he glances at me and grimaces. "No, thanks," he mouths.

I hold back a laugh, but it quickly turns to horror.

Because there's a *giraffe* in the Harrises' backyard.

I can see the head peering through the sliding glass door that leads outside, and beyond it, there are four spindly, spotted legs.

Oh, my god, Fea. What are you *doing*?

I hear her voice in my head right as Antoine asks me if I'm ready to go.

"Oh, David Bravo!" she sings. "Let me guess: My theory about Antoine was right, wasn't it?"

"David?" says Antoine, and he waves in front of my face. "You okay? What are you staring at?"

"Nothing!" I say quickly. "I thought I saw something in your backyard, that's all."

"You did," says Fea. "It was me! Giraffe necks are so *weird*, David Bravo. You should try one sometime."

No! Why is she doing this *now?*

Antoine glances out the back door. "Like . . . like a person? An animal or something?"

"An animal, yes," I say, nodding. "Maybe it was a squirrel."

"I *can* be a squirrel if you want, David," says Fea. "If that makes it easier for you to accept the truth, that is."

"Do we have time for me to use your bathroom?" I ask. "Real quick, I promise!"

"Yeah," Antoine says. "You sure you're okay?"

"Definitely!" I say, but my voice wobbles when I speak, so there's no way it sounds convincing at *all*. I head down the hallway past Antoine's room and duck into the bathroom. I shut the door behind me and lock it; my anxiety feels like it's at an all-time high.

What am I *doing?* What is happening to my life? There's a talking giraffe in my best friend's backyard. I've traveled through time more than once. And now, this shape-shifting spirit *thing* is urging me to admit my feelings for Antoine.

I can't tell him the truth. I can't risk him thinking I'm a weirdo and never being friends with me again.

"That performance was subpar," says a voice in my head.

I resist the urge to groan because someone will *definitely* hear me. I look around the bathroom but don't see any animals. I pull aside the shower curtain, but the tub is empty.

"Where are you, Fea?" I whisper.

"The sink, David."

There, sitting near the hot water knob, is a centipede.

"I've never had so many legs before!" she says.

"Fea, what are you *doing* here?" I whisper.

"David, let's not focus on me," she says, crawling around the sink toward me. "Let's focus on *you*. What are you waiting for? Tell him! Make some big grand gesture of love! You only live once, David Bravo!"

"I know that!" I whisper harshly at her. "But I'm not *in* love! I just . . . like him. It's a crush. Or something! And besides, I'm not doing it in front of his *mom*!"

"David?"

Antoine's voice is outside the door.

"Uh . . . yeah?" I say.

"Who are you talking to?"

I glare down at Fea. She snickers in my head, so I grab a cup next to the sink and turn it upside down over her.

"Hey!" she calls out. "I might run out of air in here!"

"You don't have a body!" I whisper, and then turn to the door. "Sorry, Antoine. Sometimes . . ."

How many times have I tried to cover for someone catching me with Fea by saying I talk to myself? I can't keep doing this. But also . . . I want to tell him *some* version of the truth.

"Sometimes," I say, "I get nervous and talk to myself."

He's silent for a moment, and I'm certain that I've ruined everything.

"I do that, too," he says softly. "Been doing it a lot lately."

· 171 ·

I put my hand on the door. "Really?"

"Yeah. Especially when I get anxious about running. I don't want to disappoint my dad."

I've known Antoine for six years, and I've never once heard him mention anything like this. "You get anxious, too?"

"All the time. I hide it well, I guess."

I open the door, and he's right there, standing on the other side.

"I never noticed."

"I didn't realize it about you, either."

"Really?" I say in disbelief. "I feel like it's obvious."

"No," says Antoine, shaking his head. "I always wish I was as cool as you are."

He stares at me with these sad eyes, and it's suddenly too much. I can't lose him as a friend. I can't tell him the truth. God, I don't even *know* the truth yet! All I'm certain of is that he's the best person I've ever known, and the idea of him not being my friend . . .

Ugh. It's terrible.

And so I freeze up. I just tell him we should leave soon so we're not late to school, and the moment passes. Antoine says goodbye to his parents as we leave his house, and on the short walk to Mira Monte Middle School, Antoine talks about the book he's reading, then those early-morning practices that he's supposed to start. And then he's complaining about math, which is one of our favorite things to complain about, and it's nice to have him back like this. I missed it.

At the front steps of the school, he nudges me with his shoulder. "See you at lunch?" he says.

"Always."

He holds his hand out.

"Crisscross," he says.

"Always floss," I add.

We complete our handshake.

"Always friends," Antoine says.

"To the end," I finish.

He walks away from me, and it's like he looped a string around my chest, because all I can feel is a tugging sensation in my heart. How can I ruin this? How could I possibly risk losing it?

Fea has to be wrong about my future.

MONDAY, SEPTEMBER 25
8:14 A.M.
Fea still thinks she's right.

I'm walking to Mr. Bradshaw's when I feel a cold, wet nose on the back of my leg, which makes me yelp and jump at the same time. Justin Li—who's in my pre-algebra class—turns around to stare at me.

"It was a bug!" I say. "It nearly flew into my eye."

"Okay," he says, casting me a suspicious glance. "Must have been a big bug."

"Enormous!"

Well, he's already walking away, so this is a disaster. I look behind me to find . . .

. . . I actually don't know what I'm looking at.

It's like . . . a long thin . . . otter? Sea otter. But it can't be. It's too small, and it's not in the water, and . . .

"I give up," I whisper. "What are you, Fea?"

"They really don't teach kids about the animal kingdom anymore, do they?" she says. "I'm a pine marten."

I turn back and start walking as fast as I can to Mr. Bradshaw's class. "That sounds fake."

"You sound fake."

"Unlike you, the rest of the world can see me!" I say.

Fea patters behind me on the concrete. "Doesn't make me less real."

"Can you go bug someone else? I'm not sure you can even help me anymore."

"That's where you're wrong, David Bravo," she says. "And today, I would like to actually prove it to you."

"How?" I say.

The warning bell rings.

"Do you trust me?" she asks.

"Hardly," I say.

"Wow, David Bravo. You're so cruel."

"You'll live," I say sarcastically.

"I *literally* will not," she counters. "Dead, remember?"

"Oh, right. I forgot. Sorry."

"It's actually very fitting," she says. "Because this kinda has to do with me and my death."

I scratch my head. "I'm lost."

"I think this is so difficult for you because it's all ideas. Theories. Generalizations! You need to *see* this all in action to understand it."

"Understand *what*?"

"Regret," says Fea.

The bell rings for first period, but I'm not moving. I'm staring down at a brown pine marten, which I must admit is a pretty cute animal. "What do you mean?"

"I think it's time I show you *my* truth," says Fea. "And

take you back to when I was your age. Maybe if you experience my mistake, you won't make the same one."

I crouch. "Are you offering to take me into *your* past?"

"Yes," she says. "The Powers will allow it, but we can't interact with anything or anyone. It's just to observe."

"Will you get me back early enough so I'm not late again?"

"Yes," she says confidently. "No mistakes this time."

I am not so sure that she's right about me and Antoine, but . . . I *do* kinda want to learn more about Fea's life. And if she can return me at the correct time. . . .

It's time travel! I *have* to do this.

"Show me, then," I say. "Take me back."

Fea trots forward on her tiny legs and uses my outstretched hand to climb up my arm to my left shoulder. She sits around my neck like those terrible pillows people bring onto airplanes.

Then her magic tugs deep in my stomach, and I fold over and over again, pulled back along my timeline while the events of my life flash by, spiraling above me. I don't scream like I usually do, and I wonder if that means I'm actually adjusting to this.

Seconds later, my timeline goes blank, and I'm thrust into a terrible darkness. "Fea!" I call out. "Is everything okay?"

"Hold on!" she yells back. "We're entering my timestream in three . . . two . . . ooooooonnnnne!!!"

I'm weightless for a brief moment, and then my stomach

lurches. Suddenly, images are rushing past me, all of them of someone *else's* life, but I can't really make out what it all is.

Then it's like hitting a brick wall.

We come to a stop, and the breath is knocked out of me. I stumble, fall over, and my hands and knees are on concrete, and I'm trying to breathe, gasping for air, and I look up and—

And—

Oh, my *god*.

OCTOBER 23, 1956
9:43 A.M.
Fea's story, part 1

I was gonna say that what I'm looking at is impossible, but . . . well, that word doesn't mean anything anymore, does it?

We're outside a building at the bottom of a set of concrete steps, kids rushing past us. They're all dressed in these super formal uniforms, like nothing I've ever seen, so it's definitely not my school. I can see signs on the large building and above the front gate:

FOUNTAIN MIDDLE SCHOOL.

I rub my eyes. "Fea, where are we?"

"Oh, David Bravo," she says, then I hear this high-pitched squeaking sound. I look around. It sounds like it's coming from the tall pine next to me.

Ah, I've found Fea.

She's a *squirrel*. Why, oh, *why* did I give her that idea?

"Do I need to feed you some acorns or something?" I ask.

Fea chirps at me. "Isn't that a chipmunk thing?"

"You ask me that like I know *anything* about either chipmunks or squirrels."

Fea rubs her tiny paws over her face. "Your question would have been much more interesting if you'd asked *when* we are."

"*When?*"

I turn around, and I can't believe I didn't notice before. The cars.

They're *wrong.*

They're huge, first of all. They look somehow rounder than cars in my time. A long convertible pulls up, driven by an older teenager with slicked-back black hair, his skin a darker tone of brown than my own. Two younger girls get out of the back seat wearing identical uniforms—black skirts and black cardigans over white dress shirts, with clunky black shoes—and wave to him, and he drives off, looking possibly cooler than anyone else I have ever seen.

"Fea," I say as she chirps away in the tree, "is this *your* school?"

"He finally puts all the pieces together," she says, then leaps from the trunk of the pine to my left shoulder. "You're a genius, David Bravo."

"Have you ever considered saying something nice to me?" I ask sarcastically. "Just, like . . . once?"

Fea puts her squirrel paws on my left cheek. "This eye looks *great*," she says. "Just a stellar, solid eye. Good job, David. You can observe things perfectly fine!"

I push her off my shoulder, and she scurries ahead of

me. "Well, come on!" she calls out, her fluffy tail straight up behind her. "Follow me!"

For a moment, I forget that we're just glimpsing the past. I try to push my way around some of the students in uniforms, but my hand passes *through* them. It's *weird*.

Fountain Middle School is enormous, and unlike my school, it's all in a single building. After I make it up the front steps and through the front door (like . . . *literally* through the front door), I spot Fea in the middle of the hallway to my left. She's sitting on the floor, chewing on something while watching a group of four young brown girls.

"Okay, what now?" I say. "What am I supposed to see?"

"You're looking at her," says Fea softly.

"Who? What are you—?"

Three of the girls leave the fourth next to her locker, and that's when I see the name tag on the front of it:

Juanita Flores.

The girl standing next to it looks like she wants to open the locker, but something is stopping her. She sighs loudly, then leans her head against it.

"Fea," I say hesitantly. "Is that . . . is that *you*?"

"Welcome to the world of twelve-year-old Fea," she says. "Fountain Middle School. 1956."

"Wait, your name is *Juanita*?" I say. "Why didn't you tell me before? Oh, my god, I've been calling you ugly this whole time and you had an *actual* name."

"First of all," she says, spinning around on the tile to

face me, "*you* gave me that name, and you never even asked what mine was."

"Oh. Right."

"And second . . . Fea has kind of grown on me. It's like I'm reclaiming the word or something."

"You're strange," I say. "And are you going to explain why you brought me here?" I watch as Juanita gathers a notebook and some books from her locker and then puts them in her canvas bag. "Or am I here to learn that you, too, were once in middle school?"

Another girl comes up to Juanita and accidentally startles her. Juanita slams the locker door shut.

"Maricela!" says Juanita, breathing hard. "Don't scare me like that!"

"You like it when I do," Maricela says, smiling from ear to ear.

Juanita smiles back. "Maybe," she says. "But only when it's you."

"Soooo," says Maricela, dancing from one foot to the other. "You talk to your mami yet?"

Juanita sighs. "Tonight, I *promise*," she says. "Pero, she's so strict, Mari. I don't think she's going to let you come over."

"Just tell her that every young girl needs a best friend," says Maricela. "And we can do homework together and everything. So it'll be educational!"

"I know, I know. It's just that I get scared because I know she's just going to tell me no."

"Cut the gas, Juanita," says Maricela, shaking her head. "No more excuses! If you want, I'll come home with you and we can try together?"

"I'll think about it," Juanita says, casting her gaze to the ground.

"Fea, can you like . . . pause this?" I ask. "I have a million questions."

Maricela freezes in midsentence, and now her mouth is just open awkwardly.

"I still can't believe that's you," I say. "Like . . . you're a person."

"Was," says Fea, her tone a lot more even than it usually is. She also doesn't seem that energetic anymore. "I *was* a person. Now I'm more like . . . like a soul with an almost unending homework assignment."

I make a disgusted face. "I have something I want to say."

"Oh, no," says Fea.

"It's going to sound mean, but I don't know how else to say it."

"So you're going to basically be imitating me, then?"

I have to laugh at that one. "Okay, yes. But Fea . . . or Juanita . . ."

"Fea's fine. I'm not that little girl anymore."

"Well . . . your whole afterlife sounds like it *sucks*."

Fea sighs, then climbs up my leg and my side until she makes it to her favorite shoulder. "I think I need to tell you who I am in order to explain what I think I'm here for," she says. "And it's not the happiest story."

"Okay," I say. "But if you think it will help, then I'll listen."

"Thank you," she says, and there's no sarcasm or humor in her words this time. Which kinda scares me! She's being *serious*.

"So . . . what happened?"

"Well," says Fea, taking a deep breath and then continuing. "Mari and I were good friends for years. Until we were eighteen, actually."

"But . . . ," I say. "I can hear that coming."

"But . . . I fell in love with her, David Bravo," she says sadly. "I fell in love with her by the end of middle school, but I didn't tell her then. I was in love with her all during high school, and I didn't tell her. And then I got the chance to, but I blew it, and we never ended up together."

"Wow," I say. "This is *also* gonna sound mean but: that really sucks, too, Fea."

She sighs. "It does."

"Why don't you go visit her? Is she still alive now?"

"She *is* still alive," says Fea, but then her voice drops again. "She's a mom. She has a daughter, I think. But . . . David, I'm not allowed to see her."

"What?" I say, shocked. "That's ridiculous. Just use your little magic . . . power . . . thingy. Whatever it is you use to take me to my past!"

"That's the thing," she explains. "I can use it on a person I am assigned to, and I can visit my own past, but that's it.

It's all constrained by the Power of the Bees. And trust me, I've been trying for *ages*."

"I'm sorry," I say. "I know that isn't helpful, but I really am sorry."

"Wait," says Fea. "There's more you need to see. Hold on. . . ."

There's a tug in my stomach, and I twist. I spin. It *is* getting easier, I have to say, though when I stop and my feet are on solid ground, I'm disoriented. We're indoors this time in some sort of long hallway, and it *looks* like a school again. But it's not the same one.

And then Juanita comes into view.

She's next to Maricela, and both of them are taller. Older. They're whispering something to one another, and then they giggle and duck into a room and shut the door behind them.

"Come on," says Fea. "If you're going to understand why I believe I'm here to change your future, then you need to see this."

I follow her over to the door, and before I walk through it, my own heart starts racing. I have this sense that I shouldn't see this, that it's too personal.

But maybe that's the point.

I trust Fea, and I walk through.

APRIL 28, 1961
9:43 A.M.
Fea's story, part 2

Maricela is sitting on the sink when I walk in, and she's laughing, her thick, black curls bouncing as she does. Juanita is staring at her, almost like she has stars in her eyes. Seriously. She basically looks like an anime character. It's like Maricela's laugh is the best thing Juanita has ever heard.

Is . . . is that how *I* look at Antoine? Is that what Fea wanted me to see?

"So, I wanna ask you something," says Maricela. "But you can't make fun of me."

"¿Y si quiero?" says Juanita, grinning. "I'll do what I want!"

"Shut *up*," says Maricela. "I'm being serious."

Juanita stands upright and runs her hand over her face. "Okay, this is my serious face," she says. "I'm ready."

This just causes Maricela to laugh even harder. "Stooooopp! Nita, I *swear*, you're going to make me die of laughter someday."

"Fine, fine," says Juanita, stepping closer. "I'm back to

being serious again. Tell me. What is it?"

Maricela doesn't hesitate. "Go to prom with me."

Juanita's face falls, and her eyes go wide. "What?"

"What I said. Go to prom with me."

"Are you joking, Mari?" says Juanita, raising an eyebrow at her.

"No. I told you I was being serious."

Juanita goes still, and even though this isn't happening to me—in fact, it happened like a million years before I was born—it *feels* like I'm right there. My heart is in my throat as I'm seeing Juanita like this.

Is this what I look like when indecision hits me up, too?

"Say *something*," Maricela says, her face twisting in worry. "You're scaring me, Nita."

"I . . . I can't go," Juanita says. "Because Mami is making me work at Dad's store that night."

"Oh," says Maricela. "Well, that's bogus."

"Yeah," says Juanita, and I notice that she can't seem to make eye contact with her friend anymore. "Yeah, I'm sorry."

Maricela hops down from the sink. "Well, see you in class, then?"

"Of course," says Juanita, trying her best to smile, but . . . it's not believable. I stand there, watching as Maricela leaves, as Juanita stares at herself in the mirror and says nothing. She looks *miserable*.

When Juanita freezes, Fea clears her throat. "So, yeah. I disappointed her that day, but there was still hope. It wasn't until prom itself that I made the worst mistake of my life."

"I'm confused," I say. "You liked her. Like, a *lot*."

"I did," says Fea.

"So why didn't you tell her then? Maybe you couldn't have gone to prom with her, but she seemed pretty into you."

"I lied."

I shake my head. "I don't get it."

"I didn't have to work that night. I was just . . . afraid. I wanted nothing more than to go to prom with her, but David . . . it was *such* a different time back then. The idea of going to prom with the girl I liked . . . it scared me more than anything."

Fea jumps off my shoulder, and in midair, she turns into a bat, flapping her wings furiously as she bounces around in front of me.

"I have to show you one more thing," she says.

I nod and hold out my hand. She lands on it and an instant later, I'm traveling through her timeline again.

We end up indoors once more, but it's darker. There are colorful lights spinning across the ceiling, and there's a live band nearby playing music. It takes me a second to get my bearings, but when I do, I see a school gymnasium, completely packed with dancing teenagers. They're all moving . . . weirdly. I don't know what any of this is. Why is that one girl swinging her arms like that? Do any of these people know how to count the beat of the music?

"Not here," says Fea, flapping around me. "Come outside."

I walk through the door of the auditorium and head outside, just in time to see a long wide sedan pull up. Why are all the cars in this time so *big*? Do they even fit on the streets?

A young boy, decked out in a sharp suit, his hair perfectly slicked back, gets out of the passenger seat in the front, closes his door, then opens the one behind him.

And out steps Juanita.

I actually gasp. She looks *stunning*. She's got on this fancy pink dress with a white collar and a black bow tied around her waist. She steps out of the car delicately on bright pink shoes, and the boy takes her hand, which is covered by a matching pink glove.

"Juanita, oh, my *god*," I say. "You look amazing! You made it to the prom anyway!"

But she doesn't say anything to me. No silly comments or jokes. In fact, I turn around and look above me to find her clutching the overhang outside the gymnasium, hanging upside down.

"Fea? What's going on?"

She still doesn't say anything.

"Who is that guy?"

Still nothing.

Then I find out why.

"How *could* you?"

I quickly turn around to see Maricela—in a gorgeous dark red suit with black dress shoes—storm up to Juanita.

Juanita panics. Her eyes go wide, and her date—who is pretty handsome, if I say so—looks from Maricela to Juanita and back.

"What's going on, Juanita?" says the young man.

Maricela's eyes are watering, and then the tears spill over. She turns around and walks away from the gymnasium, disappearing around a corner.

For a moment, it looks like Juanita is going to chase after her. But then she looks up at her date. "It's nothing, Marcos," she says. "Just a disagreement between friends."

Again: none of this is happening to me, but I still feel a little sick to my stomach.

"Fea, what *happened*?" I ask. "Why did you come with that boy?"

"My mom forced me to," she says, flapping down from the overhang and landing on my shoulder as more people show up to the dance. "Told me that she wasn't going to have me miss out on this experience, not after everything that she sacrificed to get us to this country. I get her reasoning now, but at the time, I knew that doing this was going to hurt Mari. But I didn't stand up for myself."

"And she probably thought you rejected her," I say. "Right?"

"But I *did* reject her!" Fea cries out. "I never told her how I felt, and so she probably spent the rest of her life believing that *she* ruined our friendship when she told me the truth. And all I should have done was tell her the truth back."

"But you fell in love again, right?"

Fea is silent.

"Right?"

"Not really," she says softly. "That's why I'm here, David Bravo. We all only live once, and I spent most of my life wishing I was with a person who never knew how I felt. I regretted it until I died, and the Powers That Be . . . well, they saw me fit for this job. Who better to help others undo their greatest mistakes than someone who made a mistake like I did?"

"Wow," I say. "That's . . . *really* heavy."

"It is," she says. "But it also means I know regret. *Really* know regret."

A sadness rushes through my chest. I think about having to live the rest of my life without Antoine. What if he stopped hanging out at lunch? What if he stopped inviting me over? What if he moved to a different school and then we never talked again?

It feels like there's a stone in my throat.

"Take me back," I tell Fea. "Please."

She doesn't fight it this time. We twist, we turn, and she takes me back to the present time.

As soon as I'm back on solid ground, Fea—in her original xolo dog form—whines at me.

"I'm sorry," she says. "I think that was harder for you to watch than I expected."

"It's okay," I say, and I wipe at my watery eyes. "I was just thinking about Antoine. And what it would be like if he wasn't my friend anymore."

Fea's tail wags. "So you'll tell him?"

I shake my head. "I really don't know, Fea! What if *that* is the thing I'll always regret? Maybe the Power of the Bees wanted me to see *Maricela*'s side of things, to show me that I'll regret it if I tell Antoine I like him."

"Well, that makes no sense at all, David Bravo!" says Fea defiantly. "What a convoluted means of getting to the point. What if I'd never taken you to my past at all? You never would have learned the truth."

The second morning bell rings out, and I pull my phone out. It's 8:15. Great. I'm going to be late!

"Fea, I have to go," I say. "Please, I just need more time to think about this."

"David Bravooooooo," Fea sings out.

"I know, I know. I only live once, right?"

"You do. And do you see where I'm going with all this?"

I sigh. "You don't want me to mess up like you did. Yes, I get that."

"Soooooo, isn't this what your heart wants? This would be like the greatest romance of all time!"

"I don't actually know that I want that!" I say. "I mean . . . you were in *love* with Maricela. That's clear."

"You don't need to be in *love*, David," says Fea, jumping around. She barks a few times. "You just have to believe it might be possible with Antoine."

It sounds nice, but . . . it's kinda scary, isn't it?

"Believe in possibility!" she says, and then she's gone.

I rush into Mr. Bradshaw's class a moment later, and he looks up from his desk and frowns. "Don't be late again, Mr. Bravo," he says as I hurry to my seat.

Gracie thankfully doesn't turn her whole body away from me this time. She actually *smiles*, even though it's a very short one. I give her one back but then wish I'd actually shown up early. Mom's advice rings in my mind. I really need to try again with Gracie. Here's someone who might be able to help me a little bit with what I'm going through.

Still, everything is so confusing. Mr. Bradshaw starts talking about the American electoral system, but my thoughts are lost in this predicament I'm facing. Fea was stuck in her regrets because she was afraid. But what if that was because of the time she lived in? I don't know that much about history, but it clearly wasn't easy to be a girl who liked other girls back then. But . . . am I a boy who likes other boys? Is that what's going on with Antoine and me? Is that who *I* am?

God, why isn't there a class about this kind of stuff?

I do my best to pay attention to Mr. Bradshaw and take notes, but I still haven't mastered that skill. All I can see in my mind is Maricela's face, full of rage and disappointment. It's so very easy to imagine Antoine in her place.

Do I tell Fea to take me to an earlier point in my life?

Do I tell Antoine that I think I have feelings for him?

Is the answer to all this bubbling chaos in my past or in my future?

I really wish someone would just tell me.

MONDAY, SEPTEMBER 25
12:35 P.M.
Fea barges into my life. *Again.*

I'm practically at the cafeteria when I hear a loud bark at my feet that can come from only one source.

"No," I say to her, and I keep walking toward the double doors.

"You have to be ready soon, David Bravo," says Fea.

"No, I actually don't."

"Come onnnnnnnnn," she whines. "It's time. You have to make a decision."

I don't respond to her, but I do stop walking. If I kept going, I'd be seated across from Antoine within five minutes. And the thought of seeing him right now . . .

I want to. But I'm also terrified. What if he *knows* what I'm thinking? What if it's obvious now?

"David, you can't ignore me forever."

"I could try," I snap at her. "Would you like to start now?"

She sighs. "I don't get why you're being so difficult. The solution to this little mystery is so obvious now! I got stuck with you because of Antoine. It's clear as day!"

"How do you *know* that? Did the Power of the Bees actually tell you this time?"

She groans. "They don't need to! You saw my past. You know why I got made into this . . . this guide thing."

"But how can you know for *sure*?" I ask. "I'm willing to admit I might like Antoine—"

At that, Fea yips and then does an actual flip. "I knew it!"

"—but! It is also entirely possible he *doesn't* feel the same as me!"

"David Bravo," she says, pacing back and forth in front of me. "It's clear that he actually wants to be around you as much as *you* want to be around *him*. Right?"

I press my lips together tightly. "Sure. I guess."

"I think he feels the same way about you."

"But you *think*, Fea!" I say. "You don't *know*!"

"David, *no one* knows the future! Everything is a guess! And if you keep living your life so frightened of what's to come, you're never going to choose *anything*!"

This is the first time I've seen Fea . . . well, *angry*, I guess. She starts panting, but she doesn't say anything.

"I'm not that bad, am I?" I say softly.

Fea whimpers. "I don't know. Maybe I'm overreacting."

"Look, it's true that it's hard for me to make choices. Especially when I don't know what will happen!"

"You're not alone in that. I *still* get scared about things, too."

I'm not sure that's all that comforting. I sigh and then slump against the wall outside the cafeteria, thankful that there's no one out here to see me wallowing. "I'm sorry, Fea."

She nuzzles up against my leg. "I'm sorry, too. I shouldn't have yelled at you."

"It's okay."

"No, it's not," she says. "I need to be honest with you, David Bravo. I have been a little freaked out recently."

"About what?" I ask.

She leaps up and puts her paws on my left thigh. "Look at my charm," she says.

I grab it between my fingers and turn it around.

Aside from one tiny sliver of red on one end, it is completely green.

"Fea, does this mean—?"

"Yes," she says. "My time as a timeline guide is coming to an end. *Soon*. I think you're my very last assignment."

There's a bench outside the cafeteria, and I sit on it. I pat my lap, and Fea jumps onto it so I can pet her.

"I didn't know," I tell Fea, running my hand over her skin. "Are you scared?"

"A little," she says. "I don't know what comes next."

"The Power of the Bees haven't told you?"

"Nope."

"Well . . . I really *do* appreciate that you're trying to help me."

"Thank you," she says. "But I think you're right, too. I'm

putting a lot of pressure on you, and it isn't fair for me to rush you into a decision like this. It *is* a big thing. And I want to give you the time you need to figure it out."

I scratch Fea along her back. "You're all right for a shape-shifting chaos demon," I say.

"I'm the best," she says. "And I think maybe there's a way to fix both your problem *and* the broken timeline."

"Really? How?"

"It would require us going back to the very first day of this school year."

"Okay," I say. "Well, what do you—?"

"David, what are you doing?"

Antoine scares me so badly I actually jump in place. I look at him, panic spreading over my face.

"Who were you just talking to? Yourself?"

"Yeah," I say quickly, then shake my head. Oh, my god, I must have looked like I was petting the air in front of me. I quickly shove my hands in my pockets. "I was practicing an argument for . . . for one of my classes."

"Like a debate thing?" he says, and he comes to sit next to me.

"Yeah, kinda like that," I say.

Fea is still in my lap, her tail wagging furiously. "Daaaaaviiiiiidddd," she coos at me. "I love this boy's tim-ing!"

I don't! I have an invisible dog in my lap who is talking to me!

"Cool," he says. "I was just wondering where you were.

You're not usually late for lunch."

"The library," I say. "Mx. Reyes was helping me."

"Oh, they're so great, aren't they?" says Antoine, lighting up. "Did you get any books? I want to know everything you checked out."

"David Bravo, we need to go," says Fea. "I promise I'm not trying to ruin this little meeting, but I really want to fix this for you."

"Uh . . . ," I say, trying to focus on Antoine, but then Fea starts jumping up and down in my lap. I yelp and try to clamp my hands down on her, but she leaps out of the way.

"What's going on?" says Antoine, knitting his eyebrows together. "Do you feel sick again?"

"Yes!" I blurt out. Then: "No!" Then: "I mean . . . I should be getting to lunch."

I stand up quickly, and I'm sure it looks completely unnatural.

"Hurry along, David Bravo!" says Fea, bouncing around at my feet. "We've got some*when* to be."

I wave to Antoine. "Okay, I'll see you at practice!" I say.

"Ummm . . . okay?" he says, weakly raising his hand to wave back.

As I head toward the cafeteria doors, I glare down at Fea. "Seriously, why are you always like this?"

"No time to discuss," she says, and she leaps forward to put a paw on my shoe. "Off we go!"

Which is the exact moment when I feel a hand on my shoulder, followed by a familiar voice:

Antoine.

"David!" he says. "I meant to ask—"

"NO!" I cry out, and then the tug is there, in my stomach, pulling me hard into myself, and I fold, ripped back along my timeline, but this time, there's something else there.

No.

There's some*one* else there, screaming alongside me.

"Whaaaaaaaattttttttttttttttt!!!!!!" screams Antoine.

Oh, *no*.

TUESDAY, SEPTEMBER 5
8:10 A.M.
The first day of middle school (the *second* time)

My feet slam down hard on cement, and next to me, I can hear Antoine's breath rush out of his lungs. He doesn't land as gracefully as I do—possibly the first time in our entire friendship that I am less clumsy than him—and I'm at his side once he tumbles over, pulling him to his feet.

"What—was—that???" Antoine gasps, clutching his chest.

He looks up.

I follow his gaze.

Oh, no. I know exactly *when* Fea has taken us.

Just a few feet from Antoine and me are . . .

Well, Past Antoine and Past Me.

"What if we just *don't* go to school?" Past Me says.

I watch as Past Antoine scrunches up his whole face as other students stream around the two of us and head up the steps at the entrance to Mira Monte Middle School.

"That's a really good idea, David," says Past Antoine. "But what are we going to do all day?"

No. NO! Antoine can't see this. He can't be here. He can't know what I've been doing because this is going to *ruin* our friendship!

"Ta-da!" says Fea, prancing around in front of me. "Welcome back to the first day of school, David Bravo! So, my theory is—"

"Uh, David?" says Antoine, his outstretched finger shaking. "Is that dog *talking*? Like, in your head? Or is that just me?"

I don't think I've ever felt panic rip through my body quite like this. Fea spins around a few times and then:

Oh, my *god*. She squats and starts peeing.

Look, I'm so freaked out myself by what's unfolding that I almost want to wet my shorts, too, but I *don't*.

Fea whines loudly, her little dog eyes darting between me and Antoine, then trots over to the two of us.

"David Bravo," she says, "is that Antoine next to you?"

I nod. "Yep."

"*The* Antoine."

She points her nose toward Past Me and Past Antoine, who are still talking about the plan to ditch school and assemble LEGO models at Target. In an instant, they both freeze. *Everything* freezes.

"You can hear the dog, too?" Antoine says, his hands on his head. "Also, why did everything . . . stop?"

"So . . . this is happening," Fea says to me after a long pause.

"Fea, you need to fix this!" I cry. "What's going on?"

"Whoa," Antoine says, stepping up to his Past Self and examining him. "What is this? Alternate reality? Time travel? A simulation?"

"Somehow, Antoine traveled into the past *with* us," Fea says. "That . . . that's a new thing. Huh."

"I'm right here!" Antoine says, whirling around to face us. "Why are you both talking about me like I'm not here?"

"You *shouldn't* be here!" I snap, then point at Fea. "You also shouldn't be able to see *or* hear her!"

"Well, I can, so what if we move on from that? Then we can talk about the fact that she just said I *traveled into the past*."

Antoine is . . . well, he's clearly shocked but also *excited*. A small burst of relief fills me. This is just like those science fiction books he reads, isn't it? Maybe he isn't going to freak out on me!

"Well, at least Antoine got on board in less than two minutes," Fea says. "Why couldn't you be more like him?"

"Not addressing that!" I say. "How on earth did Antoine travel with us?"

"Could someone tell me what's going on?" Antoine asks.

"Was he in contact with you?" asks Fea.

"Contact?" I say.

"Was Antoine *touching* you when we traveled?"

I hit my forehead with an open palm. "Yes! He grabbed my shoulder right before you yanked me back in my timeline."

"Timeline?" Antoine echoes.

"It's possible that my powers work on any living crea-ture in touch proximity to my assignment," says Fea in a low voice, like she's talking to herself. "But this has never happened before."

"Fea, are you at *all* concerned about all the mistakes you're making lately?" I ask.

"Maybe!" she says defensively. "I've . . . thought about it. Like once. Or maybe a hundred times."

"Hello???" Antoine says, and then he claps his hands together a few times. "Could *anyone* acknowledge the fact that I seem to have traveled through time and am now staring at the frozen versions of me and David?"

"Not only traveled," says Fea, "but I've instituted a tem-poral lock at the moment to prevent the timeline from barreling forward."

Antoine stares at Fea for a moment, then glances at me, a smile spreading over his face. "Cool," he says. "David, this is the *coolest* thing that's ever happened in the whole world."

I smile weakly because I appreciate his excitement, but I'm still internally flipping out over this whole scenario. What are we supposed to do *now*?

"Well, I'm glad that *someone* appreciates my skills," says Fea haughtily, and she prances around Antoine with her head held high. "Watch this!"

The world comes alive again around us. Past Antoine

and Past Me finish our Handshake and head into school.

"Is that *us*?" Antoine asks. "Like . . . oh, my god, this really is the first day of school. *Again*."

The school bell rings, and kids start rushing up the stairs. I watch as Past Me and Past Antoine disappear beyond the front gate, and it's *still* a surreal thing to witness.

"I can't believe this is happening," says Antoine.

"Fea," I say, "we need to—"

I don't finish because someone collides with my shoulder.

"Whoa, watch out, buddy!" says a tall kid with brown hair.

"Sorry," I say, and I lock eyes with . . . Tommy.

Who can see me.

And who *definitely* touched me.

"It's cool," he says, but he glares at me as he leaves.

The panic is back, and it's even worse than before. I put a hand to my chest because I'm certain my heart is going to explode out of it at any moment.

"Fea!" I say. "Did you see that? Why was Tommy able to touch me?"

Silence.

I turn around to find Fea lying with her belly on the ground, her ears folded back.

"Fea?"

"Oh, man, this is so cool," says Antoine. "So, can we change the past? Is there any way we can make it so that Tommy isn't the worst?"

"We have bigger problems," Fea whines.

"Antoine Joseph Harris, why aren't you in school yet?"

My heart drops when I look up to see Mrs. Harris getting out of her car.

TUESDAY, SEPTEMBER 5
8:17 A.M.
My soul leaves my body (but Antoine saves the day).

"Uhhh . . . hi, Mom," says Antoine.

"Antoine, what's going on?" says Mrs. Harris. She holds up a large water bottle. "I doubled back around because you left this on the front seat. Please tell me why you are standing here on the sidewalk with David and a dog when school has already started."

A dog.

She can see Fea?

None of this is making any sense at all. Indecision rages through me. Do I make up a story? How do I explain this? Should Antoine and I just run to class and hope for the best? Oh, no, that would *definitely* be a bad idea.

Suddenly, Antoine darts forward, nabs Fea, and lifts her up.

"Sorry, Mom," he says. "We found this stray dog running around the parking lot, and we got caught up trying to save her."

"A stray?" Fea says in my head. "Excuse *me*, but I smell like a freshly bathed dog."

A new wave of terror crashes over me. Can Mrs. Harris hear Fea? She doesn't react to what Fea said, so I guess not.

Antoine doesn't let it phase him, either. He holds the dog out. "I was going to take her into the front office so that animal control could deal with her."

Mrs. Harris narrows her eyes at Antoine. "That right, David?"

"It is!" I say, my voice shaking, fully terrified that I've just told a lie to Mrs. Harris. I've never done it before, and I plan to never do it again.

"Well, that's a good thing to do," she says, stepping closer and petting the top of Fea's head.

"I like her," says Fea. "Make her keep petting me since you barely ever pet me, David Bravo."

I have a small desire to chuck Fea onto the roof of the school, but instead, I smile at Mrs. Harris. "Would you like to come with us?" I ask her.

"Sure, David," she says. "I'm sorry I came in so hot. I misread the situation at first."

"I know, Mom," says Antoine. "I wouldn't want to disappoint you, but this poor dog needed some help."

He gestures to her to lead the way up the steps. Then he quickly glances at me. "What are we doing?" he whispers.

"I don't know!" I whisper back. "I was following your lead!"

Fea barks loudly in our heads. "Do you two have a plan? I can just disappear if you like."

"That will definitely make things worse!" I say softly.

We walk into the front office, and a slim, tall Black woman with long locs greets us. Her nameplate says, "Ms. Hayes."

"Good morning!" she says cheerily. "And what do we have here?"

Ms. Hayes makes a beeline for Fea and starts petting her. Fea eats it *up*. "This might be the best day of my afterlife," she says. "I'm not used to all this attention!"

"Afterlife?" says Antoine, his eyes wide.

"What?" says Mrs. Harris.

"Nothing!" he says quickly. "Just . . . talking to myself."

This is a disaster, I think. Mrs. Harris explains the situation to Ms. Hayes, who promises to get us passes to our classes so we're not marked as late. "Don't want *that* on the first day of school," she says.

"No, we don't," says Mrs. Harris, casting me and Antoine a still slightly scolding glance.

"Well, thank you for saving this cute little dog!" says Ms. Hayes, clutching Fea close to her chest.

"She thinks I'm cute," says Fea. "Tell her I'm in love."

I am not all that worried about Fea when we leave her behind. This is partially her fault anyway, and I'm sure that her powers will allow her to escape from the arms of Ms. Hayes. Antoine gets a hug from his mom before she ushers us off to class.

"No more dog saving, boys!" she calls out.

Once we're far enough away from the front office, Antoine and I break into laughter. I have to hold myself up against a wall to stop from falling over. Antoine has tears streaming down his face, and I can barely breathe.

"Did that just happen?" chokes out Antoine. "I can't believe it."

"You were amazing," I say. "You thought up that story so quickly!"

He bows, and then we break into laughter again. Once I'm able to breathe, I stand up and wipe at my eyes. "This was too stressful," I say.

"It was," says Antoine. "But it would have been worse without you here."

My heart leaps in my chest at that. Does this mean Fea is right? *Does* Antoine feel the same way about me as I do about him?

Antoine smiles at me. "So, what are we supposed to do now?"

"I'll handle that," says a voice, and there, at our feet, is Fea.

"Fea!" I say. "I'm glad you're okay. Why is everything going haywire?"

"Oh, it's *still* a mess," she says, and she shakes her head back and forth like she's soaking wet and trying to dry off. "Do you know how hard it was to get away from Ms. Hayes?"

I roll my eyes. "I'm sure you did just fine."

"Okay, *yes*, I did," she says. "But I couldn't disappear or change form. None of my powers were working!"

"What powers?" asks Antoine. "I still haven't had this explained to me."

"Soon," says Fea. "Let's get you back to your current timeline first."

"But, Fea, none of this should have happened!" I say.

"Later, David Bravo, I promise!"

Is she even going to be able to take us back to our original time? What if *all* her powers aren't working?

"So, what do we need to do?" asks Antoine. "To travel back, that is."

Then Fea *laughs*.

"David. Antoine," she says gravely. "You need . . . to take each other's hands. So I can transport you both."

Oh. *That's* why she laughed. I frown at her, but I do as she says.

Antoine interlocks his fingers with mine. His hand is soft and warm. I look down at it, and I like how it looks in mine. But as my heart races, I'm not sure I should look at Antoine. What if this makes him uncomfortable?

I glance up at Antoine. His face is . . . I don't really know. He's kinda smiling, but he also looks . . .

Scared.

"Here we go, boys!" says Fea, and soon, all three of us are twisting through the timeline, heading back to the present day.

MONDAY, SEPTEMBER 25
12:40 P.M.
Back to the future! Or the present. Both?
Time travel is really hard.

When we land outside the cafeteria, I'm *slightly* jealous of the fact that Antoine does not appear to stumble or sway in place like I do when I travel. In fact, it looks so *natural* to him.

And then he starts jumping up and down.

"Oh, my god, David," he says, "you can travel through *time?*"

"Shhh!" I say, putting a finger to my lips. "Antoine, you *have* to be quiet. Someone else could come out of the cafeteria and hear us!"

He puts his hands on my shoulders. "You realize this is the best day of my life, right? All those books I've read over the years, and it turns out my very best friend in the world can actually *travel* through *time?*"

I can't ignore how infectious his joy is. I smile back at him. "Okay, it *can* be cool, but it's also a lot more complicated than that."

"You mean complicated because you have a telepathic dog companion?"

"Actually, I'm not a dog," says Fea. "I only look like one!"

I start to say something, but Antoine crouches to Fea's level.

"Okay, so I have about one thousand questions," he says.

"But—" I say.

"Shoot," says Fea.

"Are you corporeal?"

Fea barks loudly. "I am *not*, Antoine Harris! An excellent observation."

"Are you physically affected by the constraints of time, or do you exist outside of it?"

"Wow, you really *did* come prepared for this," says Fea. "The Powers That Be and all their agents like myself exist outside of time. Also . . . non-corporeal. So no aging or anything like that."

"The . . . who?" Antoine says. "Bee . . . Powers?"

"I call them the Power of the Bees," I say.

"Think of them as the ethereal beings who were here before everything else and will be here long after," says Fea.

"Okaaaaayyy," says Antoine. "I'll come back to that later. Can you assume any physical form you want?"

"As long as it is a living creature," says Fea. "I usually

appear as a human when I'm helping others, so—"

"Wait!" I say. "Then why are you always an animal with me?"

"Because . . . it's fun?"

"You're like a cursed Disney movie companion," I say.

"Wow," says Antoine. "What else can you do?"

"Who knows anymore?" I say. "Fea, I really think something *is* wrong with your powers. You've made mistakes before—"

"Only a few!" she says, her ears drooping.

"But today was . . . That was a lot. What if we had changed my timeline too much?"

"Changed?" says Antoine. "Was something supposed to?" His eyes go wide. "David, are you trying to *change* the past?"

I sigh. "Fea . . . do you want to handle this one?"

The bell marking the end of first lunch rings, but Fea just freezes time, then sits down in front of Antoine. "Antoine Harris, I am a timeline guide, sent out into the world to help humans by offering them a chance to do a part of their lives over."

"Wow," he says. "That's . . . that's so amazing."

"I'm sure you have more questions—"

"Like four billion more," Antoine interjects.

"—but for the time being, all you need to know is that I'm trying to help your friend David Bravo."

Antoine looks to me, then nods. He lifts his chin in the

air. "Well, count me in," he says. "I want to help."

I'm panicking. *Again.* "Um, I'm not sure you can," I say.

"Oh, nonsense!" says Fea. "The more the merrier!"

But I know why Fea really wants Antoine to get involved. What if she pushes Antoine too hard? What if she messes up our friendship?

"However, Antoine Harris: you have discovered the secret of the timeline guides," says Fea, her voice grave and serious. "Can I trust you to keep our existence to yourself?"

Antoine nods. "Yes, absolutely."

"Wait," I say. "Why didn't I have to make that pledge?" I ask.

"Because I knew you wouldn't tell anyone," says Fea. "You barely accepted it yourself, so it was obvious you weren't gonna go blab about it to the universe."

"Wow," says Antoine. "A real time traveler. A non-corporeal guide! This is the best day ever."

"Glad you think so," says Fea. "Now, I think I need to pay a visit to the Powers and find out why my abilities are malfunctioning. Can I trust you two to behave?"

"You won't be disappointed," Antoine says.

"I like him already," says Fea. "Don't you agree, David?" She pops out of existence, and the world unfreezes.

"Yeah," I sigh. "I guess I do."

"I want to hear the whole story!" Antoine says. "Where else—*when* else—have you visited? Tell me *everything*!"

I wince. "I don't think it's as exciting as you think," I say. "It's not like Fea and I are traveling all over the world or going way into the past."

"I still wanna hear!"

I decide to sacrifice part of my own lunch to give Antoine all the details. I'm filled with warmth as I tell him about Fea's first appearance, but I leave out the *why*. I'm not sure I know it, first of all, and I *definitely* don't tell him about Fea's current theory.

By the time we get to his class a few minutes later, I've given him a *very* short summary of what's been happening to me, and Antoine looks like he's going to explode from excitement.

"So, you haven't found the right moment," he says. "What about that time you kicked a ball into George's face in third grade?"

I laugh. "I forgot about that. But that didn't really affect *me*. Maybe George is traumatized by kickballs now."

"Good point. What about when you and I had that skateboarding accident at the park?"

"We are definitely not meant to be skaters," I say. "But no, that can't be it. Fea says it has to be something *big*."

Antoine is quiet for a moment. "How early can it be?" he says.

"Early?" I raise my eyebrows. "What do you mean?"

"Well . . . do you think it's about you being adopted?"

My stomach sinks. There's been so much happening

lately that it's been easy to *not* think about Tommy, Project David, and the anxiety that's been slowly growing in me. But what other big event in my life *is* there?

"Maybe," I finally say, "but Fea says the only thing I can change is something *I* chose, not someone else. She had this theory about her changing my future—"

I stop. I can't explain that one to him, either. All of this involves him!

"I don't know, Antoine. It's all so confusing."

Antoine nods. "You know, this does explain a lot," he says.

"What do you mean?"

"The strange way you've been acting," he says. "You were dealing with all this stuff and trying to fix your timeline, and I had no idea. I was just really, really worried you weren't going to be my friend anymore."

I impulsively reach out and grab Antoine's hand. "Never," I say.

His hand lingers in mine.

I pull away, heat burning my face. "Anyway, yeah, there's been a lot going on, and I'm trying to fix it all."

"You have to tell me more," he says. "After school? If Dad doesn't make me practice more, that is."

"Yeah," I say. "And . . . thanks for being so cool about all this."

"No problem."

He reaches out, and we do our Handshake.

"Always friends?" he says, more of a question this time.

"To the end," I tell him.

Antoine heads into his class. There's a new feeling deep inside me, though, that I didn't expect. This one I actually welcome.

I'm *relieved*.

Because someone else finally knows what I'm going through.

TUESDAY, SEPTEMBER 26
2:40 P.M.
Antoine's request

Unfortunately, Antoine and I don't get to spend any real time together until practice the next day. His dad keeps him for extra running on Monday afternoon, and then we both have way too much homework. Mom says that sometimes, I need to do things I don't want to in order to be responsible. "You'll regret it later if you don't do your homework now."

I hate when she's right! Why can't she let me be irresponsible?

So I'm anxious to see Antoine on Tuesday, but at practice, I'm surprised when he *willingly* runs slower to stay with me on our five-mile course for the day. I keep thinking he's going to dart off and hang with the faster runners, but it never happens.

And the whole time, he's asking me *questions*.

It's like I'm being interrogated or something. Antoine wants to know everything about timeline guides, time travel, my existing timeline, and everything else. I tell him as much as I can, dancing around the truth of why Fea thinks she's supposed to change my future, but then Antoine asks something I don't know the answer to.

"How much extra time have you lived?"

"Huh?" I huff. I do love that Antoine wants to spend time with me, but also . . . this is quite possibly the worst time to ask me questions. I can barely breathe!

"Well, you've looped back on yourself at least twice," he says. "Meaning you've basically lived 'extra' time that the rest of us *haven't*."

I wipe sweat from my right temple. "Oh. That's a good point. It doesn't feel like it, though. Especially since I didn't actually experience those blocks of time myself, you know? I basically have to figure out what changed from *other* people."

"That sucks," says Antoine. "If I was one of the Power of the Bees people, I'd design a better system. Theirs is super inefficient."

"I guess," I say. I don't want to get into that, because I still don't know why they sent Fea to me or why they believe my life is off track. Or *will* be, if you believe Fea. Which I don't.

Antoine falls silent for the remainder of our run, but he does stay with me the whole time, much to Coach Williams's frustration. Once we're done, we've both got our hands on our heads, trying to catch our breath.

I glance over at Antoine, and his eyes look all . . . sad.

"What's up?" I say.

His mouth twists up on one side.

"You're acting weird, Antoine."

"Sorry, it's just that . . . I was curious about something else."

I look around at our other teammates as they finish, and I gesture to the sycamore tree on the far side of the field where the team's duffel bags are gathered. "We're going to go stretch!" I call out to Coach Williams, and he nods his approval at us.

I grab Antoine's arm and pull him along as I jog over to the tree. "We can't talk about this in the open," I say.

But Antoine doesn't say anything. He shifts his weight from foot to foot.

Then, finally, he asks, "David, can you . . . summon Fea?"

"Like right now?"

He nods.

"I don't know. Sometimes. She is incredibly unreliable when it comes to being summoned."

"Ah, okay," he says, and he turns away from me for a moment.

I sense that Antoine needs . . . comfort. I think. Should I hug him? Ask him again if something's wrong? How do people *do* this? Maybe I could call Mom and ask her how to deal with someone else being sad or upset. She's a therapist. She'd know the answer!

But I don't.

So I reach out to Antoine, thinking I'll grab his hand,

but then I jerk it back. Uncertainty creeps into my heart. "Hey," I say instead. "Are you okay?"

Antoine turns, and there are tears pouring down his cheeks. "Can I have a hug?" he asks.

For a moment I don't move at all. I've never seen Antoine cry before, and I'm suddenly able to see a new side of him as his face twists up.

Then I just *act*. I stretch my arms out and Antoine leans into me, and even though he's not really moving, I can tell he's still crying.

Antoine pulls away, and his eyes are red and puffy. "I'm sorry," he says. "You got me thinking about a lot of stuff, and it all just . . . came out."

"It's okay," I say. "You know, my mom says that it's better to release emotions rather than keep them inside. They always get worse if you push them down."

Antoine laughs, more a nervous thing than anything else. "Yeah, I think she's right."

"Not that I'm good at that," I say, smiling.

"I don't know, you always seem so emotional to me. I like that about you."

My face warms. Wow, that really *does* happen around Antoine a lot.

I can hear Fea's voice in my head, pushing me to tell Antoine what I feel, and boy, do I wish I was thinking about something else.

"What's going on?" I say.

Antoine wipes at his face again. "Okay," he says. He

takes a deep breath, then lets it out. "I think I need Fea and her powers."

Just like that, Fea appears between us and yips *very* loudly. "Fea, your friendly timeline guide, at your service," she says.

"Antoine can summon you like *that*?" I say. "Why do you always ignore me?"

"He's in a state of distress!" explains Fea. "Can't you see that, David Bravo?"

"And I'm *not* in distress other times?"

"Actually, I don't know," says Fea. "I didn't hear Antoine at all. I just happened to show up now."

"What's going on?" I ask.

"There *might* be a problem," she says. "With my powers. And *the* Powers."

"That's so vague!" I yell.

"*You're* so vague!" she yells back.

"Do you two do this every time you talk?" asks Antoine.

We both turn to him and say in unison, "YES!"

"Fea, why don't you tell us what the problem is?" he says.

"Well, since you asked so nicely . . . ," she says.

I stick my tongue out at her.

"The Powers wouldn't take a meeting. At all. In fact, they appear to have stopped all communication with me."

"That seems bad," says Antoine.

"It is definitely unprecedented," says Fea.

I can't escape the realization that comes to me then: Is

all this stuff that's never happened to Fea before happening now . . . because of *me*?

Is there something wrong with me?

"Are you doing okay?" Antoine asks.

"Well, never mind me, Antoine Harris," she says. "Are *you* okay?"

He is quiet for a moment, and then: "Can I ask you a favor?"

"Certainly," says Fea. "You have graciously kept the timeline guides' secret. What is your request?"

Antoine sighs. "I want you to fix my life."

"I'm sorry, *what?*" I say.

"David, you're my best friend," says Antoine. "And I've wanted to tell you for a long time, but I was afraid to. Not because of anything you did, but because . . . well, it feels so enormous. Like it's impossible."

"What are you talking about?" I say, my heart thumping faster in my chest.

Antoine takes a deep breath. "I need to have won that placement run," he says.

"What?" I say. "The one where you sprained your ankle?"

He nods. "That exact one. I have to get on the varsity team because then I won't be disappointing my dad."

Fea blows air out her nose. "I don't get it. What does that race have to do with your dad? Besides, David already tried—"

"—tried to change that day because I got sick," I say,

cutting Fea off and then giving her a dirty look.

"Right," she says. "Definitely."

"But maybe that's because *I* need to make a choice," says Antoine. "Maybe it was never David's decision to make."

"I don't know," says Fea. "I mean, that technically sounds possible, but I can't just snap my finger and make things happen. I'm not like the Thanos of wishes."

"How do you even know who Thanos *is?*" I say. "You've been dead forever."

"I pay attention to things!" she says to me, then turns back to Antoine. "You're not my assignment, so I don't think I can help you."

"But you owe me one," says Antoine.

"What?" says Fea. "I owe no one anything!"

"I'm keeping your secret," he explains. "You made me swear and everything."

She scoffs. "Antoine Harris! You would threaten to disrespect the sacred secret of the non-corporeal timeline guides?"

"No!" he says quickly. "I didn't mean it like that. I just . . . I need the help, Fea. It's getting really bad. My dad is giving me such a hard time about missing all those practices because of my injury, and this morning . . ." Antoine sighs. "Coach Williams said he already picked the varsity team, and now I'm not on it."

My heart sinks. All of this is because of *me.*

"I'm sorry," I say.

"I am, too," says Fea. "But you seem to be forgetting that even if I wanted to help, my powers are a huge mess."

"Please?" says Antoine, and I realize I've never seen him like this. He must be in a lot of pain, the kind you can't see, the kind you bury deep inside. I think back on my interactions with him over the course of these past few weeks. It was right there, and I didn't pick up on it once. I know that his dad's always been very intense about running. But there was also all that stuff about how I did him a favor and how he was thankful that he'd be getting a break. . . .

It feels weird to think that we have both been keeping the truth from one another at the exact same time. Antoine was brave enough to finally tell me.

Should I do the same for him?

The thought is still too scary to me, but I feel like I have to do *something* for him.

I crouch in front of Fea. "Fea, I know you're supposed to be helping me," I say. "And we can still do that. But I believe Antoine, and I think this is the best thing for my friend right now."

I stand up and face Antoine. "I'm sorry I didn't notice it until now," I tell him. "I think you were telling me the truth in your own way, but I was so stuck in my own world that I didn't realize what you were saying."

"It's okay," says Antoine, smiling. "I couldn't find a way to tell you how bad things got. I really think if I got on varsity from the beginning, Pop wouldn't be so harsh on me."

"Wow, you two are really pulling on my heartstrings," says Fea, and she rolls onto her back and whines. "Someone should make a Hallmark movie about you two. They still make those?"

"Well, my mom watches—" says Antoine.

"Nevermind!" Fea shouts, leaping up and interrupting him. "You've convinced me. It is entirely possible that we are now closer to the true intentions of the Powers than ever before."

"Wait," I say, "what do you mean by—"

"Please remain in contact with each other while I attempt to initiate travel!" she says quickly.

Antoine and I stand there, looking at one another, then back at Fea.

"Ugh," she groans. "Must I explain everything? Hold hands! Duh!"

There is only a slight hesitation before Antoine reaches over and grabs my hand forcefully. "I won't let go," he announces. He sounds proud.

My heart patters. I'm nervous again. But I don't get time to think about it before Fea bounds forward, lands on Antoine's foot, then cries, "Away we go! Maybe!"

To the surprise of everyone, we fold in on ourselves, twist, and turn, flashing back across Antoine's timeline while Fea yells, "What a plooootttt twiiiiiissstttt!"

And then we land on the grass of the infield of the track, managing to stay on our feet.

"I did it, I did it!" Fea exclaims. She could not sound more thrilled with herself. "Antoine Harris, welcome to your past!"

TUESDAY, SEPTEMBER 12 (FOR THE . . . SIXTH TIME? WHO'S COUNTING ALL THIS?)
2:44 P.M.
Antoine's do-over

Fea, Antoine, and I have landed in the middle of the field, and the runners from both teams are warming up around the track. Antoine squeezes my hand really hard.

"David, look!"

He points across the field, and there we are, sitting across from each other, stretching.

"Wow, this is never going to stop being cool," Antoine says.

I twist around to see Mr. Harris—decked out in his very professional coaching gear—come toward us. I don't move, though Antoine panics and tries to hide behind me.

Mr. Harris moves past us as if we aren't even there.

I gotta admit, even I'm relieved.

"My powers are functional!" Fea exclaims.

"So, it's like a transfer of consciousness, is it?" Antoine asks her. "A shifting of temporal perspective?"

"You know way too much about time travel, Antoine," she says, and when I look down at her, I see she's changed form again. She's now a long slender dog with gray fur.

"What are you?" I ask Fea.

"A greyhound," she says. "They're racing dogs, so I figure it's appropriate."

The three of us walk over to Past Me and Past Antoine, and it's clear very shortly that we're in a timeline where I ate the spinach. I look awful, like my skin is made of wax, and I think I am sweating out of every pore in my body all at once.

"David, you look worse than I remember," says Antoine.

"Thanks," I say. "I don't know how you're going to get out of this one."

"Watch," he says, then kneels in front of Fea and starts petting her. "I'm ready. Do your thing, and I'll show you I can change my future."

"Gladly, Antoine Harris!" she says, wagging her tail. "In a moment, you will feel a sensation similar to timeline travel, only this time, your consciousness will be in your past self's body, okay?"

He nods, like everything Fea said makes perfect sense.

"Once you're there, you'll be able to interact with the real world. Make your decision, and when you've done so, I'll pull you back here."

"Perfect," he says. Seriously, it's like she told Antoine she's going to give him a high five. Why is he so casual about all this?

Maybe I need to read more of those books he likes.

"Your enthusiasm is inspiring!" Fea says. "Go change

your timeline, Antoine Harris!"

He then disappears. Literally. The Antoine standing next to me is gone, and then I see Past Antoine open his eyes wide. He looks in the direction of where we're standing, but . . . whoa. It's so weird. It's like he's looking through us.

"He can't see us," Fea explains.

"This is all still so very weird," I say. "Is this what it's like for you when I travel?"

"Yep," she says. "And Antoine isn't so far off about how it all works, either."

Fea is silent for a moment as we watch the past unfold.

"I really like him, David," says Fea. "And I think he really likes you."

"Whatever. We're not here about that."

I watch Past Antoine and Past Me talk while stretching, fully expecting the same outcome. Past Antoine leaves with his dad. I stand, looking like I'm lost and have never been on this field in my entire life. The race begins without me, I continue wandering about, heading straight for the collision with Antoine, and— I can't watch this again. I've lived it and seen it too many times already.

"This is pointless," I say. "It's all the same, Fea!"

"Just wait," says Fea.

Seconds before Past Antoine reaches me, he slows down, and Jesse Sánchez, who always tries to beat Antoine but never does, pushes past him, a hunger on his face, and *he* is the one who crashes into me. Antoine, now a few feet behind us, takes a leap over my body, which is splayed out over the track.

"Fea!" I cry out. "Are you seeing this?"

"Shush!" she says. "Let's see if he actually finishes!"

To our great amazement, just over fifteen minutes later, he does. Antoine crosses the finish line after completing the three laps around the school, and Mr. Harris rushes over to his son, screaming in excitement and hugging him. "That's my boy!" he cries out. "Excellent pace, and way to deal with that obstacle!"

Antoine's chest is heaving as he tries to catch his breath, but his face is lit up with joy. He looks so happy, but it lasts only a second. As soon as his dad says "obstacle," the smile is gone. "Where's David? Is he okay?"

A second later, Antoine is standing next to me, watching himself. "It worked!" he exclaims. "I won!"

"Well, it looks like you were right," says Fea, wagging her tail. "Doggone it, Antoine, you were right!"

"That was amazing," I say. "The way you just leaped over me!"

Antoine winces. "But are you going to be okay? Can't I go back into my body and help David?"

"I already got helped off to the locker room," I say. "I'll be fine in a few hours, if this goes like it did before."

"Thank you," he says to both of us. "For helping. You have no idea how much easier it's going to be at home now that I didn't hurt myself in this race."

Then Antoine collides with me but on purpose. He

wraps his arms around me and squeezes, and when I hug him back, I can see Fea over Antoine's shoulder.

She's got her tongue out, and she's wagging her tail faster than I've ever seen it go. I know she's got something sarcastic to say to me about Antoine, but she thankfully keeps it to herself.

"Okay," says Antoine, pulling away. "Now what?"

"I take you back to the present," says Fea. "Who knows what ramifications your choice will have?"

"Well, I'll definitely be on the varsity team," he says. "And it'll mean my dad isn't disappointed in me. That's all I wanted!"

"Perfect," she says. "All aboard!"

Antoine reaches down.

He grabs my hand.

My heart flutters, and my stomach drops.

And then Fea takes us back to our new timeline.

TUESDAY, SEPTEMBER 26
3:59 P.M.
Back home

When Antoine and I land on the field at school, I finally feel like an expert. I manage to bend my knees just a bit so I absorb the shock of the hard ground beneath my feet, and I am not out of breath, gasping for air, or splayed out on the ground.

"Wow, that is still the coolest feeling," says Antoine.

"Congratulations!" says Fea, still a greyhound. She runs a mean circle around the two of us, which is precisely when I notice the problem.

There's no one else around.

We're definitely next to the sycamore tree, and I shiver as a breeze flows over my skin. The track is empty, except for two duffel bags on the ground. They're definitely mine and Antoine's, but . . .

"Uh, Fea?" I say. "Did you mess up again?"

"What?" She freezes in place. "I never mess up!"

I glare at her.

"Okay, I *rarely* mess up!"

"Where is everyone?" says Antoine. He dives down and digs in his bag until he finds his phone. "Oh, it's almost four! Fea, we're *late*."

"Only by a few minutes!" she says. "I did the best I could, but your present time felt so slippery. I couldn't grab ahold of it."

I find my own phone and pull it out of my backpack, and sure enough, I have two texts and a missing call from Mom. "Oh, great," I say. "I probably missed my ride home!"

As I dial Mom, Fea whines. "Sorry!" she says. "I did the best I could."

"It's okay," I say. "I know this is out of your control."

Mom's voice is sharp when she answers the phone. "David Bravo, where *are* you?" she says. "I drove by the track, but Coach Williams said you were with Antoine?"

"Yes," I say, wincing. "Sorry, he wanted . . . to . . . you know, run longer."

"We'll talk about you and this practice thing later," she says, and I can tell she is *angry*. "I'm at the front of the school. When can you be here?"

"A minute or two!" I say, gathering my stuff. "Sorry!"

"Dad just texted me that he's on the way," says Antoine. "He said he isn't far, so he'll be here soon."

"Then all is well!" Fea announces. "Antoine, you've made a new choice in your life and changed your timeline. From here on out, it's up to you to live life as you see fit. I, for one, am proud of you for being bold enough to suggest the unexpected!"

Antoine smiles, and I'm pretty sure he's blushing. "Aw, thanks," he says. "I'm glad you could help me. This is gonna make things so much easier."

"Oh, David Bravo!" sings Fea. "What if this was it? What if this whole time, I was connected to you so I could help Antoine?"

She sounds excited when she says it, but her words sting. *Could* all of this have been just for Antoine? What about me? Do the Power of the Bees or whoever they are not care about all the problems I'm having?

But Antoine is so *happy* right now. I can see it all over his face. So I don't spoil his joy. Instead, as his dad approaches us on the track, I wish him well. "Text me later," I say. "If you need help figuring out how things changed, I'm around."

"Of course," he says, and then . . . he lingers. It's like he wants to say something to me.

But he shakes his head. "I'll see you soon."

When I pass Mr. Harris on my way to the front of the school, he waves at me. "Good to see you, David. You thinking of coming back?" he asks me.

"Uh . . . sure?" I say to him. I want to ask what he means, but he's already past me, and I keep moving, not wanting to make Mom wait much longer.

Coming back to what? I wonder.

"I'll return shortly," says Fea. "Just need to check on a few things!"

She disappears without another word.

Mom's car is sputtering in the front parking lot, and Mom is . . . Well, let's just say it's clear that this is going to be a very awkward ride. As soon as I get in the passenger seat and buckle up, I glance over at her, and she's full-on glaring at me.

"David," she says.

"Hi, Mom."

"What have we discussed about impromptu plans?"

I grimace. "Not . . . to . . . have them?" I guess. Because I don't actually know! *Have* we discussed this in this time-line?

Oh, I definitely do not like this part of time travel.

Mom frowns deeply. "David, you need to *tell* me about things like this. If you're going to start hanging out with Antoine again and going on these runs, I have to know about them."

"What?" I say.

Because . . . no. I didn't hear that right.

"I'm serious," says Mom. "Just shoot me a text, let me know, and that way I don't have to waste any time."

She pulls the car away from the sidewalk and then waits to turn out of the parking lot. "Thankfully, I was able to do a quick session over the phone with a client, but some days, it's not that easy."

I know she's speaking, but the words don't make any sense. Did she say that she thought I was going to *start* hanging out with Antoine again?

What does *that* mean?!

My phone starts buzzing in my pocket, but I know if I pull it out right now, Mom will only get more irritated. "I'm sorry," I say to her. "I guess I just got caught up."

"Is it because of this morning?" she asks. "Is that why you did this?"

My stomach drops. Like, I'm pretty sure it just exited the car and is now behind us on the road.

"I don't know," I say. "Why do you think that?"

Mom sighs. "I don't know what's been going on inside your head lately, honey," she says, her voice low and sad. "Sometimes, it's hard to know why you do the things you do, but I want you to know it's okay to tell me whatever you're feeling. I know what we talked about this morning is a big change, and if you want to stay, we can discuss that, too."

Stay?

Stay?

"I'm confused," I say.

"That's okay, too. I promise."

Oh, god, but that's not what I'm confused about! How do I get Mom to reveal to me what we apparently talked about this morning?

Even though the air is on in Mom's car, I start sweating. A *lot*. I wipe at my hairline, and my fingers come away damp.

"Do you think I should stay?" I ask her, hoping this will

get her to give me some sort of clue about our conversation.

Mom grips the steering wheel tightly. "I know it's been difficult," she says. "What with Antoine pulling away at the start of the year."

No! I think. *That happened* again?

"And you've had so many troubles in school this year, too."

I want to groan. What troubles?

"So it's a hard decision, and I know you have a lot of things to consider. Are you having second thoughts?"

I take a deep breath to calm the rising fear in me. I have absolutely no idea what Mom is talking about! It doesn't help that I can't force down my bubbling nerves while my phone continues to buzz repeatedly in my pocket.

"Mom, I don't want to be rude, but I think something happened. My phone keeps vibrating. Can I check it?"

This time, she smiles. "Of course, David. Thanks for asking."

I try not to seem too desperate as I yank it out of my pocket, but then I nearly drop it when I see that I have *thirty-three* texts.

And they're all from Antoine.

"It's Antoine," I say.

Mom nods at me. "Go ahead and take a moment."

I open my phone and go to my texts, scrolling back up them to the first one Antoine sent me, and my heart nearly bursts when I read it.

SOMETHING IS WRONG!

Then:

David, Fea messed up.
SHE MESSED UP.
Help me, I don't know what to do.

I'm already alarmed because Antoine *never* uses all caps.
I am trying to read all the texts, but more are coming in
faster than I can keep up. I reach another one in all caps:

OMG MY DAD JUST SAID HE IS OUR ACTUAL
COACH NOW.

What? I think. *How is that possible?*
And then, four texts in a row that I have to read twice
to fully understand:

DAVID, LOOK AT THE DATE.
PLEASE SUMMON FEA.
SHE WON'T APPEAR FOR ME.
SHE HAS TO FIX THIS!!!

The date.
The date???
I shut my screen off, then tap it. Once it comes to life, I

read the date. Over and over and over again.

March 26.

March.

THE TWENTY-SIXTH.

Fea has sent Antoine and me *six months into the future.*

MONDAY, MARCH 26
4:15 P.M.
I try to piece together my life!
(Spoiler alert: I CAN'T.)

I gulp down a wad of fear and send off a quick text to Antoine:

I'll come over in a few minutes!

Then I stuff my phone back in my pocket.

March 26.

March 26.

"Is everything okay, honey?" says Mom, glancing over at me.

I want to scream: NO, IT ABSOLUTELY IS NOT.

But I don't. I smile weakly at her, then say, "Yeah, of course. I think things are getting better with Antoine. He wants to do some homework before dinner."

"That's wonderful! I'm glad to hear it. I think your father will be, too."

I don't know what else to say. I feel like I'm sitting in a

puddle of my own sweat right now. My hands are damp. My underarms are, too. Even my *legs* are sweaty.

This is awful. Six months. SIX MONTHS. If her powers are messing up this badly now, is she even going to be able to fix this?

When Mom pulls into the driveway, Dad's pickup truck is there, his tools still in the bed. He must have just gotten home, which normally would have excited me. But now? I'm afraid to see him. I'm afraid to find out some new twist in my timeline. And most of all, I'm afraid to learn what decision they're waiting for me to make.

I hop out of Mom's car. "I'll be right back!" I call out, then I dart across our lawn to the Harris house before Mom can say anything else. I'm at Antoine's front door seconds later, pounding on it.

Mrs. Harris answers the door, and her eyes widen in shock. "David?"

"Hi, Mrs. Harris. Is Antoine in? He texted me and asked me to come over."

"Well, isn't this a surprise?" she continues as if I haven't said anything at all. "David, we haven't seen you over here since last year. How are you doing?"

"I'm . . . fine," I say, because I really can't answer that question truthfully. "You know, just doing school and all."

"Well, I'm glad you're committing to something this year. I know we were all sad when you stopped doing cross-country."

I honestly feel like a semitruck just hit me. I stand there, completely unable to say anything, my mouth hanging open.

Mrs. Harris raises an eyebrow at me. "You all right, David? You look a little sick."

I recover before I pitch forward and become one with the entryway tile at the Harris residence. "Sorry, I'm just a little tired. I actually went running with Antoine today."

Now it's Mrs. Harris's turn to be taken aback. "You did?"

"Yeah," I say, because apparently that's what I did. (Don't remember it, of course.)

"Well, I'm sorry to tell you this, David," she says, "but Antoine went off with my husband to see a trainer across town for some stretching routines. You know how hectic Antoine's schedule has been ever since his state placement last year."

"His *what*?"

"It's been amazing seeing his progress," she says, continuing on as if I'm *not* currently melting in panic on her doorstep. "But I'll let him know you came around, okay?"

She goes to close the door, then pauses. "It was really nice to see you, David. Don't be a stranger."

The door shuts in my face. It takes me a moment to muster up the strength to head back home, but I finally do, unable to escape the sinking sensation in my heart.

Antoine has become exactly the athlete his father wanted him to be. I'm sure Mr. Harris is thrilled. But in the process . . .

It sounds like Antoine and I really *are* no longer friends.

When I head inside my house and kick off my shoes, Mom's in the living room, drinking a mug of tea while Dad sits nearby. "That was quick," she says. "What happened?"

"He's busy," I say. "Got his schedule mixed up today or something."

Dad frowns. "You okay, mijo?"

I nod. "Yeah. I'm gonna go do my homework in my room."

My parents don't say anything. In fact, they continue to avoid the subject throughout dinner until the last possible minute. As I'm helping Dad clear the table, he lays a hand on my shoulder.

"Tomorrow," he says.

"Tomorrow?" I say.

"Why don't you give us an answer tomorrow?" He smiles real big at me, then looks over to Mom. "We'll support you regardless of what your choice is."

"Sure," I say, but an ice-cold terror runs down my spine. I know that if Fea were here, she'd make fun of my epic indecision, but this? This is *worse*. Because I'm having indecision about something I know nothing about!

The anxiety crawls over my skin, and I excuse myself

to my bedroom, where I try something I know isn't going to work.

I summon Fea.

I think about her. I beg her to show up and bring her annoying, wacky powers with her, because she has to fix this. There's no way that the Power of the Bees will allow this to stand! It's broken! It has to be repaired!

But Fea remains silent.

. . .

School the next day confirms that this is the absolute worst timeline of them all.

Gracie doesn't ignore me when I cautiously say hello to her in Mr. Bradshaw's class. Instead, she stares at me like I'm a mysterious creature from the deep ocean. It's a mixture of surprise and horror.

"What?" she says.

"Hi," I say. "How's it going?"

She actually looks around the classroom before gazing back at me. "Are you talking to me?"

"Yes," I say. "Why wouldn't I?"

Gracie shrugs. "I didn't know you spoke," she said. "You've barely said anything all year."

Okay, maybe I'm not on Tommy's or Walter's level, but that doesn't sound like me at all. When they enter the class—Tommy literally shoves Walter inside, and the two of them are cackling loudly—I brace myself for whatever comment the two of them are going to throw my way.

But they don't speak.

They don't even *look* at me.

By the end of Mr. Bradshaw's class, no one has spoken to me or glanced in my direction or acknowledged me in any way.

Somehow, I've become *invisible*.

. . .

I figured there would come a point during the day when things would start to feel normal again, but I'm standing in the middle of the cafeteria with my tray, staring at one of the lunch tables like a weirdo, because what I'm seeing makes no sense at all.

Antoine is sitting at a different table.

It's in the center of the cafeteria, and he's surrounded by other kids. I recognize some of them from cross-country and track: Phuong. Jorge. Caitlin. Some of the other track team members, whose names I don't know, and a few boys from the football and baseball teams.

And on either side of Antoine: Tommy and Walter.

Antoine appears to be telling a story. His face is lit up, and people are leaning in as he talks. I don't hear what he says, but the table breaks out in laughter.

He doesn't even look my way.

I think about walking over and seeing if someone would let me in. I even imagine that Antoine would ask someone to scoot to the side so I could sit across from him. But when another round of laughter breaks out, I see how happy he is. This is exactly what he wanted *and* more.

And he's done it all without me.

I dump my tray in the garbage and leave.

. . .

I discover that my sixth period, which would have been Track and Field since it's spring, is now free, so I end up sitting on the front steps until the school bell rings. I fall into silence because that's all there is in my life now. No one talks to me; no one seems to want to be my friend. Is this what Mom was referring to when she said my year had been "difficult"? I'm not on any team anymore, Antoine has "pulled away" from me, and I don't think I've ever been so alone.

How is this fair? How can this possibly be what the Power of the Bees want for me?

Mom pulls up in her car a few minutes after the final bell has rung. I didn't expect Dad to be with her. I climb in the back seat. "What's going on?" I ask.

"A surprise," Dad says, and a grin spreads over his face as he turns back to me. "You earned it."

It doesn't matter how many timelines I've been through; I still don't like surprises! But I give Dad the biggest smile I can, then stare out the window as my school passes by.

Do any of the other students here even care what's been going on in my life?

Does *Fea*?

She came into my life and promised to fix my past.

Then, she promised to fix my future. Now, everything is a wreck, and I don't know how to fix any of it. I have no idea where I came from or where I'm going. I don't know where I fit in or what to call myself.

Am I ever going to?

Moments later, we pull into the small strip mall a couple blocks from home and I perk up. There's a convenience mart here, as well as a laundromat, a tiny coffee shop, and then . . .

"No way," I say.

"Yes, güey!" Dad says back, and then laughs so hard he's crying.

"I don't get it," I say.

"It's a Spanish joke. I'll explain it later."

"Mom, are we here for Yolanda's?"

She nods. "This is the only time in your youth that you will be allowed to have dessert before dinner," she says. "And Fernando, you are *not* to steal one of the tiny spoons."

"I have never stolen anything!" he says, offended. But then he hides his face with his hand so Mom can't see him. "I'm taking two of them this time," he whispers.

"How come I'm getting ice cream?" I say, taking off my seat belt.

"Well, we figured it would put you in better spirits while we talk about your decision," says Dad.

And just like that, my mood is crushed.

Right. Dad said I had to choose by today.

Unfortunately, I still haven't figured out what it is I'm supposed to make a decision about. I fidget in the back seat, and my mind scrambles to come up with *anything* that'll get one of them to tell me what they want me to consider.

"I know it might have been fun to spend time with Antoine yesterday," says Mom, breaking my silence, "but it's also true that his life is on a different path."

Oh, you have no idea, I think.

"It happens sometimes," says Dad. "I remember how crushed I was when Mom packed us up and took us to Hawai'i. I thought my life was over."

Hawai'i?

Wait.

Wait.

"Are we moving?" I ask softly.

Dad's face immediately twists up. "What? No. No, we discussed this. I'm just giving an example."

"David," Mom chimes in. "I promise, if you decide not to stay, we're still not going anywhere."

"Stay?" I say.

"Stay at Mira Monte," she says, then she narrows her eyes. "Like we discussed?"

My heart feels like it has erupted in my chest.

Dad reaches out and puts his hand on my leg. "It'll take some maneuvering on our end, but your mom and I worked out that next school year, if we put you in La Sierra Junior High, the two of us can switch dropping you off. That way you won't have to take the bus."

"Unless you *want* to take the bus!" Mom adds. "It's all what you want, David."

No, no, no. I'm not hearing this. Change schools? They want me to go somewhere *else*?

"I don't understand," I say. "I don't get why I can't just *stay*."

"David, honey," says Mom. "I know it's a scary decision to make, but we know you've had trouble making friends."

"It's been a big adjustment for you," says Dad, agreeing with Mom. "And having to do most of it without your best friend? Well, that made it even harder."

Mom's the one to deliver the worst blow, though. Her face looks so sad when she says:

"David, *you* were the one who asked us to send you somewhere else, remember?"

I can't hold back the tears in my eyes anymore. They spill over and onto my cheeks, and I'm shaking my head. "This isn't happening," I say. "I don't want to leave. I don't want to go to a new school."

"Perfect," says Dad. He grabs my hand and starts caressing it. "That is totally fine, and we can stay here!"

"We can bring back Project David, too!" Mom says excitedly. "Anything to help you find your place."

"I don't need a *project*," I snarl. "I need to know how to fix my life!"

"David, please don't raise your voice," says Mom. "I understand you're upset, but there's no need to yell at us."

"Mom, I'm not one of your patients!"

As soon as the words come out of my mouth, I know they will sting. Mom recoils and Dad lets go of my hand. "David!" he yells. "What on earth was that?"

"Why would you even *let* me consider leaving school?" I cry out, fully aware that I should not be doing this, but I can't hold it back anymore. "Why would I go to La Sierra? It's so *far*."

"We just wanted to do what is best for you," Mom says.

"By sending me *away*?"

Now Dad looks furious. "Don't say that, David. Ever. That's not funny."

"Well, my birth parents gave me away," I say, "so it's not like it's impossible."

Both Mom and Dad are shocked into silence, and Dad's mouth hangs open a little. Mom wipes at a tear on her cheek, and I wonder if there's any truth to what I said. Are they trying to get rid of me? Is my life just going to be people leaving me?

I don't think about it. I grab the handle on the door and shove as I open it, and then Mom and Dad are screaming at me, but all that time I spent running has finally paid off, because I pull away from my parents, sprinting as fast as I can down the street, then turning right, and I keep running and running and running and running.

TUESDAY, MARCH 27
5:55 P.M.
I finally make my decision.

I didn't intend to end up there, but I find myself in the park near my house. It's small, and the entrance is tucked in between two homes. I keep running until I reach the other end, but I don't know what I'm doing. I wish Antoine was here. I wish he was still my best friend.

I wish I knew who I am or where I'm supposed to be going.

I collapse where I'm standing and lie on the grass, staring up at a cloudless sky, and I breathe in deeply, trying to calm my racing heart and fried nerves. I don't know what I've just done, and I certainly don't know how to fix it. But that's the story of my life right now! Everything is broken!

"Ugh, Fea!" I cry out. "Why can't you help me?"

A mosquito buzzes in my ear, and I slap at it, then yelp when I don't hit anything but myself. This is the cherry on top of the worst sundae ever made. That thought makes me even angrier because I blew up at my parents before I could get ice cream.

"Way to go, David Bravo," I say to myself, right as the mosquito buzzes near my ear. I go to swat it when I hear someone yell at me.

"Watch out!"

The voice is loud. Close.

Oh.

Real close. Like in my head close.

I sniffle. "Fea?"

"Down here," she says.

I sit upright and look around but don't see anything.

"Ugh, hold on!"

There's a loud thumping sound in front of me, and there Fea is on the grass in her xolo dog form.

"That's the last time I try out a mosquito," she says. "Like, I knew they were annoying, but it's even annoying *being* one."

"Wait," I say. "Was that you?"

"Yes, it was. I like to stay adventurous in my elder age."

"You don't even age," I say, lying back down in the grass.

For once, Fea doesn't have a witty comeback for me. She curls up against my side, and we stay that way for I don't know how long. I don't mind the quiet. What do I even say to her? How do I summarize everything that has happened to me in the last twenty-four hours?

Fea is the first to speak. She rolls over on the grass so she's belly-up.

"I think we have a lot to talk about, David Bravo."

I sigh. "That barely covers it."

"I know."

"But *do* you?" I say, sitting up. "Do you know what's happened?"

Fea whines softly. "Yes, David. I actually hitched a ride in the car."

"Really?"

"Yes," she says. "I thought about annoying you like I usually do, but it was clear that my usual shenanigans were not going to help in that situation."

"So you heard everything."

"Every word," she says, then licks my hand. "I'm sorry I made everything worse by helping Antoine."

"You couldn't have known that would happen," I say, petting her head. "I don't think *any* of us could have predicted this."

"Still, I messed up. I shouldn't have told you that the Powers put me in your life to fix Antoine." Fea stands to attention. "But I am here to help *you*. My charm still has one red line left. You're the last one, and I'm here until we both figure this out!"

I feel the weight of that press down on me. The last one. Meaning that Fea has helped more humans than I can possibly count, and yet . . .

I was the only one she couldn't fix.

I shake my head at her. "It's okay. I don't think it's worth it."

"Don't get all down in the dumps," says Fea. "I know this is a *huge* setback, but there's gotta be a way to keep Antoine happy while also improving your life."

"No," I say.

"Why not?"

"Because you can't help me, Fea. You can't change my life to make it better."

"I've been *trying*," she says. Her tail starts wagging. "We just haven't found the right decision in your timeline. We could—"

"No," I say again, shaking my head.

"Come on, David! It's just a temporary setback. Together, we can figure this out."

"No," I repeat. "There's nothing else, and I'm tired of repeating my school year. I'm tired of being dropped into a future where I don't know what happened in my past. I *already* don't know my past, Fea! I don't know where I came from, and every time your powers get all wonky and overshoot the present day, it's like a big reminder that I'll *never* know what my own past is."

Fea is quiet for a long time. "I'll make it up to you," she finally says.

It all feels so wrong, but I don't know what else to do. Fea is going to stick by my side until I figure out why my timeline is messed up, and in the meantime . . . what? Does my life just keep getting worse? Do none of my decisions actually matter?

"Please?" she begs, and her tail curls under her.

"How, Fea? What else is there to change?"

"You just need to take a bigger risk. That *has* to be it. Think bigger!"

"Except I have already! I even asked Antoine about it, and the most he could come up with was a couple embarrassing moments. What else could possibly be bigger than all *this*?"

The same anger that bubbled up in Mom's car is threatening to overflow once more. I stand up and pace away from Fea and back.

"There's nothing to change," I say, my heart thumping in my chest so hard I wonder if it's going to leap out of my body. "Nothing!"

"Come on, David Bravo," Fea says, wagging her tail. "Remember, you only live—"

I don't let her finish. I loose a scream at her. "AAAAG-GGGGGHHHHHH! No! Don't say it!"

Fea winces.

"I know I only live once! You keep telling me that, but I've now lived *four* versions of my first month at this school! So what you're telling me is a LIE!"

I'm steaming. I can feel the heat in my face, and it's like I can't stop.

"David Bravo, maybe you should—" Fea begins.

"You keep telling me what I should do," I say.

And what did that get me? I tried to find where my life

went wrong. I tried to stop hurting Antoine. I tried to give my presentation *my* way. It left me without friends and without answers.

Maybe Antoine was right. Maybe I haven't gone back far enough.

I kneel in front of Fea. "You want something risky? Something big? Something that'll change my whole life? Then take me back to the moment I was adopted and *change it.*"

For once, Fea is quiet. I'm so used to her constant talking that I know I've made my point.

"Well?" I say.

"Oh, no. No, no, no."

She bounds away from me, then comes back. Away. Back. Away. Back.

"No, that is a bad idea. We can't do that. Can we? Will the Powers That Be allow that? No, this is absolutely out of the purview of Regulation 12.A7.9. And the very basic point of what I do! David, *you didn't choose that.*"

I wave my hand in front of Fea's face when she paces back toward me. "Who cares?"

"David Bravo, there are rules for a reason," she says. "Some of which I have come dangerously close to breaking with you. But I can't take you to that pivotal moment in your life. Not only am I not allowed, but I'm pretty sure I *couldn't* do it."

"Why not? You helped Antoine, and that wasn't part of the agreement."

"I can't explain that," she says, a desperate tone to her voice. "And even if I could do what you wanted . . . well, David Bravo, I wouldn't do it."

"What? But I asked you to!"

"I don't think it's a good idea! I know you're upset, but that . . . that was someone else's choice. I can't change it. Your birth parents chose to have you be adopted, and there's nothing I can do."

"Then what good are you if you can't help me?"

I always knew puppy dog eyes were a thing, but it's a completely different experience to watch them happen on a dog like Fea. What I've just said must have felt like a slap in the face, because Fea's eyes are wide and . . . sad.

She looks *sad*.

"You know, I had a whole life before I was made into this," she says. "And most days, I get to see my powers change a person for the better in a way I *never* did when I was a living, breathing human. It's a wonderful feeling, David Bravo, to know you actually made an impact on someone."

"I'm sorry, Fea, but—"

"No, let me finish." She bares her teeth at me. "I got why this happened after I died, and I've certainly had difficult assignments. I've seen some *soul-crushing* things, but you know what? I helped people make those things *right*."

I look away from her as embarrassment turns my face red.

"So why can't you believe that I'm trying? That I do

actually want the best for you?"

"Maybe I don't deserve the best," I say, after some silence. "Maybe I'm so broken that I'm not worth the help."

I feel the hot tears come back.

"Maybe I shouldn't have been adopted at all. It would have made Mom's and Dad's lives easier. I mean . . . they practically want to get rid of me by sending me to another school."

"You know that's not true," says Fea.

"Well, I wish I could see what it would have been like if I hadn't been adopted."

"David Bravo," says Fea, her voice shaking. "Please don't say that. I know everything is hard, but your parents *love* you."

She comes forward, quick at first, then slowly over the last few feet until she's nearly touching me.

"I am promising you now: I am not leaving your side until we figure out why the Powers That Be sent me to you. I don't care how long it takes, even if it is forever."

"Forever?" I say. I smile and wipe away my tears. "Am I going to be immortal now?"

"Who knows?" Fea says, laughing. She puts her paw on my foot gently. "You only live once, David Bravo, and—"

And I don't understand it, but I immediately twist and turn, and I'm screaming, and *Fea* is screaming this time, too, and images flash by, not just of the last six months, not just of the last six years, but of *everything*—it's all going by.

Elementary school. The time I broke my arm falling out of a tree, Antoine screaming for his parents, the last time I went to Hawai'i, our first trip to Hawai'i, the day I started kindergarten and cried because I didn't want to be away from my parents.

And then I'm seeing things I don't remember. Mom changing a diaper. Dad feeding me. Mom and Dad, sitting in an office and signing a paper, both crying.

And then—

Poof.

We're on a floor. It's carpeted. Fea immediately falls over, then bounds back up. "David, are you okay?"

I rub at my eyes, nausea rolling in my stomach. "What did you do?" I ask. "Where did you take me?"

"Nowhere!" she says, looking around. There's a giant crib made out of white wood to my left. The walls are painted a light green, and there are cute decals of animals parading horizontally across it.

"Whose room is this?" I say. "I don't recognize it."

A baby gurgles in the crib, then starts babbling.

"¡Te escucho, Beto!" a woman calls out. "¡Ya voy!"

"Someone's coming!" I hiss at Fea. "Get us out of here!"

"I can't!" she cries back. "My powers aren't working!"

"Aren't working?" I scream. "But you sent us here!"

"David, *I didn't do this*!"

My stomach drops. I can hear footsteps in the hallway.

"Will they be able to see us?" I ask.

The footsteps get closer. Closer. Closer.

"I don't know!" Fea says harshly.

Oh, no.

We're going to be caught.

????

There's a closed closet door on the opposite wall, and I rush to fling it open, but my hand passes *through* it.

"Fea, what is *happening*?" I say, yanking my hand back.

"Well, that's good!" she says. "We're safe! If you can't interact with anything, we *must* be hidden."

My breath catches in my throat as a young woman with brown skin and black wavy hair appears in the doorway. And Fea's right: she doesn't seem to see us. She quickly makes her way to the crib and reaches inside. "Aw, Beto, estoy aquí, papito. Te prometo."

She clutches the baby to her chest and begins to rock it back and forth.

"This is all very cute and touching," says Fea. "But do you have an idea who these people are?"

The woman continues rocking the baby—who looks super young—as I turn to give Fea a worried look. "I know exactly as much as you!" I say.

"Excellent! Then we're on the case together."

"I'd prefer not to be here in this stranger's house at all! Why aren't you worried about this?"

"Well, the fact that you can't interact with the physical world around you means this is *just* like when I take any human to view the past. It's my magic preventing you from mistakenly altering history. Lots of measures put in place, you see, because humans are such unpredictable chaos demons, and we don't want a repeat of . . . well, a lot of things. Some plagues, a few missing ships—let's not have you accidentally start the apocalypse today, okay?"

"That's a little disturbing," I say, "but I'm most bothered by you calling people chaos demons. Isn't that what *you* are?"

"Moving on," she says, holding her head high. "I think we need to simply . . . observe."

I twist around and decide to approach the woman and the child. They can't see me, right? When I get closer, I see that the baby has light brown skin and a little tuft of hair.

But I'm transfixed by this woman. The way she looks at this child—*her* child?—is giving me goose bumps. She's got such *love* in her eyes, like there's nothing in the world that could ever get her to break her gaze. She's tender, too, like when she runs her thumb over the child's forehead a few times.

"You're my precious one," she coos. "Te amo mucho, Beto."

A voice rings out from another part of the house. "¡Yamira! ¡Unas de tus amigas están aquí!"

The young woman—who I now know is called Yamira—smiles down at the bundle in her arms. "Okay, Mami!" she calls out, then lowers her voice. "Did you hear that, Beto? Some of my friends are here. Will you be okay while I'm gone?"

Yamira lays Beto in the crib, and as soon as she does, I'm pulled away. The twisting hits me hard this time, knocking the breath out of me, and Fea howls alongside me.

"What! Is! Happening!" I manage to scream.

"Enjoy the ride!" Fea screams back.

There are no images this time; it's just a terrible, unending darkness until I see a pinpoint of light. It grows and grows, until it swallows the two of us.

We are suddenly deposited in a *new* room, this one a little bigger than the last. My vision blurs at first, and I nearly fall over, but the sight before me makes me freeze.

It's Yamira. She's kneeling across the room—painted blue, with decals of race cars and soccer balls along the wall—and there's the same child, only older and bigger, waddling toward her.

"That's right, Beto!" Yamira coos, her face lit up with joy. "Come closer!"

The kid nearly stumbles, and Yamira makes to catch him, but he actually stays upright. He finishes the journey across the room, and Yamira is so *happy*. "You did it, mijo!" she cries. "I'm so proud of you!"

The child babbles happily at her.

Something strikes me then: the strangest sensation that

I've been here before. The hair rises on the back of my neck.

"Fea, what's happening?" I say.

"I'd guess that this child finally walked on his own," she says.

"No, not that." I look down at her with wide eyes. "What's that feeling called, when you think you're repeating a part of your life again?"

Fea scratches at her ear. "Déjà vu?"

"Yes! That thing!"

"Are you experiencing it?"

"I am. Which is—"

"—impossible," she finishes. "I can't believe you got me to say that, by the way."

I move closer to the kid, staring at his wavy black hair and his dark eyes, and it comes to me all at once.

"Fea," I say, my voice shaking. "I know who this is."

"Beautiful, my fellow detective!" she says. "Would you kindly share it with me?"

I turn back to her, and my vision blurs with tears. "Fea, that's *me*."

????
(I STILL DON'T KNOW
WHAT YEAR IT IS.)

There is no doubt anymore: This is what I looked like when I was really young. I've seen photos on Mom's phone from when I was a toddler.

The weirdness of what I'm seeing overpowers me, and emotions rush to the surface: joy and sadness and confusion, all at the same time, all of them pushing tears out of my eyes and a smile onto my face.

"Fea, this is me," I say, my voice shaking. "This is *definitely* me."

And I—eleven-year-old me, that is—can't believe what I'm seeing.

"But . . . if this is you, who is Yamira?" asks Fea.

"I have a ridiculous theory."

"You know I love all things ridiculous," she says. "Give it to me."

I take a deep breath.

"Fea, I think the Power of the Bees granted my request."

"Noooooo," she says. "There's no way."

"But what else could this be? If I'm right, then . . ."

I walk up to Yamira, to the woman with the thick curls and the long lashes and the golden-brown skin.

"Oh, David Bravo," Fea says softly. "I think I know what you're about to say."

"This is . . . this is my mom, isn't it?" I say.

"Maybe," says Fea, who is surprisingly subdued. She actually starts to back away from me. "Are you sure, David?"

"This kid is named Beto. Maybe that was my name before my parents gave me away."

Fea growls low and deep. "I'm not so sure."

"Why aren't you more excited about this?" I ask. "This is exactly what I wanted to see!"

"Because I don't know what this *is*!"

"Well . . . use your magic! Do your powers work at all?"

"Maybe I can still put you into your body," she says. "See if you can, like . . . I don't know. Walk around? Babble like a baby? Oh, if this works, I may laugh for an hour straight."

Fea licks my shin.

Nothing happens.

"And . . . go!" she says, then bops me with her nose on the back of my leg.

"I don't think it's working," I say.

"That's very helpful, David Bravo," she says sarcastically.

I feel the pull a moment before it hits, and then we're gone, spinning away from the scene. This time, images *do* flash by, none of which I can make out, and then . . .

A school.

I'm standing on a sidewalk, and there are kids everywhere, and for a second, I think I'm being swarmed. I cry out and one kid, holding his backpack in one hand, rushes toward me and—

Oh, right.

He goes *right through me.*

I don't feel anything when he does, but that actually makes it *weirder.* I turn and watch him run to the front steps of the school, and I would probably be freaking out more about the numerous kids who run through my body, but the sign in the parking lot is way more distracting.

MORENO VALLEY ELEMENTARY SCHOOL.

Moreno Valley? That's *so* close to Riverside; it's like the next city over!

"Fea!" I call out. "Fea, look at this!"

But she doesn't answer. I look for her at my feet, assuming that she's still a xolo dog or some other animal, but I don't see her.

"Fea?" I call out again, much more hesitantly. I step into the parking lot and run so I don't get hit by an oncoming car. Though wouldn't it go right through me, too? Probably, but I'd rather not test that out. "Fea, where are you?"

"Over here, David!"

I groan. "Fea, describe where you are," I say. "Your voice just sounds like it's in my head, remember?"

"Oh, right," she says. "Um . . . third row of cars. Black sedan. Hurry!"

What's a sedan? I think. But I don't need to ask that because once I cut through the cars—actually through them, which ends up being even weirder than people running through me—I see a xolo dog sitting behind a black car.

"What is it?" I say.

"Inside."

That's all Fea says. I get closer to the car and—

Oh, my god.

I see me in the passenger seat. I'm a few years younger than I am now, but it is unmistakably me. I crouch and peer through the window and see that I'm . . . *crying?* Yamira is sitting next to me, and she looks concerned.

I know this is going to be possibly the weirdest thing I've ever done, but I stick my head right through the door so I can hear what's happening.

"Beto, please," says Yamira. "Tell me what's going on. You were so excited to start school yesterday!"

"No one's going to like me," Beto says. "I'm never going to make a friend."

"That's not true at all," says Yamira. "Not for someone as bright and funny as you are. I bet you'll have like *five* new friends by the end of the day."

Beto wipes at his nose. "You think so?"

"I *know* so."

I pull my head out of the car. "Fea, try and put me back into my body again."

"I've *been* trying!" she says. "Not a single one of my powers is working! I can't freeze time, I can't transfer your consciousness, and I can't contact the Powers or any other timeline guides!"

The door swings open and like everything else, it passes right through my body. Beto steps out, but before he shuts the door, he turns back to Yamira.

"You promise everything will be okay?"

I feel the tug right as Beto asks that question.

"No, *no!*" I say. "Not again—"

But we're already twisting and turning.

A moment later, I'm actually *sitting*. It takes me a moment to get my bearings, but I figure out I'm on a bench. I look around and see that I'm outside. . . . Oh. Wait.

There's a jungle gym nearby, a seesaw, a set of monkey bars. . . .

A bell rings, and a bunch of tiny children come pouring out of two sets of doors of a nearby building. They're screaming and laughing. Some of them immediately head for the playground, but most of them—carrying colorful lunch boxes—swarm the benches near me.

But not *my* bench.

One lone kid comes to sit there.

Beto.

I don't think Beto is any older than when I last saw him. So . . . is this the same day? Why are Fea and I here?

"You know, I travel like this all the time," Fea says, and I twist to the side see her panting at my feet next to the bench. "And I also don't technically have a body, but I gotta say: I think this is going to make me sick."

"Now you know how I feel," I mutter, staring at Beto. He nervously glances around, then pulls a small plastic container out of his lunch pail. He eats it with his eyes on the other kids. Wow, I guess I'm nervous even in this timeline?

But then another boy sits across from him. He's Black, he's got these short dreads in his hair, and when he sits down, a smile flicks across his face. "That smells good," he says. "What did you bring?"

Beto looks up, surprised. "Um . . . well, my mom made it. It's called chile relleno. It's like . . . like a big pepper stuffed with . . . stuff."

"Cool," the other kid says. "My mom made me oxtail stew. They don't really sell it in places around here."

"What's oxtail?" Beto asks.

"It's a part of a cow. My mom says it's the actual tail, but it doesn't *look* like a tail, so I think she's just making it up."

Beto puts a forkful of food in his mouth, and before he's done swallowing it, he says, "My name is Beto."

"I'm Anthony," the other kid says. "Let's be friends."

"Cool," says Beto.

Anthony?!

"Hey, Fea?" I say, my voice raising in alarm. "Fea, who is that? I've never met that person before."

But Fea is growling again. "This is why I thought this

· 272 ·

was a bad idea," she says. "We don't know what we're dealing with here or how it's going to affect the timeline!

Before we can make sense of it, we twist.

We turn.

We are *both* yelling.

We're in a room. A bedroom. There's a dim lamp on in a corner, and Beto sits on the twin bed, writing in a notebook. He's a little bit older than in the last glimpse we got.

I'm doubled over, my stomach cramping. "Fea, can you make this stop?" I ask.

"I'm trying!" she yells back.

The door is torn open—by Yamira, who immediately slams it behind her.

"I'm an adult, Mami!" she yells. "You don't get to make decisions for me!"

Beto looks up at her, confused.

"Sorry, papito," she says. "I didn't mean to yell."

"It's okay," he says. "Why do you and your mami fight all the time?"

Yamira sighs. "We don't *always* fight."

"You fight a lot," says Beto, then turns his attention back to his homework.

Yamira sits on the edge of the bed. "Mi amor, sometimes it's hard to live with your parents. I'm working really hard, though, and I think we can have our own place next year."

Beto glances up at her. "Really?"

"Si, papito," she says, running her fingers through his black hair. "A *whole* house."

He smiles. "That would be cool."

I'm still bent over, and I'm now soaked with sweat. Then the tugging sensation hits again.

"Oh, come *on*!" I manage to say.

We twist.

We turn.

I'm out of breath when Fea and I are deposited on concrete. We're in a park of some kind. It's bright and hot out, and I'm out of breath once again.

"Fea," I manage to gasp. "Fea, you have to stop this! I don't know how many more of these jumps I can take."

Fea's tongue flops out of her mouth as she pants. "David, I am not doing this! I promise!"

I see two boys riding their skateboards down the sidewalk in our direction. One of them wobbles a lot as he rides, but I also can't judge them. I haven't ridden a skateboard in years, not since Antoine and I tried and failed to become professional skaters in a single afternoon.

As they get closer, they come to a stop just short of me and Fea, and they're staring at us, their eyes wide.

It's Beto and Anthony. They're still younger than I am, but not by much.

"Fea," I say, "do you have any theories as to why this is happening?"

Before she speaks, someone else does.

"What's up, buttfaces?"

I have two simultaneous thoughts:

1) Who says "buttface" anymore?

2) Someone is about to walk through me again, isn't he?

The second thought comes through as a third boy on a skateboard does, in fact, pass right through my body. It . . . tickles. That's the only way I know how to describe the sensation. Well, it's also disturbing. Why could I feel something this time, but not before?

The newcomer has on a helmet, which he takes off to reveal bushy dark brown hair. He's the same age as Anthony and Beto, so maybe he's their classmate?

"Hi, Tommy," says Anthony softly.

"*Tommy?*" I say. "No, Fea, this isn't real! Who is that?"

"What are you two up to?" he asks.

"Just . . . skating around," says Beto.

"I bet you aren't as good as me," says Tommy, who, by the way, *isn't* Tommy at all. Who are these imposters?

Beto sighs. "Probably not," he says. "I just started a few months ago."

"Can you do this?" Tommy says, and he pushes down the sidewalk and executes a perfect ollie, landing smoothly and twisting the board around so that he comes to a stop.

"Not yet," says Anthony.

"That's because you suck," Tommy sneers.

"Yeah, we *know*," says Beto. "We already established that."

"Well . . . maybe if you hadn't been adopted, you'd be

normal like me," says Tommy, and then he skates off.

If I was in pain before, it's nothing like the gut punch that hits me then.

Tommy's words ring out in my head: *If you hadn't been adopted.*

Which means Yamira isn't my birth mother.

I sink to the ground as Beto and Anthony skate off. "Fea, help me understand this," I say. "How am I *still* adopted in this timeline?"

"I am not sure you're going to like my answer," she says softly.

"Just say it."

She makes a grunting sound. "I think the Power of the Bees interpreted your request how *they* wanted. They're just showing us what your life would be like if someone *else* had adopted you."

"What? How is that possible?"

I feel the pull coming right then.

"Oh, no," I whine. "Can—"

We twist.

We turn.

We appear in yet another new location, and my vision blurs into darkness around the edges. I can't even remember what I ate last, and yet I can feel something heading up from my stomach, so I hunch over once more.

"Fea, *please*," I cry. "Make it stop!"

Fea is hacking up a storm, and it sounds so loud in my

head. "Powers!" she cries out. "Okay, okay, I get it. You've taught us a lesson! Take us home!"

Nothing happens. I stand upright and discover that we're in a dining room. Whose? I have no idea, at least not until Beto—now just a little younger than I currently am—comes stomping in and loudly pulls a chair out from the table.

"Beto, I *really* don't need a temper tantrum right now," says Yamira, who follows after him. "Especially not after finding out you *fought* someone at school!"

"Well, *he* started it," says Beto, and he puts his head down on the table.

"Maybe," says Yamira, "but we've talked about this, papito. There are other ways to resolve problems than punching someone."

Beto doesn't respond, and Yamira stands next to him, waiting.

"Why are we being shown this?" I ask Fea, but she doesn't answer.

"Beto," says Yamira. "I'm talking to you."

"I'm a table now, Mami," he says.

She sighs. "No, you're not."

"I have become the table. It is my destiny."

Fea paws at my leg. "That certainly *sounds* like you," she says.

I frown at her. "So . . . the Powers wanted to show me that I'm still the same person in two different timelines?"

I feel the tug.

The twisting.

The turning.

It's bright again. We're outside, and the sun is too bright. This time, I collapse, falling to my knees as tears blur my eyes. My stomach aches something fierce, and I can hear Fea's whines in my head.

"Please, Powers . . . stop," she begs.

There's a loud popping sound, and my head snaps up.

Wait.

We're on a field. Not just any field, but one encircled by a track!

I can see runners coming around the near corner, and I push myself to my feet. That sound must have been the starting gun! The track is one of those all-weather ones made of red rubber, like the one over at Poly High School. I don't recognize the team colors, though. One team has yellow-and-black jerseys and black shorts; the other is all green.

"Fea, look!"

Coming around the corner is Anthony. He's clearly in the lead, his dreads bouncing as he runs. He almost looks like he's flying over the track.

"Fea, how is it that Anthony is an entirely different person but *still* runs track?"

Fea yips loudly. "Alternate timelines . . . they can be a surreal thing to experience, David. But what do I know anymore? None of this should be possible!"

Anthony maintains his lead as he rounds the next corner of the track, and that's when I see him.

Beto.

Standing on the inner field, his hand over his mouth.

Suddenly, he darts forward, and my stomach does flips inside me.

"No!" I call out, because I know exactly what's about to happen.

Beto lurches forward and steps onto the track, and as he does so, Anthony collides with him.

"You're kidding me!" I scream. "How?"

"This is too much," says Fea, sitting next to me. "I've seen some ridiculous things as a guide, but *this*?"

Anthony goes sprawling onto the track, and then he's clutching his ankle, rolling around in pain. Meanwhile, Beto crawls to the side as two runners from the other team narrowly avoid him, then finish in first and second place.

"Even in a whole separate life," I say, "it all *still* happens."

"What?" says Fea.

I see a coach—not my Coach Williams, though—run to Anthony. I hear him yell at Beto.

"It's all the same," I say. "Please, take me *home*!"

Fea trots over to me. "Let me try something," she says. "Think of home. Anything and everything about home, David Bravo!"

Think of home? What does that mean? Am I supposed to just think of things at my house?

I do exactly that because I need to get home *now*. The images appear in my mind: Mom. Dad. A pot of noodles on the stove. Dad's blue pickup truck.

Fea puts her paw on my foot.

And then we twist and turn, and I feel like I'm being wrung out by time travel, like someone is squeezing out every part of my body over the sink.

When I land, it is surprisingly comfortable. It helps that the Powers have deposited me and Fea on a bed this time, especially since my mind and stomach are spinning at a million miles an hour.

"David," Fea gasps. "David, where are we?"

I push myself up, hoping that the Power of the Bees have heard my wish.

If they have, they don't care.

I'm not home. I'm in someone else's bedroom.

I fling myself off the bed and make for the door, and because of everything I've just been through, I assume that I can walk right through it.

I can't.

I smack my head against it. *Hard*.

"No!" I cry, clutching my forehead. I spin around to find Fea in the middle of the room. "Where is this?"

"I asked you the same question! I don't know!"

"What am I supposed to do *now*?"

Fea doesn't answer, and my stomach sinks to my feet.

We're in the wrong timeline, and we're completely lost.

TUESDAY, MARCH 27
4:34 P.M.

Fea sniffs the air a few times. "This room smells like you," she says.

"That's . . . weird," I say. "Also, I'm standing right here. Maybe you just smell me."

She leaps off the bed and then dives headfirst into a pile of laundry. Her head pokes up, and she's got a dirty sock over her eyes.

"Nope," she says. "This is definitely you."

"No, it's not," I say. "This isn't my house!"

My phone vibrates, and when I pull it out, my heart sinks.

Mom, it says.

"My mom's calling!" I say as the phone continues to vibrate.

"Well . . . are you going to actually answer it?" asks Fea, the sock now in her mouth, and she shakes her head from side-to-side before flinging the sock across the room.

As she bounds after it—ew, *gross*—I wonder if I should

pick up the phone. Before Fea and I were sent on this trip, I basically ran away.

I decide *not* answering it is a much worse option.

"Hello?"

"Where are you?" says a voice on the other end.

A voice that *isn't* my mom's.

"Who is this?" I say.

There's a momentary silence. "Did you just ask your own mom who she is?"

Wait. That voice . . .

No. *No!*

This isn't my mom. This is . . . this is Yamira.

"My who?" I say.

Which is absolutely a mistake. "Beto, this isn't funny. You told me to pick you up, and I took an hour off work to get here, and now you're not at school."

"I'm at home," I blurt out, and then immediately face-palm.

"You're at home."

"Uh . . . yeah."

"You're not at school."

"No."

"But I'm at school."

"I guess?" I say, because I don't understand this! How am I interacting with Yamira?

"David, I think you should hang up the phone," says Fea.

"Beto, I'm sorry you're having a hard time at school,"

says Yamira, "and I'm sorry that Anthony stopped being your friend."

A jolt of anxiety pierces my heart. This . . . this can't be real.

"But you are making me very, *very* upset with your behavior."

I can't take this. I hang up, and seconds later, the phone is ringing again.

It says Mom on the screen again.

"Fea, how?" I ask.

"Something is horribly wrong," she says. "None of this should be possible. You shouldn't be able to interact with a past timeline at all! There are protections in place!"

But those protections must be gone, because now I'm fully in my alternate self's timeline. I turn away from Fea and wrench the bedroom door open.

I'm in a completely different house. It's not neat and organized like mine; there's stuff everywhere. There are two paintings on the wall in the dining room of a gorgeous beach scene, complete with palm trees and a blue ocean. The stove is silver, not black, and the sink has just one basin instead of two. Even the refrigerator is completely different.

I can hear Fea's nails clicking on the tile behind me. "Fea, am I stuck here?"

"I don't think so," she says. "But . . . my powers didn't work like they were supposed to. You thought of home, right?"

I whirl around. "Of course I did! And this isn't my home!"

"So then what are the Powers That Be trying to tell us?" Fea says. "There's got to be a message here! Nothing is an accident, David Bravo!"

"Except when I got Antoine hurt in EVERY TIME-LINE," I say.

"Funny," she says. "Maybe you'll grow up to be a comedian in this timeline!"

"I don't want to be here!" I shout.

Fea's ears fold back and she whimpers.

"This all feels like the worst joke ever told," I say. "Even in another timeline, my life is the same, isn't it? I'm still getting picked on, I'm still losing my best friend, I'm still getting in trouble all the time."

"We've only seen a little bit of your life," Fea says quietly. "Just pieces of it."

"And it's enough. Enough for me to know that my life *always* needs to be fixed. I'm cursed in every timeline, aren't I?"

"Don't say cursed!" she says. "No one is cursed, no matter how unlucky or unfair things are."

She huffs for a moment, then says, "You know, I would have done anything for parents like yours."

I freeze in the middle of this strange dining area. "What did you just say?"

"You saw only the tiniest sliver of my life," says Fea. "You saw bits and pieces of Mari, you saw me betray her, you saw me refuse to stand in my truth."

"I know," I say. "And I'm sorry that happened."

"Me, too, David Bravo," she says, and her tone has a sharp edge to it. "But what you didn't see was everything else around it. I couldn't be who I wanted to be when I was your age. The idea that I could go to the dance with a girl I liked? Now *that* was impossible."

"But I don't—"

"No, stop!" she says, baring her teeth at me. "This isn't about Antoine, it isn't about regret, and it really isn't even about me. This is about *you* being unable to see what you already have!"

I know dogs can't cry like humans, but Fea sure is making it look like it's possible. "I know it's confusing and scary that you don't know where you came from," she says. "And I get why this whole Project David thing feels ridiculous to you. But can't you see how much your parents love you? I know for a fact that whoever you end up being, they will accept you. Why can't you see that?"

This time, when the sensation tugs at me, I groan loudly. "Stop it!" I yell, hoping that whoever is doing this can hear me. "Just take me back!"

Twist.

Turn.

Flash.

And then I'm back.

I'm really back.

Fea and I are crumpled on the floor of my room, and she

rolls off me, then shakes herself.

"Is this it?" she says. "Is this your place?"

My head aches, and it hurts to look at any source of light, so I squint as I sit up.

That's my bed. The tiny desk I use to do homework and read. The hamper I put my dirty clothes in.

"I think so," I say. "It looks like it."

"David, is that you?"

It's her voice. My mom's voice.

"Fea, what time is it? Like, what day?"

"I don't know," she says, and I can hear the scowl in her voice. "Do I look like a calendar?"

"You literally travel through time!" I whisper fiercely. "How do you not know what time it is?"

"Fernando, it sounds like him," I hear Mom say.

"But he ran off down the street!" Dad whispers back. "How could he be back here?"

"Honey!" Mom calls out. "Are you here? We just want to talk!"

I glare at Fea. "*Now* you send me back to exactly when we left?"

"I didn't do any of this!" she hisses. "Remember?"

"Who are you talking to, David?" Mom asks. She sounds so close!

I rush to the door and grab the handle just as it starts to turn.

"David, open the door, honey," she says.

"Just a second!" I call out, then glare at Fea. "Fix this. NOW!"

"Fix what, David?" says Dad.

One of them jiggles the handle again.

"What am I supposed to do?" says Fea. "You have to give me a place to go!"

"Take me to the beginning!" I yell.

"David Bravo, please let go of the door and let us in!" Mom yells. "This is your last warning!"

"The beginning?" asks Fea. "What does that mean?"

I turn around and press my back against the door, still clutching the handle. "I know what I'm supposed to do," I tell her. My face flashes hot with frustration. "I know where all my problems started."

The handle stops jiggling. "What problems?" says Mom, her voice nowhere near as angry as it just sounded.

"Perfect," says Fea. "Then tell me when!"

"When you showed up!"

Fea's ears droop. "What?"

"David, who is in there with you?" Dad asks.

"No one!" I call out, and now I'm crying again. My voice breaks when I speak. "I'm—on the phone! I promise I'll explain everything in a second."

There's silence on the other side of the door, and then:

"Okay, David," says Mom. "You promise you're not going to run off again?"

"I promise," I say, sniffling. "I'm not going anywhere.

You won't have any problems with me."

I am met with silence as Fea whines in my head.

"David," she says, "you can't mean that."

I shake my head. "My life wasn't perfect, Fea. I know that. But if I learned anything from all this—especially from what we just saw—it's that it's never going to be perfect. I can't keep doing this. There's nothing in my past to fix. I have to accept this."

"Accept what?"

"That I won't always be best friends with Antoine," I say, and hot tears spill down my cheeks. "That I'm never going to know anything about my birth parents or where I came from."

"Oh, David Bravo," says Fea.

"But it's okay. Because you're *right*. I still have *my* parents, and I love them, and they love me. If I can just . . . do this again, all the way from the beginning, I can at least fix *that* part of my life."

She whines again. "But . . . I don't think I can do that," she says. "If I did, that would mean . . ."

I nod at her. "I'll forget you. None of this will have happened."

Fea howls, long and hard. "Please, David Bravo, I'm sorry. I'll do better. Please don't send me away. I need to solve you, or I can't move on."

"That's not true," I say, and the tears fall harder once I see it. "This is exactly what I'm supposed to do."

"But what about Antoine?" she says, her ears perking

up. "If you do this, it'll erase his changes, too. I don't meet him if I don't meet *you*!"

"This isn't fair!" I cry. "You're always hounding me about making decisions for myself. 'You only live once, David Bravo,' you say. And now I've made a choice for *me*, and you want me to *not* make it because of someone else?"

I point to the charm around her neck.

"Look."

The infinity charm is glowing green.

All of it.

"No," she whines. "No, that can't be true."

"It is. You have to do it, Fea. Just let me live my life."

I hate seeing her like this. It doesn't make sense, but it's like I can feel her sorrow.

"I'm sorry, David Bravo. I'm sorry I wasn't good enough."

"It's not your fault," I tell her, crouching and petting her head. "I promise. I just can't do this anymore."

I stand back up. "That's my decision. Take me to . . . to . . ."

I'm not sure at first. There have been so many overlapping timelines. Where could I start over *again*?

But I know it. It comes to me, and I know it's right.

"The steps of Mira Monte," I say. "The first day. Can you take me there and reset everything?"

"I think so," she says quietly.

She curls up at my feet. "Thank you for letting me try," she says. "And for giving me one heck of a final assignment."

"I hope you get to . . . I don't know what you do next. Take a nap?"

She laughs. "Sure, David Bravo. I hope I get a very long nap."

Her powers tug deep in my stomach.

I twist. I turn. I land perfectly, and there, before us, are Past Me and Past Antoine, frozen, staring up in anticipation at the front gate to Mira Monte Middle School.

"Do it," I tell Fea. "Put me back in my body."

Fea says nothing as her magic hits me, and I'm back in my original body. I look down at her while the world is still frozen.

"I'm sorry," I say. "I wish this could have ended differently."

"Me too," she says, and her voice sounds . . . broken.

"Goodbye, Juanita," I tell her, a terrible sadness growing in me.

"Goodbye, David Bravo."

And then . . . it all snaps back.

TUESDAY, SEPTEMBER 5
8:10 A.M.
The (last) first day of middle school

"What if we just *don't* go to school?"

Antoine Harris, my very best friend in the whole world, is standing next to me, his thumbs looped behind the straps of his backpack. His mom has just pulled away from the curb and left the two of us there.

Antoine scrunches up his whole face as he stares at the steps that lead to the entrance of Mira Monte Middle School. Other kids are rushing up them before the first bell rings, but the two of us? We're not moving at all.

"That's a really good idea, David," he says. "But what are we going to do all day?"

I scratch at my chin. "We could walk to Target," I say, and then . . .

Something nags at me. I turn around to glance behind me because I've got this feeling that I've forgotten something important. I look at my feet, as if I'm expecting something to be there.

"David?" says Antoine. "What's up?"

I shake my head to snap myself back to the present. "Sorry. I feel like I forgot something."

"Well, it's only the first day of school," he says. "You can bring it tomorrow, right?"

"Sure," I say, but the feeling lingers for a bit.

"I wish we had actual classes together," says Antoine.

"Whoever made up the idea of middle school is evil," I say.

He laughs at that. "How about this?" he says. "Let's regroup at lunch. At least then we don't have to become clichés and worry about where we're going to sit."

"Excellent plan," I say. "No after-school specials about us."

And then:

The Handshake.

We slap the back sides of our hands against each other's twice.

"Crisscross," we say in unison.

A dap, mine on top first, then his.

"Always floss."

We grip each other's hands, but only at the fingers.

"Always friends."

Then we pull our hands apart, so fast that it makes a little snapping sound.

"To the end."

Then . . . we both linger there for a second. Antoine looks like he's about to say something to me, and I can't escape this weird feeling.

"You feel that?" says Antoine, and then he squints at me.

"I think so," I say. "What was that?"

"I don't know, but . . . man, this is wild, but have we done this before?"

I shake my head. "Nah, it's probably just nerves. I'm sure my mom could explain it with her therapy stuff."

"Right," he says, but he stays there unmoving for another moment. "Let's go."

Antoine bumps his shoulder against mine as the two of us ascend the stairs to Mira Monte Middle School. I don't know what our first day holds at this new school, but I feel comforted by my best friend's presence. I honestly don't know what I'd do without him.

It's a weird thought. He's been by my side for so long! I literally can't imagine him *not* being my friend. When I try to, there's a gnawing pain in my stomach.

Yeah, I don't think I'll do that.

Antoine veers off from my side, waving as he does, and heads to a different class than mine.

I have this urge to chase after him, but I don't follow it. *No, David,* I tell myself. *You just have to make it to lunch.*

I can do that.

I think.

I have to face this. There's no running away from it!

I breathe in. I breathe out.

I step into the uncertain and the unknown.

TUESDAY, SEPTEMBER 5
8:15 A.M.
The first class

It's weird navigating a campus I don't know *and* doing it without Antoine by my side, but I finally figure out where Mr. Bradshaw's social studies class is—room 213—without getting hopelessly lost.

I am immediately faced with my first big choice of the school year.

Where do I sit?

More than half the desks are empty, and the teacher steps out from behind his own desk as I survey the room.

"Welcome, students," says Mr. Bradshaw, a tall white man with a shiny bald spot in the middle of his gray-and-white hair. "Please choose where you sit carefully. That will be your seat for the remainder of the year!"

More students shuffle in, and I don't want to be left without a good seat. Almost like I'm on autopilot, I head to the far corner and sit next to an Asian girl who slams a notebook shut as soon as I turn to her.

"Hi," she says, a nervous edge to her voice. "Gracie. I wasn't doing anything."

I blink a few times at her. "Okay," I say. "I'm David."

She smiles, then turns away.

I glance down at the notebook. "Do you draw?" I ask. "Or is that for writing?"

Gracie turns back. "What?"

"Well, your little notebook. It's cool. I like that color."

"Oh," she says. "Thanks."

Then she gently opens it and flips through a few pages. "I'm not very good," she says, then stops. "Yet. I'm not very good *yet*."

I smile at that. "But you're practicing, right?"

Gracie nods, then holds the notebook up toward me. There's a pencil sketch of a dog leaping off a couch, and I gasp as I examine it.

"Wait, *this* is what you're not very good at?" I say. "Gracie, this is . . . Wow."

She raises an eyebrow. "You think so?"

"Absolutely! I can't even draw a good stick person."

And just like that, she doesn't seem so nervous anymore, and you know what? Neither do I.

Did I just make a new friend?

Wow. This is a lot already, and class hasn't even started.

The bell rings, and right as it does, two kids come tumbling into the class. I don't need to be an expert to know that I will *not* be friends with them. They're slugging each other in the shoulder over and over. The taller and browner of the two—who honestly looks like he's at least in high school—sneers at the other. "Man, you're *weak*," he says.

"Please take a seat, gentlemen," says Mr. Bradshaw, gesturing to the only two open seats . . . which are of course right in front of me.

"Where should we take our seats?" says the other kid. "Should we take them outside?"

He's the paler one, and he's got this long, stringy blond hair that looks like he's part scarecrow.

"Yeah, let's go sit right outside the windows," says the tall kid.

Mr. Bradshaw's mouth curls up on one side. He doesn't exactly look happy. I glance over at Gracie, and she slams her notebook shut again and smiles.

O-okay.

As Mr. Bradshaw calls out our names and marks us down on his "map" of the classroom so he can do attendance easier in the future, I learn that the almost-late kids are Tommy Rodriguez and Walter May.

Tommy flashes two peace signs when Mr. Bradshaw calls out his name. "That's me," he says. "What are you gonna teach us, Teacher?"

Mr. Bradshaw frowns. "This is social studies, Mr. Rodriguez."

"Dope," says Tommy. "You gonna teach us about Twitter?"

Our teacher narrows his eyes at Tommy. "What?"

"You know," says Tommy. "Like . . . social media?"

Mr. Bradshaw sighs. "This is going to be a long year," he mutters, then, much louder, he says, "I'll explain everything once I'm done taking attendance."

There are so many other kids in the room. I don't catch all of the names—I remember Wunmi Onyebuchi, though, because . . . have I heard her name before? I'm not sure. Anyway, I'm pretty sure she's cooler than me. Mr. Bradshaw makes a comment about Gracie's sister that makes no sense, but I don't have time to ask her about it.

Finally, after Tommy and Walter interrupt way too much, Mr. Bradshaw introduces his class to us. He tells us that we're going to learn a little bit of history about the world, but we're also going to spend time "expanding our horizons."

"It's my job to teach you about this wonderfully diverse and complicated world," he explains. "And I can't image a better way of doing that than assigning you homework."

The whole class groans in unison.

"Homework *already*?" says Tommy.

I don't even like Tommy, but I can't disagree with his complaint.

"Yes, *already*," says Mr. Bradshaw. "But it's going to be an easy A. I believe everyone here can start the year off with a perfect score."

Okay, sounds easy enough. I wait attentively as he scans the room.

"Each of you is going to introduce us to the cultures

of your home," says Mr. Bradshaw. You will give a short presentation—all oral, under two minutes—and explain what cultures make up your home and make you *you*."

This might be complicated, I realize.

"Tell your fellow students about where you and your parents come from! Do you have interesting cultural practices or traditions in your home that you'd like to share?"

I'm not so sure about this. I start thinking about my mom. My dad. Where they came from, what "cultures" exist in my home, and then . . .

Well, who *am* I?

"I'll start," continues Mr. Bradshaw. "My family is originally from Boston, and I was born outside Cambridge, Massachusetts. But my grandparents are actually from a place called Rotterdam, which is in the Netherlands, just south of Amsterdam! Have any of you been to Amsterdam?"

There are a lot of head shakes and a few kids softly mutter, "No." I almost want to blurt out that most of us haven't even left California before. The Netherlands?! I don't even know where that is on a map!

I also don't know where on a map I'm from.

Well, I was born in Los Angeles, I know that. But being adopted always makes this hard. Well, hard for other people, I guess. I confuse people sometimes because I sort of resemble my dad, who has a Mexican mom and a Brazilian dad, but I look nothing like my Japanese mother.

But . . . that's not *my* problem, is it? So what if I look

different? I can already feel the irritation rising in me, since I know exactly the kind of questions I'm going to be asked. It happens all the time. Where were you born? Who were your parents? Why did they give you up?

Well . . . I don't think anyone has actually asked me that last one. Why did I think that?

You'll be fine, I tell myself. *Just tell them the truth.*

Will I be fine, though? I know I have a problem with indecision, and this presentation feels like a big choice to make. How much do I tell the class? Should I keep being adopted to myself? I don't know the best path for me to take!

I spend the rest of my first class of the year buzzing from my rattled nerves, feeling . . . I don't know how to describe it. It's like everything is just a little bit crooked.

TUESDAY, SEPTEMBER 12
8:40 A.M.
The moment of truth

It sucks that Antoine isn't in any of my classes, but I still see him at lunch and during cross-country practice. We even did our first week of homework together, too. But I still have the presentation for Mr. Bradshaw's class hanging over my head the entire time. I'm not always super nervous about it, like I was at the end of that first class, but I can't seem to find a way to push it out of my head.

Over the weekend, my first attempt at the project was to make two columns on an index card with Mom on the left and Dad on the right. I wrote down where they were from, where their grandparents came from, and then started listing some of the things they'd taught me. It seemed like a good start, but . . .

It wasn't quite the truth, was it? I still thought that maybe I shouldn't admit to being adopted. It wasn't like anyone from Underhill Elementary was in the class, so if I simply skipped over the adoption part, no one would know.

Then there'd be none of the weird questions or comments about me and my parents.

By the time Gracie Lim's name was called on Tuesday morning, I had mostly convinced myself that it wasn't worth it to tell the class that I was adopted. This was just a short presentation for an easy grade. Why was I stressing myself out over it?

I put my index card down to listen to Gracie. She stands nervously at the front, swaying back and forth.

"Hi, my name is Gracie Lim," she says, and her face flushes red as she looks out over the class. "I initially had a hard time thinking about what I was going to say to all of you because my family is kinda complicated."

Probably not as complicated as mine, I think smugly.

"The truth is that I was born in Korea, and while I do have a Korean mother, she's actually my adoptive mom. One of *two* of them, actually!"

My jaw drops.

Wait.

Gracie is *adopted*? How did I not know that?

That thought feels like it belongs in someone else's mind. I barely know Gracie! We've only talked before class for a few minutes over the past week. Of *course* I don't know a lot about her.

I still listen, though, as she describes her unique circumstance: she has an older sister who is her *actual* biological sister, only six years older. "I feel lucky that the agency my parents adopted me through kept us together. So while my family might look different to outsiders, I am happy that my sister and I get to be in each other's lives."

The class breaks out into light applause, and I'm sitting there feeling like I can't even breathe. What are the odds that there's another adopted kid in my class? And somehow, I also chose to sit next to her!

But then that *thing* happens again: a thought that makes no sense appears in my head.

You shouldn't have said those things.

I even get that sinking feeling that comes with guilt, like I did something horrible to Gracie.

What? I barely know her!

I shake off the weird thoughts and turn to Gracie. I smile at her and tap her arm. "That was really good," I say.

She blushes again. "Thanks, David."

"Excellent work," Mr. Bradshaw says. "Up next, we've got David Bravo," says Mr. Bradshaw. He gestures to the front of the class.

"Thank you," I say to Gracie. "You made this easier for me."

She gives me a look of confusion, but it's the truth. No one asked her any strange questions; no one made her out to be a weirdo. I don't think I have anything to worry about!

I breathe in deep and stand up, which is also when Tommy decides to open his mouth.

"What kind of last name is Bravo?"

"It's mine," I say quickly.

Tommy looks taken aback.

"Please, Mr. Rodriguez," says Mr. Bradshaw. "Let David present first, okay?"

I make my way up, ignoring Tommy and Walter, who are giggling at me. I stand at the small wooden podium Mr. Bradshaw teaches from and clear my throat.

It's a weird feeling, to have all the eyes in this room staring at me.

I look to Mr. Bradshaw, who nods at me.

"Hi," I say, and my voice comes out a little shaky, so I breathe in again and speak more clearly. "My name is David Bravo. I was born in Los Angeles, and I have a really different kind of home life. Well, not *that* different, as I just learned. Like Gracie, I am also adopted."

Gracie's entire face lights up when I say this, and it's honestly the best thing *ever*.

I keep going. I explain my family to the class, telling them where my parents came from, and what it was like to be raised by them. I think I'm going too fast. I don't know. The whole thing is kind of exhilarating! Like I'm on a ride at Six Flags. Mr. Bradshaw is actually smiling at me when I finish. "Wonderful, David," he says. "That's really interesting!"

"Thank you," I say, lowering the index card and letting out a breath of relief.

"But what do you consider *yourself*?"

His question catches me off guard. "Huh?"

"Well, we know your parents' cultures, but what are *you*?"

"I'm . . . David Bravo?"

I'm not trying to be sarcastic, but Walter snickers anyway.

"Yes, but what would you say you are? Where do *you* come from?"

"You mean . . . like, do I consider myself Japanese?" I scratch at head. "Or Mexican or Brazilian?"

"Sure," says Mr. Bradshaw.

"Well, I'm not really sure," I say, and even though a jolt of fear pulses through me, I keep going. "I had a closed adoption, which means that there's no info on my birth parents. But I've always thought of myself as Latinx. It's just the best word to describe me."

"I didn't know that was a thing," he says. "Thank you, David Bravo! I'm glad I got to learn something today, too."

Tommy whispers something to Walter, and this time, Mr. Bradshaw turns on them.

"Excuse me, gentlemen," he says sharply. "You're being rude. Do you have something you'd like to ask David?"

Tommy gives one glance to Walter, then smiles at me. "Did your parents give you up because they didn't want you anymore?"

I hear someone gasp near me. I think it's Wunmi. My mouth drops open.

"No," I say. Then: "Well, I don't know. I don't know anything about them."

"Maybe we shouldn't ask such invasive questions, Mr. Rodriguez," says Mr. Bradshaw.

"Or such *rude* questions," says Gracie. She's got a scowl on her face.

"I don't know why my original parents gave me up," I say, and I can hear my voice shaking. I don't want to give off the appearance that I'm rattled, but . . . well, I kinda *am*. Tommy's question was so mean! "It's not like I can ask them."

Gracie puts up her hand, but then she doesn't even wait for Mr. Bradshaw to call on her. "I don't know anything about my birth parents, either," she says.

"Ms. Lim, thank you, but—"

"But it's true!" she says.

"Jeez, sorry," says Tommy, and he tries to look away from me, only to find that Gracie *and* Wunmi are glaring at him.

"Okay, then," says Mr. Bradshaw. "Let's get things under control. Terry Jimenez, you're up next."

I go take my seat, and Gracie is practically vibrating next to me. "I'm sorry," she whispers. "I just couldn't help it."

"Thank *you*," I whisper back. "I'm glad you said something."

Gracie tears a page out of her notebook. "I drew something for you," she says.

She drops a small square of paper onto my desk.

I pick it up and unfold it.

Oh.

It's *me*.

Gracie drew me giving my presentation to the class! It looks like she spent an hour on it, not just two minutes; she even got my dark eyes and my wide nose.

"Thank you, Gracie!" I whisper just before Terry starts, tucking the drawing in my notebook.

Gracie turns red again. "Adoption buddies," she says.

I nod. "Adoption buddies."

It's not until we're leaving class that I realize I've just made my first friend at Mira Monte.

TUESDAY, SEPTEMBER 12
12:35 P.M.

I slide my tray down the counter in the cafeteria, and Norma Gutierrez—one of the cooks in our school—smiles at me. She's got the same color hair and skin tone as I do.

A thought pops into my head: *Am I secretly related to her?*

It's not the first time I've had the thought, but now I wonder if Gracie does this, too, whenever she sees someone who resembles her. Or is it different for her because she *knows* she has a sister?

"Hola, mijo," Norma says. "How are you, David?"

I can't really explain it, but there's something about the way she calls me "mijo"—despite that I'm not her son—that makes me feel all warm inside. So I smile back at her.

"I'm good," I say. "I think I did well on an assignment today."

Norma glows when I tell her that. "¡Felicidades! Then let me make your day a little better." She puts two peanut butter cookies on my tray first. "My treat. What else would you like, David?"

I point at one of the chicken sandwiches, then a fruit cup, and then, knowing we have that scrimmage race that afternoon for cross-country, I decide that I probably need something else that's supposed to be healthy. I gesture at the spinach. "That's supposed to give you energy, right?"

Norma makes a face, then shakes her head.

"No?" I say. "Bad idea?"

She looks around like she's going to share a secret with me. "I don't think this is our best batch," she says. "The spinach smelled a little weird this morning."

There it is again: a little tingle up my spine. The hairs along my arm rise up.

"David?" says Norma.

I stare at her, convinced that she has told me this already. Which is ridiculous! But . . . something tells me Norma wouldn't warn me unless she was serious.

"I'll pass on the spinach," I say.

"Next time," says Norma, and winks at me.

I find Antoine at the table we've decided is our meeting place, since our lunches only overlap for fifteen minutes. He's there with Samrat, this kid with brown skin and braces that he has a class with.

"How'd your presentation go?" Antoine asks as I sit down.

"Not bad!" I say. "You're not gonna believe it, but the girl who went before me also happens to be adopted."

"Whoa," says Antoine. "That's wild. What a coincidence!"

"Yeah, she's cool, too. Didn't you have a test today?"

"Unfortunately," he says. "And I'm pretty sure I failed it."

"Mrs. Valdez?" I say.

He nods.

"She's tough," I say. "I feel like she expects us to know all these math things she has *literally* not taught us."

Antoine throws his hands up in the air. "Right? Wouldn't that defeat the whole purpose of being in school if we knew it all?"

I chuckle awkwardly because . . . man, I can *swear* Antoine has told me that joke before.

Huh.

"I actually like math," says Samrat, "but she's not a fun teacher."

"Thank you for the solidarity," I say to him, and give him a fist bump.

He accepts it, then waves as he leaves the table. Once he's gone, I notice that Antoine's bouncing his leg up and down.

"You seem nervous," I say.

"A little," he says. "I know our race today isn't a *real* race, but I'm still freaking out a little over it."

"Why? You'll make varsity without a problem, Antoine. You're the fastest one on the team."

"Yeah, but . . . well, Pop is always going on and on about how I have to treat every practice like it's a race."

"But . . . it's *not* a race," I say. "At least not yet."

Antoine looks away from me for a moment. "I hope if I get on varsity, Pop won't be so harsh on me."

I grip the edge of the table in front of me, stilling myself as a jolt runs through my body.

Because I have *definitely* heard that before.

I remember: I'm standing across from Antoine, whose eyes are red and puffy. I think he was just crying? And then I crouch in front of—

Wait . . . that didn't happen. I've *never* seen Antoine cry. So how can I remember it?

I realize I've zoned out. I snap back to attention, then look up at Antoine. He's staring at me with wide eyes.

"David," he says, "are you okay?"

"Yeah, sorry, just spacing out," I say.

The image of Antoine crying pops back into my mind.

"Are *you* okay?" I ask.

"I don't know," says Antoine, shaking his head. "It's just . . . hard. I'm so used to seeing you all day and having the same friends, and everything here is . . . different."

"Yeah, I know what you mean," I say.

"You know, Isaiah once told me that this is when everyone changes," Antoine says. "That by the end of middle school, all his friends were different people than when he started it."

"Yeah, but Isaiah is old. Are you sure you wanna listen to a senior citizen like him?"

Antoine laughs. "You get what I mean."

"Maybe he's right, but . . . I'm not going anywhere, Antoine."

"You're not gonna get new friends and disappear on me, are you?"

It's there again, right at the edge of my consciousness: the odd sensation that I have lived all of this before. I push past it. "No," I say, and I hold up my hand for our Handshake.

"Crisscross," we say in unison.

A dap.

"Always floss."

We grip each other's hands.

"Always friends," says Antoine, a smile lighting up his whole face.

"To the end," I say, blood rushing to my cheeks, but as we're finishing up, the thing I was ignoring is rushing back, the bell signaling the end of first lunch is chiming, and someone's words are echoing in my mind:

I want you to pay attention to what you're feeling! Like, when he talks to you or asks to spend time with you.

I watch Antoine leave, wondering whose words I'm remembering.

Think about what happens when he smiles at you.

Think about what you feel if he happens to touch you.

And think about how you feel when he leaves.

When Antoine leaves, I want him to come back. I want

him to sit with me and talk and tell jokes with me. I hate that we don't have classes together, sure, but . . . it's not just that, is it?

I really like Antoine.

Maybe more than I've ever admitted to myself.

I sit in silence while I think about my little realization, but I don't know what I'm supposed to do with it.

Even worse:

Why am I remembering things that haven't happened?

TUESDAY, SEPTEMBER 12
2:42 P.M.

Antoine beat me out of the locker room, so I find him out on the infield of the track, where he's stretching by himself. I'm already pouring sweat everywhere; the sun is clearly not ready for summer to be over in a couple weeks. As I go through my stretches on the ground with him, I notice that Antoine is still shaking like he was at lunch.

"You okay?" I ask, bending at the waist and reaching for the bottom of my foot.

"I'll be fine," he says. "Just nervous."

"You're gonna be great, Antoine. No one on this team is faster than you. Jesse likes to *think* he is, but you outlast him every time."

I look up when I hear someone call Antoine's name, and I notice that Mr. Harris is jogging our way.

"You all stretched, son?" Mr. Harris asks Antoine, then nods at me. "Hey, David!"

"Hi, Mr. Harris," I say. "We're doing okay. Just a little nervous, I guess."

"Well, don't let it be infectious," he says. "Keep your head in the race, Antoine. Pace yourself! And remember—"

"'Every run is a race against yourself,'" Antoine finishes. "Yeah, I remember, Pop."

"You need any last-minute stretches?" Mr. Harris asks.

Antoine looks to me. "Yes," he says. "David said he'd help me, though."

Mr. Harris gives me a look like he's trying to determine if I'm up to his standard. "Okay, son," he says. "Meet me at the other end of the track when you're ready."

Antoine's dad jogs off, and once he's out of earshot, Antoine lets out a breath. "He can be so intense sometimes," he says quietly.

"Yeah," I say. "I've . . . noticed."

He bends at the waist and grabs his ankles with his hands, pulling himself lower to the ground. But then he jerks upward quickly.

"Antoine?" I say.

"I have a bad feeling about this race," he says.

As if it is contagious, a sense of dread passes over me.

It's going to happen again. You can't change it.

"Hey, Antoine," I say, certain—*finally* certain—that I have to say something about this, that whatever is happening to me shouldn't be ignored.

His eyes dart up to me. "Yeah?"

"I'm sorry if I'm wrong about this, but . . . do you feel like this has happened before?"

Antoine gulps. "How did you know that?"

"What you just said! About having a bad feeling about the race. I feel like you shouldn't do it."

His eyes go wide. "Me, *too*. And it's like . . . we've never been here before. How could this be a memory?"

I notice that he's sweating a lot, too. Even worse, most of our teammates have wandered over to the starting line, so we don't have that much time until our placement run begins.

"I don't think I should do this," Antoine says, and his eyes are red and glassy, like he's about to start crying.

But he *has* to run. If he doesn't, his dad is going to be disappointed. And . . . well, I don't want that for Antoine. I want to see him happy.

Because that makes *me* happy.

I swallow down the fear and indecision rising in me, that's telling me not to do this, that's telling me I should have minded my own business. Something Mom told me once comes back to me. There are times when people need help, but they're too afraid or too ashamed to ask for it. But if you're paying attention, you can tell.

I can tell he's upset. I can tell that he needs help.

So I go for it.

"Can I hold your hand, Antoine?" I ask. "Just to help you calm down."

For a moment, he hesitates. Then he sticks his hand out. "Sure, David."

I take it in my own. It's warm and soft, and before I do

anything, Antoine twists his fingers so that they're interlocked in mine.

I look into his eyes.

And I remember:

Antoine and I are standing outside school, right at the front steps, and I'm looking down at his hand in mine, and I like how it looks, and when I gaze up at Antoine, there are two emotions in his face, mixed up in each other.

It's the same expression I see now.

He's happy.

He's afraid.

As the two of us hold hands, right here, right now, Antoine squeezes mine harder and more images flood into my mind.

I'm on my back porch, holding a soggy bag of trash, staring at a dog.

I see a giraffe in Antoine's yard out of the sliding glass door.

I'm standing outside a high school, decades and decades ago, watching a teenage girl get out of a huge car, her flowing pink dress matching her shoes and gloves.

I'm staring at my mother in another timeline.

I'm talking to a dog.

I yank my hand back from Antoine as tears fill my eyes.

Oh, my god, I *remember.*

I remember everything.

Fea. Magic. Time travel. Other timelines.

And from the look on Antoine's face—shock, confusion, relief—I think he does, too.

"You remember," he says, his lower lip quivering.

"All of it," I say.

"There was . . . there was another timeline, wasn't there?"

I nod. "More than one," I say.

"How?" says Antoine.

"Fea," I say, and it feels like it's been a million years since I said her name.

I feel warm tears rolling down my cheeks.

"The dog," he says. "She . . . she helped us, didn't she?"

I shake my head. "Antoine, I think I messed everything up."

He shakes his head. "How can you say that?"

"Something happened. And I was upset, and I . . . I told her to erase everything. *Including* my memory of her."

This time, Antoine reaches over and grabs *my* hand. "It's because of me, isn't it? Because of what I chose?"

I shake my head. "Not really. I mean . . . maybe."

"But you made the right choice!" Antoine says. "I found out *real* fast that after I won this race and got on the varsity team, every part of my life was dedicated to running. I couldn't even text you back after I realized Fea had sent us into the future; Dad *immediately* took me to another practice. I couldn't hang out with anyone else, I couldn't *do* anything else, all because Pop was convinced I was going to be the next Olympic champion."

Antoine sighs dramatically. "It was terrible, David. I thought it would make me happy, but my life was *worse*."

I can't help it. I just start *laughing*. It's tearful laughter at first, but then Antoine pitches over, and I fall on top of him, and we're laughing so hard I can barely breathe. Coach Williams calls out to us to get our butts over to the starting line, but we don't care. How can that matter after everything we've been through?

"Should we go run?" he says, catching his breath. "Or will you run into me and then throw up everywhere?"

I laugh really hard. "Probably. Wonder what happens if we both do *nothing*."

"I don't even know how this is possible!" says Antoine. "If you erased everything, why do we both remember Fea and what she did?"

"Because we're *time travelers*!" I say, and we fall into laughter again.

"Yo, we traveled through time with a talking *dog*," says Antoine.

"Um, *excuse me*!" says a voice in my head.

I jump up *immediately*. Antoine does, too, and we spin about until we see—

Oh, my god!

"I'm not a *dog*!" says Fea.

There stands Fea, appearing as a xoloitzcuintli, her tail wagging furiously from side to side.

Antoine and I . . . well, we dogpile her, which is a weird thing to say since she *looks* like a dog. Also, where did that term come from? Are dogs known for forming piles?

"You're lucky I don't breathe," says Fea. "You two would be suffocating me."

"Fea!" I say. "You're here!"

"And *you* remember me!" she shoots back. "Both of you."

"How?" I ask. "How is that possible."

"Because somehow, I'm *still* not done with you."

TUESDAY, SEPTEMBER 12
3:07 P.M.

"You're kidding me!" I say.

I shoot upright and notice that Coach Williams is frozen in his spot about ten feet away, his face twisted in irritation.

"Fea?" I say, gesturing around us. "Did you do this?"

"I did," she says.

"So your powers are . . . back?" says Antoine. "Are they working again?"

"They are, which is strange, because . . . Well, boys, I am *done*."

Fea sits in front of me and lifts her head. I kneel and grab her infinity charm.

It's still green.

"I was your last assignment," I say.

"You were," she confirms.

"So how come you haven't . . . moved on?"

"Okay, I'm confused," says Antoine. "David, I don't

think you ever explained this part to me. Is that some sort of talisman, Fea?"

"Talisman?" Fea's ears stand straight up. "How do you know that word, human?!"

"I read a lot," Antoine says, shrugging.

"Well," says Fea, "I was on my way to my final meeting with the Powers, and I heard you mention my name, David! Your voice traveled through the ether, and I thought I was imagining it. But then I felt *you*!"

"Felt me?"

"I could feel you thinking about me. You *finally* successfully summoned me!"

"I am on a roll today," I say, beaming at Fea.

"Which leads me to what I need to say next," says Fea. "Because I think I was wrong from the start."

"Wrong about what?" I say.

"Will you be mad if I say everything?"

I roll my eyes. "So I was right, then."

"Maybe there was a lesson from the Powers in all of this," she says. "I always relied on the same thing: change a person's past, and it fixes their present. Why? Because that's what I wish I had. If I could go back in time and redo everything with Maricela, I wouldn't hesitate."

"Who's Maricela?" Antoine asks.

I look at Fea with concern. "I never really told him," I say. "It didn't seem like my story to share."

"I appreciate that, David Bravo," she says, and she

stretches out on the grass, then places her head between her paws. "Antoine, have you ever known someone who makes you happy? Like, every little thing they do makes you laugh or makes you think or makes you feel like there's someone who just gets you?"

She says these words, and all I can think about is one person:

Antoine.

"I don't know," he says, and he pulls up some grass and rolls it into a ball. "Maybe."

"Well, maybe you know someone who gives you that funny feeling of butterflies in the stomach," she says, and gives me a knowing look while Antoine is still inspecting the blades of grass between his fingers.

"Or who makes you blush or go hot in the face when you look at them. Or maybe you haven't, because you have a long, full life ahead of you, Antoine, and you could find someone like that much later, or maybe you find out that that isn't what you want at all."

I stare at Antoine, hoping his face will reveal the truth to me. Has he ever felt this before?

Has he ever felt it about *me*?

"I found my someone a long time ago," Fea continues, "and I let her go. I regretted it my whole life. And I could have prevented it if I'd just been honest. If I'd done that . . . Well, you only live once, after all, and I feel like I wasted my chance."

I know that I feel these things about Antoine, but sitting there, watching as he picks more grass and doesn't look at me, I start to worry. He has no idea what she's talking about, does he?

"So," I say, breaking the uncomfortable silence, "what does this have to do with your new theory?"

"David Bravo, over this entire adventure with you, you made difficult decisions. You disagreed with me when you thought I was wrong. You defended your friends. You believed in me, even when I gave you no reason to. I may have been a little annoying at times."

"A little?" I say, raising an eyebrow.

"We're moving past this moment as a unified force," she says. "Because, David, I think it's finally time for you to choose yourself. What do you want more than anything? Don't think of timelines or time travel or magic or powers or anything. What do you want?"

What do I want? I stare at Fea, who looks up at me with anticipation. Her tail wags softly.

I look to Antoine, and suddenly, the butterflies are back.

So is the warmth in my face.

So is the desire to reach out and hold his hand.

What does that mean?

Oh, who *cares* what it means???

"Antoine," I say, "if I don't say this now, I will probably never say it, and I believe Fea when she says that we all only live once."

Fea lets out a soft bark, and Antoine finally looks up from the grass.

He looks scared, but you know what? I am, too.

"Even though you and I got to have more than one timeline," I continue, "in every one, the worst thing that happened was . . . was not being your friend."

"I hated that part, too," Antoine says. "I know we didn't spend all that long in my new timeline, but it was like . . . like the universe didn't want me near you."

"But I'm also scared," I say, "because I have to tell you something, and there's a chance that you won't want to be friends with me after it."

Antoine shakes his head. "That's impossible. Always friends to the *end*, remember?"

The tears that spill out of my eyes are different this time. They're entirely because I'm scared. "I want to believe in that," I say, "so I'm going to believe in it while I say this."

I breathe in deep.

And I make a choice.

"Antoine, I think I like you. Like . . . *like* like you."

He doesn't say anything, but his eyebrows go up a little bit.

"Really?" he says.

"Really. And I've never liked someone like this, and I don't know what to do about it or what's supposed to happen next, and I don't even know what it means for me as a person. Do I like boys now? Have I always liked them but never noticed?"

I'm shaking my head. "But none of that matters now. I

don't *need* to know any of that. All I know is that I like you a whole lot, Antoine."

"You mean that?" he says, and his eyes are full of shock.

"Yes," I say, nodding. "I really mean it."

Antoine raises his left hand.

Puts it in my right hand.

Then slides his fingers in between mine, and it's . . . weird. But not weird in the bad way. We've held hands before, but . . .

This time, Antoine holds my hand because he *chooses* to.

"I like you, too," says Antoine, smiling.

When I look back to Fea, she has rolled over on her back, her tail is wagging furiously side-to-side, and her tongue is hanging out of the side of her mouth. "About time," she says. "I feel like I aged eight hundred years waiting for you to do that."

"You don't age, Fea," I say. "Remember?"

She flips back over. "A mere technicality."

"I'm not done, though," I say, my heart flipping and flopping as I think about my epiphany. "There's something else, and I think it's what you and I have been searching for this whole time, Fea."

"Oh!" she says. "David Bravo, you are reclaiming your destiny! I like this version of you."

I have figured out the answer to one of my big questions, and the answer is the hand clutched in mine. But the other . . . it still feels huge. Frightening. Maybe even a little impossible.

I have to *try*, though. I only live once, right?

I breathe in deeply, let it out, and then:

"I want to find out who my birth parents are, Fea."

Fea's tail stops wagging. "I'm sorry," she says. "Did you say you want to find out who your birth parents are?"

"I did," I say.

"Do you not remember that whole thing about how I can't just take you to any ol' time you want?"

"Of course. Fea, I'm not asking you to take me to them with your magic."

"Oh," she says. "Then . . . what are you talking about?"

"After seeing my life with Yamira, I'm more curious than ever," I say.

"Hi, confused again," says Antoine, raising his right hand. "Who is Yamira?"

"Oh, right! You weren't there," I say. "Before I chose to undo all this, the Power of the Bees showed us something. Something . . . kinda messed up."

"Okay," he says. "Like what?"

"Well, I asked Fea to show what it had been like if I hadn't been adopted, and instead, they showed me what would have happened if someone *else* adopted me."

Antoine's mouth drops open. "What?"

"Yeah," I say. "It was . . . interesting. I had a different name, I lived in Moreno Valley instead of Riverside, but weirdly, some things were the same? My best friend was named Anthony, but he wasn't you—though we did both run cross-country. Oh, and Tommy was kind of there, but he was also a different person? Somehow just as annoying."

"That's so weird!" says Antoine. "So it was like a parallel universe version of this world."

"Kind of! But honestly, it got me thinking: Why *can't* I find out more about where I came from in this timeline? Maybe it really isn't possible, but it can't hurt to try, right?"

"Do you want me to *try* using my powers?" Fea asks.

I smile. "No, I think I need to do this *without* magic. And it has to involve my parents. My adoption was closed, so I'm assuming there's gonna be stuff I need their help with."

Fea bows her head at my feet. "You are very wise, David Bravo."

"I still want you there!" I say. "If that's possible. I just need to talk to my parents first."

"We both do," says Antoine. He lets go of my hand and points in the direction of Coach Williams. "Look who's behind Coach."

It's Mr. Harris, frozen behind Coach as he bounds across the infield toward us.

"Ugh," I groan. "How are we going to get out of this race? I don't want to do it at all."

"To be honest, neither do I," says Antoine. "So . . . why don't we just *say* that?"

"Huh?" I scratch my head.

"I think I need to be as brave as you are, David," he says.

"I can't be so afraid of telling the truth."

"Antoine, I—"

"No, let me finish," he says. "I don't know if this will make any sense to you, but . . . sometimes, it *hurts* to keep a secret."

Yeah.

That makes a *lot* of sense.

"And I've been letting my pop think I want the same things as him, that I want to train like he did, that I want to be the best runner on the planet. I actually *like* running, but he's ruining it for me because I don't have a choice about it!"

"Okay," I say. "Then . . . the truth. We just tell Coach and your dad the truth."

Antoine gives me one of those butterfly-inducing smiles. "I would like that a lot."

"Summon me when you need me," says Fea. "Just call my name out to the universe, and I'll be there. I promise we'll figure this out together."

"Thank you, Fea," I say. "I'm glad you're back."

"We're going to solve this, David Bravo," she says, then adds: "Together."

Antoine and I nod at her. "Do it," I say.

Fea disappears right as the world comes back to life. Coach Williams is *furious*, and he stomps the rest of the way to the two of us.

"Antoine, David, what gives?" he says. "Did y'all not hear me calling your names?"

"Son, what's going on?" says Mr. Harris, coming up behind Coach.

Antoine puffs up his chest, a look of worry on his face. "I'm not running," he says.

"*What* did you say?" says Mr. Harris.

"Not today," he says, and I glance down. Antoine's arm is shaking again.

I reach out to steady it, and Antoine looks to me. Then, to my great surprise, he holds my hand.

In front of Coach and his dad. The two of them exchange a look of shock.

"I don't feel good," Antoine continues. "And I haven't for a while, but I was scared to tell you, Pop."

"Antoine . . ." Mr. Harris's whole face *changes*. The anger and frustration are gone. It's like he's melting. "What's going on?"

"Not here," Antoine says. "Let's go home, okay? I want to tell Mom, too."

There is a moment where I think Coach Williams is going to start arguing, but Mr. Harris reaches out a hand and puts it on Coach's chest.

"Okay," he says. "Of course, son."

Antoine turns to me. "Text me later," he says. "When you know more about . . . you know. The thing."

As I watch Antoine and his dad leave, Coach Williams is scratching his head. "I assume you're not running either, David?"

"Not today," I say.

"Go change, Bravo," says Coach Williams. "But I expect to see you back on the road as soon as you feel . . . better. Even if that's tomorrow!"

"Yes, Coach!" I say, and I head for the locker room. When I get there, I send a quick text to Mom, who might be doing a session from home.

> Practice is over early. I'll be waiting out front. Can I talk to you and Dad tonight?

Mom's reply comes quicker than I expect.

> Of course, honey. See you in 15.

Tonight. I'm telling them both what I want.
And it's the first time I know I'm on the right path.

TUESDAY, SEPTEMBER 12
4:30 P.M.

After Mom picks me up, she tells me that Dad's already on his way home. "Let's order delivery for dinner, okay?" she says. "So we can give you all our attention."

"Cool," I say. "Can we order from that phở place?"

"Of course!"

Once we get home, I manage to kick off my shoes at the entrance and trudge to the couch, where I promptly plop down. "I know I'm supposed to go do homework," I say, my face buried in a cushion, "but can I rest first? I am pretty sure I don't have an active brain cell left in my head."

Mom basically throws herself down on the couch next to me. "Welcome to every day of adulthood," she says.

"Glad I have that to look forward to."

She laughs. "It's not *actually* always like that. I also had a tough week so far, and it's only Tuesday."

"Let's pretend to be amoebas for a while, then. I learned about them from my science teacher."

"That sounds like the perfect plan," Mom says. "I'll

order food once your father's here. In the meantime, let's just lie here and do nothing."

"No thoughts," I say. "Just pseudopod vibes."

And we don't talk. I think Mom falls asleep briefly, but I just lie there and . . . exist.

It's nice. I'm glad I have a mom I can do this with.

. . .

"So, David," says Dad, slurping up some of his phở. "What did you want to talk to us about?"

We're at the dinner table, and the savory smell of Vietnamese food is filling the room. However, I feel like all my organs are doing a synchronized dance routine in my body. Why is this so scary to me? I've traveled through *time*.

I guess it's the unknown. That's what it always has been. It's why I have had such a hard time with big decisions. I don't like not knowing what's coming.

But this time, I've seen other futures and other pasts. I know that things could be a lot worse than they are now. I also know that if I don't do this, if I don't tell my parents what I want, then things also can't get *better*.

"Well, I didn't run today," I say. "I didn't feel good."

"So you were sick?" says Dad.

"No, not that. I mean . . . I had a weird day."

(Which is totally the truth!)

"And it made me realize something."

"What did it make you realize?" Mom asks, leaning forward.

I tell them about the presentation I had to give in Mr.

Bradshaw's class. The one in *this* timeline, that is. I don't hold anything back: not Gracie, not Tommy's question, and not how it all made me more curious than ever.

"I want to ask you guys for something," I say once I've described it all. "But I need you to know I'm not asking you this because you're bad parents or I don't like you or I want to replace you or anything."

"Oh, honey, we don't think that at *all*," says Mom.

"Yeah, and you're legally stuck with us, David," says Dad, grinning. "Good luck trying to give us the boot."

I stick my tongue out at him. "Funny, Dad."

"You might not be my biological son, but you *definitely* got your humor from me," he adds.

"Anyway," I say, right as Mom playfully swats at him, "I want to know if we can find out more about my biological parents."

I expect a long dramatic pause. I expect Mom and Dad to share a knowing look, that thing they do where they seem to have a whole conversation without talking. I expect Mom to turn on her Therapist Voice.

Instead?

"Oh, sure," says Mom. "I don't know how much we'll be able to find out, though."

"Okay," I say. "But we can still try, right?"

"We can," she says, reaching over to me and grabbing hold of my left hand. "I'm proud of you for asking, David."

"Why don't we show you your adoption papers?" says Dad, and then he gets up and heads out of the room.

"Really?" I say, gazing at Mom. "You guys don't mind showing me this?"

"Of course not!" she says, and she almost looks offended. "David, your past shouldn't be a secret."

I can hear Dad coming back, and I turn to see him holding up a large orange folder.

"But . . . *isn't* my past a secret?"

"Oh," she says. "I see your point."

"Well, let's look at these together," says Dad. "As a family."

And then Dad slides the folder over to me.

It's all official-looking papers inside. I don't know what a lot of them are, but Mom and Dad do their best to explain. I see my birth certificate for the first time, as well, and I'm realizing . . . I could have just *asked* to see this stuff. But it never occurred to me!

Or maybe I was just too scared to do so.

I point to a box on the birth certificate. "Your names are on it," I say.

"It's something that happens during adoption," Dad says. "They amend your birth certificate to say we're your parents so that there isn't any legal confusion later on."

"Cool," I say. I pick up a thick stack of papers that's fastened with a gnarly clip. "What's this?"

"The actual adoption agreement," Mom says. "That sets out all the rules and whatnot. In this case, it says your father and I are your legal guardians and parents, and that your original parents hold no legal rights as parents."

"Sometimes, there are adoptions where the two sets of

parents actually share custody of a child," explains Dad. "One thing we learned through this process is that there are so many different ways a family can look." He spreads his arms wide. "And ours looks like this."

I point at a name at the top: Queen of Angels Home. "What's this?"

Dad leans over and examines it. "Ah. That's the adoption agency. It's where you lived after you were born until the adoption went through."

"It's an actual house?" I ask.

"Yeah, more or less," says Dad. "It's actually where we visited you for the first time when you were an infant."

The idea is building in me. If it's a real place . . .

"Could we visit the agency?" I blurt out. "Maybe they know something about me!"

This time, Mom and Dad *do* exchange the knowing look I anticipated earlier.

"What?" I say. "What is it?"

"I mean . . . we could *try*," says Dad. "But I don't think that they can tell us much because of how closed adoptions work."

"Well, it's something, right?" I say. "Even if all that happens is I get to visit the place, at least I'll know where I *literally* came from."

"I like that idea," says Mom. "Maybe just call them and see what our options are, honey?"

Dad nods and stands up. "I'll be right back."

He disappears into the back of the house with the

adoption agreement, and it's not long before I can hear his muffled voice on the phone.

"This is a big moment, David," Mom says. "And you didn't freeze up when making this decision. I'm really impressed."

"Thanks, Mom," I say. And even though she won't get it, I add: "I had a lot of practice this time around."

That doesn't mean I'm not afraid. Oh, I very much am. I don't even necessarily know what I'm afraid *of*. It's possible that this is a dead end, and I'll never know anything about my birth. That's a little scary. But what if this does lead to some huge revelation? Am I ready for that?

I hope so. But as I sit there, waiting for Dad to come back, I know that Fea's mantra makes a *new* kind of sense to me.

I am only going to have *this* life, and I can't be afraid to live it.

Mom starts talking to me about school, and she tells me how happy she is that there's another adopted kid I can be friends with. It's not long, though, before Dad finally returns. When I see him walking toward us, my heart rate spikes.

"Well, I have some bad news that might be canceled out by the good news," he says.

He sits at the table and lets out a long sigh. "I'm sorry, David, but Queen of Angels closed a few years ago."

My heart sinks. Well, that was one of the possible outcomes, wasn't it? I smile weakly at Dad. "It's okay," I say. "Thanks for trying."

He puts a hand up. "Now hold on there," he says. "I kept trying after that! I managed to talk to someone who works at the agency that replaced it, and *she* passed me on to another agency run by a woman named Ms. Ramos. Now, Ms. Ramos's *mother* used to work at Queen of Angels. She couldn't promise anything, buuuuuttttt . . ."

"Yes?" I say. "What???"

"She said that her mother will meet with all of us this Saturday to tell us what she can!" Dad says.

"No way!" I say. "Really?"

"Yes, really," says Dad. "Now I'm sure your mom has given you the proper preparation about all this, but David, this might come to nothing. It's possible that Ms. Ramos's mother won't even remember you. They see so many children over the years, okay?"

But I'm already moving past that. This *has* to be the right path. "Can I invite Antoine?" I ask. "Make a little road trip out of it?"

"I don't see why not," says Mom. "Do you want him there with you, no matter what the outcome is?"

There's no hesitation on my part. "Yes, I do."

"Well, let me call Barbara," says Mom. "Make sure it's okay with the family."

"Yes!" I cry out.

"Let's not get ahead of ourselves," says Dad. "One thing at a time!"

Not much later, I get confirmation from Mom that Antoine can come along. Apparently, Antoine's parents thought it was a great idea, and Mrs. Harris mentioned that her family had just had a tough conversation, too. "Barbara said that she wanted to make sure that Antoine had the freedom to make more decisions on his own," Mom says. "Sounds like both you boys are learning what it means to grow up."

Maybe Antoine's brother is wrong about growing up. I think it's turning out to be pretty great.

• • •

That night, I summon Fea, and she appears immediately as a bear cub. "You're always full of surprises," I tell her.

"I can't resist," she says. "It's how I show love."

I tell her everything that's happened. "So, you'll come with me this weekend?"

She growls. "I wouldn't miss it for the world! Plus . . . I'm still here. I'm clearly not done. So, I think you *have* made the decision the Powers were guiding us to."

"What if it turns out to be nothing?"

"David Bravo," says Fea, "there is no situation with you that I could possibly describe as 'nothing.' This whole experience has been chaos from the start."

"That's mostly been your fault."

"You do bring out the best in me."

The truth is that I think I can finally say the reverse, because I wouldn't be where I am without Fea.

SATURDAY, SEPTEMBER 16
9:05 A.M.
Road trip!

Antoine comes over on Saturday morning, and his dad accompanies him. "Thanks for taking Antoine with you, David," he says to me. "This might be an important moment in your life, and I'm glad you want my son there with you."

"Thanks, Mr. Harris," I say. "Me and Antoine had a long talk this week about priorities, and he helped me understand some things I previously did not."

"Sounds like it's been a big week for all of us," says Dad. "We'll let you know when we're headed back, Jamal. Sound good?"

"Take your time," says Mr. Harris. "My son deserves the day off."

Mr. Harris hugs Antoine before heading out, and I notice he has a big smile on his face. It's not that I haven't seen Antoine's dad smile before, but something is different about it. It has to be because Antoine told him the truth.

And I'm so happy it seems to have worked out.

"You nervous?" Antoine asks me.

"No," I say.

He tilts his head to the side and presses his lips together.

"Okay, *yes*, of course I am!" I say.

He cackles at me. "It's okay if you are," he says. "I kinda am, too."

"It'll be fine whatever happens," says Dad. "Promise."

Mom comes rushing toward us and glances over at Antoine. "Good morning, Antoine! Glad you could join us."

"Good morning, Mrs. Bravo," he says. "Glad to be here."

"We ready?" says Dad, holding up the keys to the pickup.

I let out a long breath. "Yeah," I say. "You only live once, right?"

Mom looks impressed with me. "Exactly!" she says. "Let's go live, David!"

Dad actually remembered to clean out the back seat, so Antoine and I pile into it and put on our seat belts. "We just need to make one stop," Dad announces. "Your mother and I woke up late, and we can barely function without coffee."

"Can I get a tea?" asks Antoine.

"Of course," says Mom. "Our treat!"

Dad backs out of the driveway, and when he does, my heart leaps in my chest. This is really happening. I might just have made the biggest decision of my whole life.

"Fea," I mutter under my breath. "I need you."

Antoine gasps when a small robin appears in the truck

and lands on my dad's headrest. "I promise to behave," she says.

I raise an eyebrow at her.

"Some of the time."

Oh, Fea.

"Is everything okay back there?" Mom asks, turning around.

"Yeah," I say. "Just a little nervous."

"You doing okay, Antoine?"

He looks over at me, then reaches for my right hand and grabs it.

"Yes, Mrs. Bravo."

Mom does a double take, but . . . she doesn't say anything. She just looks down at our hands, clasped together, and then smiles and turns back.

Yeah. Everything's all right.

Dad drives us to my destiny.

SATURDAY, SEPTEMBER 16
9:44 A.M.
Moreno Valley is just a copy-pasted Riverside.

Getting coffee takes a little longer than expected because there's a long line at the drive-thru of the local chain we go to. I get an iced chai latte with oat milk—truly the best drink on the *planet*—and Antoine sips on a chamomile. After that, we get on the freeway to head out east. Dad says that Ms. Ramos and her mother don't live all that far from us. "Just a couple cities over," he says.

Mom and Dad chat with each other, but Antoine and I are silent in the back. I don't even know what I could talk about right now because an electricity is flowing through my veins. Even Fea is uncharacteristically silent. Maybe she's thinking what I'm thinking: Is this *it*?

Will Ms. Ramos or her mom have the answers I want?

Will I finally know what happened to my birth parents?

The possibilities seem endless. They could be dead. They could be alive. I could find out why they put me up for adoption; it could be a mystery for the rest of my life.

It could be . . . anything.

Wow, I don't think I've ever experienced something so scary and so exciting at the same time.

That's what is spinning through my mind when we exit the freeway thirty minutes later in the city of Moreno Valley. It doesn't look all that different from Riverside. Lots of colorful houses sit next to large collections of apartments and condos that all look the same. There are mountains and hills in the distance. The streets are all super wide.

It's basically Riverside.

But I know it's not. We pull off the main road into a neighborhood with nice lawns and big houses, then there's a huge gated community. Then we turn again, and I can feel the car slowing down, and I know this is it. We're close.

Am I close to the answer I need? Or want? Or will I come away with nothing?

Dad comes to a stop in front of a beige house with white trim. There's no car in the driveway, but beneath the windows, there's a massive flower garden, full of blooming flowers in reds, yellows, and pinks.

"What a pretty yard," Mom says. "Don't you think so, David?"

When she twists back to look at me, I'm sure she's alarmed by what she sees. I am already sweating, and I'm frozen in place.

Am I really going to do this?

What if the worst happens?

What if Ms. Ramos's mom doesn't want to talk to me?

What if she changes her mind and turns us away?

What if—?

"Honey, we're here for you," Mom says, reaching back and patting my free hand.

After taking a big breath, I say, "I'm ready."

Antoine lets go of my hand—which he held the entire car ride—and we get out of my dad's truck. It's just as warm here as back home, but it feels too bright, like the sun has risen one whole foot from my face. I'm dizzy, too, but Antoine grabs my arm and steadies me.

That's when I feel tiny feet on my left shoulder. Fea.

"We're all here for you," she says. "Whatever happens . . . you're not alone, David Bravo."

Antoine puts his hand in mine, and I think it's his way of silently agreeing with Fea.

"You ready?" Dad says, putting his hand on my back.

"No," I say, "but you only live once, right?"

I take a deep breath.

"So here goes."

I walk up the driveway, then cut around a bush to follow the path up to the front door. It's plain. White. There's nothing else on it.

What's on the other side?

I raise my hand and knock on it three times, then step back.

And wait.

And wait.

And wait.

I can hear footsteps approaching.

I think my heart's going to explode in my chest.

The lock clicks.

The door opens.

And an older Latinx woman appears. Her hair is cropped short and graying, and her face is wrinkled and dark brown.

"¿Sí?" the woman says, looking at my parents first, since they're eye-level with her.

"Ms. Ramos?" Dad says.

The woman nods but looks suspicious.

"No," says Fea softly.

"What?" I say under my breath.

"This is impossible," Fea says in my head, her voice trembling. "David, what is this? Is this a joke?"

"No!" I say, but it comes out way too loud. Ms. Ramos looks down at me and then makes a face. A *disgusted* one.

"Nieto, ¿qué estás haciendo? ¡Pensé que saliste con tu mamá!"

I don't know a lot of Spanish, but I know that this woman just called me *grandson*.

"Excuse me," my mom says, "but . . . um . . . we were *told* to come here? I think we spoke to your daughter."

"What is going on?" I ask.

Fea is busy hyperventilating next to me, which is a million times more distracting than you can possibly imagine. Have you ever heard a *bird* hyperventilate?

"David, I don't believe it," she moans. "David, *how*?"

"How *what*?" I say, which is a mistake, as there are

· 345 ·

currently three other people around me who cannot hear or see Fea.

"David, you okay?" Dad asks, and he puts his hand on my left shoulder, which goes right through Fea, sending her into an even worse fit.

"Ohmygod, ohmygod, ohmygod," she repeats, huffing and puffing.

"I'm really confused," says Antoine.

"Yo también," says the woman, then focuses her laser-sharp eyes on me. She switches to English, and she's got a thick accent. "Why did you come back? Where is your mother?"

"*I'm* his mother," says Mom, looking up from her purse. "Who are *you*?"

"I know her," says Fea.

"How do you know her?" Antoine whispers, which is when I find out that Antoine isn't that good at whispering, because we *all* hear it.

"I *don't* know her," says Mom.

"Señora, ¿es usted la Señora Ramos con la que hablé por teléfono?" Dad asks. "¿Quién es usted, Señora?"

"You are at *my* front door," she says. "I will not explain myself. You will tell me who *you* are and what you're doing with *him*!"

She reaches down and grabs my arm and pulls me toward her, which is when my mom nearly goes nuclear, yelling at the woman to get her hands off me, and Antoine looks like he's going to cry, and Fea is telling me that I need to leave, that she needs time with me alone, and it's all too much for me to stand.

"Everyone shut *up*!" I scream.

My mom actually gasps. "David," she says softly. "I don't care what's happening, we do *not* speak like that."

I hope Fea knows that she now has an opening to speak, but when she says nothing, I decide I have to. "Will someone *calmly* explain what's going on?"

The older woman looks down at me with confusion in her eyes, but thankfully, Fea recovers enough to say something.

"David," she says, "that's Maricela."

My mouth drops open. "Maricela?" I say.

The older woman now looks furious. "Excuse me, that's *abuela* to you, Beto."

"That's not his name!" Dad snaps. "He's never met you!"

Beto.

Beto.

Beto.

No. I stare at Antoine, who has a look of horror on his face. "David," he says to me, "how is that possible?"

"How is *what* possible?" says Mom. "Do you boys know something that I *don't*?"

There's a loud slam behind us.

We spin around.

I see her.

Her long, wavy black hair.

Yamira.

Yamira *Ramos*.

But that's not what surprises me. Nor is it the complete shock on her face.

No, it's the other thing.

I step forward, past my parents and Antoine, Fea sobbing on my shoulder, and I look at the boy getting out of the passenger seat of the small green car.

It's *me*.

SATURDAY, SEPTEMBER 16
10:23 A.M.
The real truth

He steps forward.

His hand is on the hood of the car, and he stares at me like I am impossible. Because this *is* impossible.

My first thought is:

Did I do this?

Did I break the world this badly because I couldn't choose the right thing? Did that create another version of myself here, in *my* timeline?

He steps forward.

His eyes are searching me, up and down and all over, and his mouth is open just a bit, and he looks just like me.

Is he me?

No. No, wait.

He steps forward.

His right eyebrow is different. There's a small line through it, and when he is so close that I could reach out and touch his face, I realize it's a scar.

I never had a scar there.

(In this timeline.)

But . . . what if this has nothing to do with timelines?

What if I didn't conjure him at all?

"I knew it," Beto says softly. "Mami, remember? Remember what I said?"

I finally look up at Yamira, whose eyes are red and watery. "Yo recuerdo, Beto," she says.

Beto.

This isn't me at all.

When I look back at Beto, he's ready to cry, too, and then he puts the pieces together for me.

"I always told Mami that I thought I had a brother," he says, "and it turns out I do."

And then his arms are around me, and he's hugging me, and it all makes sense. Finally, *everything makes sense.*

Beto isn't from another timeline; I never witnessed a life where I was adopted by someone else.

The Powers showed me that *I have a twin brother.*

SATURDAY, SEPTEMBER 16
10:44 A.M.
Returning the gift

It takes a moment for the chaos to die down.

We're invited inside, and then there's a lot of apologizing. A *lot* of it. After Maricela gets done hugging me and kissing me and thanking whoever or *what*ever helped reunite me and Beto, she tells my parents she's sorry. "I honestly thought you had, like . . . kidnapped Beto," she explains. "And somehow, he'd been smart enough to bring you back here."

"It's my fault," says Yamira. "I mentioned it to Mami, and she knew someone was coming to talk to her, but then I thought I could slip out and get some coffee before you arrived."

"Well, imagine how *we* feel," says Dad. "We showed up on your doorstep, basically holding your grandson hostage."

They all laugh. Well, all of them but Fea, who has been completely silent the entire time. To be honest, I can't even imagine what this is like for her. The Powers prevented her from even seeing what Maricela had been up to since they fell out of contact, and now Maricela is here, in the flesh, while Fea is . . .

Not.

Maybe she's just processing. Maybe she'll finally chime in once she knows what to say.

Maricela excuses herself to make a few calls about me and Beto, and then Beto turns to me.

"Can I take David to see my room?" Beto asks.

Yamira gazes at the two of us. She studies my face.

"My god," she says. "There are two of you."

I look at Beto again. He has my face. Or . . . I have his?

This is all a *lot* to deal with.

Yamira shakes herself out of her stupor. "Yes, mijo, go ahead," she says.

"I'll be right back," I tell Antoine, but I'm looking at Fea, who is sitting silently in his lap.

I get a brief tour from Beto, and as he talks, I notice slight differences between us. His voice is definitely deeper than mine, which I hadn't picked up on from when the Powers showed me a glimpse of his life. He walks differently than me, too, which seems like such a weird thing to pick out, but . . . it's just *different*.

The Ramos house isn't much bigger than ours, though it has three bedrooms, where ours has two. They have a *lot* more stuff on the walls; Mom and Dad like keep things clean and organized. But here, it's much more chaotic, just like I'd seen in my glimpse of Beto's life. I glance at the paintings of the beach in the dining room, then Beto leads me farther into his place. A poster for a band called Depeche Mode hangs in the hallway, as do some old Christmas decorations. There are lots of framed photos, too. In each of them, there's a smaller version of myself, which I know isn't really true, but it's hard to look at Beto when he was younger and not see me.

Beto's room is even more chaotic. I'm pretty sure Mom and Dad would *actually* give me up if I ever let my room get like this. But Beto doesn't seem to care. He rushes around the room and starts showing me things, like the *Star Wars* LEGO set he started putting together but hasn't finished and the pile of books in one corner.

"My friend Antoine out there loves reading," I say. "You should show him all those."

"Antoine?" Beto says, looking at me with alarm. "Did you say your friend's name is Antoine?"

I nod. "Yep."

"My best friend's name is Anthony!" he says, his eyes wide.

"I know," I say.

Which is immediately a mistake. I know it as soon as the words leave my mouth.

"How could you know that?" he says, giving me a suspicious look.

I shake my head. "Sorry, I don't know why I said that. I'm just nervous. This is . . . It's a lot."

His mouth curls up on one side. "Yeah, it is," he says.

"We have a lot to catch up on," he says. "Like . . . our whole lives."

I nod. "I still can't believe all this. I actually have a twin brother. I'm not an only child anymore."

"I mean . . . technically we are?" Beto says.

"What do you mean?"

"We each have our own families, and we're only children in those."

"Good point," I say. "But still, I have a lot of questions."

"Me, too," he says quickly, smiling.

"I might be kind of annoying."

"Annoying is okay. I've never had an annoying brother."

"How'd you get your scar?"

"Fell off a slide a few years ago," he says. "I made the mistake of trying to go down the one at the park down the street in the middle of summer. It burned my legs, and then I tried to stand up *on* the slide, and I ended up falling off it."

I laugh. "Why do they make slides out of metal? It's like they *want* us to get hurt."

"Right? It should be illegal or something."

"Are you . . . are you pretty anxious?"

He nods, and one side of his mouth curls down. "Kinda."

"Me, too," I say, and then the question I've been burning to ask is on the tip of my tongue. "Beto, what about our—"

Mom calls out my name.

"To be continued?" I say.

"Yeah," says Beto, nodding, and I think . . . I think he knew what I was going to ask.

Me and Beto rush back out to the living room. When we arrive, Dad waves us over.

"Yamira was just telling us about their family," he says, "and I thought you'd want to know this stuff, too."

I plop down next to Antoine as Dad gives me a recap. It's just the three of them here. Maricela and her wife adopted Yamira because Maricela worked with adoption agencies and foster kids. It just seemed natural to them. Yamira's other mom passed years ago, but when Yamira wanted children of her own, she decided to adopt, too.

Maricela is speaking in another room, but I can't make out what she's saying. Her words are fast and sharp. I try to ignore it as I sit between Antoine and Beto.

"I'm sure this is the question on everyone's mind," Dad finally says. "But . . . *how* were Beto and David separated?"

"That's why Mami is on the phone," explains Yamira. "She's reaching out to all her contacts in the foster and social work community. She gets like this when she has a problem to solve. Just jumping on the phone, calling every-one. But I hope she solves this problem because . . . this doesn't make sense." Her eyes start watering again. "They should have been kept together."

"*We* should be together," Fea says softly in my head.

She must also be speaking in Antoine's head, because he

suddenly squeezes my hand *very* hard.

"I can't even imagine what sort of mistake happened to keep them apart," says Dad.

Fea sighs. "I know *exactly* what mistake kept me away from Maricela."

I'm squirming now. It doesn't help that I can feel Fea's little bird feet on my shoulder and they tickle. I try to be subtle and reach up to scratch where she's standing, and thankfully, she flies off.

And then lands on my *other* shoulder.

"It could be anything," says Mom. "It happens. When I first started as a therapist, I had a patient who had recently been reunited with her twin sister."

I lean forward on the couch and swat at my right shoulder. "How had they been separated?" I ask.

Fea lands on the coffee table in the center of the room. She's staring up at Yamira. "I've known separation my whole existence," she says. "Why now? Why reunite us *now*?"

"Well, confidentiality, David," Mom says, "I can't tell you personal details of my sessions, but I will say that theirs was a case of a mix-up at the hospital."

"My *heart* is mixed up," Fea says dramatically.

I can feel Antoine wincing beside me, so I stand up suddenly. "Hi, can I go talk to your mami, Ms. Ramos?" I blurt out. "Like . . . maybe alone?"

"David!" says Dad. "Don't you want to stay here and learn these things? There's so much we have to talk about!"

"Yes!" I say. "I definitely want to hear everything. I just . . . have something I need to talk to Ms. Ramos about. I promise it will be short."

"These kids and their ideas," says Mom. "Shouldn't you wait until she's off the phone?"

"It's important," I say. "It can't wait."

Yamira nods at me, but she's also clearly a little suspicious. "I'll take you," she says.

Yamira takes my hand. I glance over at Beto, whose face is twisted up in confusion. Antoine, however, is looking at me with pity. He can hear Fea, too.

But I have to do this. This might be my only chance to help Fea.

When we pass by the first bedroom, I can hear Maricela arguing with someone. "That wasn't what we were told!" she yells.

Yamira opens a door to a *very* neat room, one with a flowery comforter over a large bed with four wooden posts. It smells like flowers, too, and sunlight falls over the room from the huge bay window on the far wall.

It feels safe here.

Which I need, because I see that Maricela is sitting on the edge of her bed, her face twisted with frustration. She seems *really* worried.

I don't know if I can do this, but I think I have to.

"Mami," says Yamira, "David here said he really needs to talk with you."

Maricela looks up at me. "Ay, por supuesto, nieto," she

says, and then says into the phone: "Ernesto, give me ten minutes. I'll call you back."

"I'll give you two some privacy, okay?" says Yamira. When she leaves, she closes the door to the bedroom gently.

For a few moments, Maricela just stares at me and I at her. My memories of my trip to her past resurface, and I can see the younger Mari in this woman's face.

"This is weird for me," says Maricela. "I feel like I am looking at my grandson, but . . . you are not him. You are an entirely separate person. So please forgive me if I can't stop staring."

Fear washes over me.

But I push past it.

"I have to tell you something," I say. "And it's going to seem very weird and very impossible, but I need you to let me finish, okay?"

Maricela's brow is still furrowed, but she nods at me. "Okay, David," she says. "What is it?"

That's when Fea shows up. She appears at Maricela's feet as a xolo dog, and her sorrowful whine rings out in my head. "What are you doing, David Bravo?"

"I'm doing what you can't," I say aloud. "You can't appear to her, but I'm here."

Maricela frowns. "David, who are you talking to?"

"Someone you used to know," I say, then glance down at Fea. "Fea, I never would have found the rest of my family without you. You've spent so much time with me, doing everything you could to help me. It's time for me to help *you*."

"Nieto, you're scaring me," says Maricela, standing up. "Who helped you find us?"

Fea whimpers. "But how? How can you help me?"

"Will you let me try?" I ask Fea.

She whines once more.

I take a deep breath.

"Will you let me try to talk to her, Juanita?"

Maricela gasps, and seconds later, tears are pouring down her face. "David, how do you know that name?"

"I met her," I say. "Sort of."

Her hands go to her mouth. "Ay, David, I haven't heard that name in *years*," she says. "Pero . . . I think of her all the time."

Once she says that, Fea breaks out into a terrible howl, and it is the saddest thing I've ever heard. It's a howl of years and years of regret and sorrow.

I crouch in front of Fea. "I'm sorry you had to go through this," I say.

"David," says Maricela, kneeling next to me. "Is she here? Is that who brought you here? Did Juanita help you?"

I nod at her. "She did. She changed my life. She taught me to think of life as a gift and that I shouldn't doubt myself so much that I don't *live* it."

"But how?" says Maricela. "I haven't seen Juanita since I was nineteen. Where is she? How are you talking to her?"

I realize suddenly that what I'm about to do is impossible—at least to Maricela.

Instead of answering her, I reach out and pet Fea, my

nerves threatening to freeze me up. "You were a good person, Juanita," I say. "You *are* a good person. And if I really am your last assignment, I'm proud to be the one to help *you* move on."

"I don't understand!" cries Maricela. "Who are you talking to?"

The hairs on my arms stand up, and Fea pops out of existence. I fall back in shock, which makes Maricela gasp. She reaches for me and helps me up, and then I feel—

No.

NO!

The tugging. Deep in my stomach.

"No!" I cry out. "Leave me here! Don't do this again!"

"David, what is *happening*?" Maricela says, her hands on my shoulders, her watery eyes locked with mine.

But then they aren't.

She's looking behind me.

"Dios mío," she says.

I turn quickly and—

There's a woman standing there in Maricela's room. She's tall, with thick, graying curls and light brown skin, and she's crying.

"Hi, Maricela," she says. "I don't have much time, but I wanted to see you before I left."

Maricela reaches her hands out. "Is that you, Juanita?"

"Yes," Juanita says. "It's me."

SATURDAY, SEPTEMBER 16
11:24 A.M.
I get dust in my eye. Yes. Totally have dusty eyes.

Juanita pulls Maricela in for a hug, and they hold one another for a long, long time, crying as they do. I feel like I should leave, like I shouldn't be watching this, but when I make for the door, Juanita pulls away from Maricela.

"Stay," she says to me. "Please, David Bravo."

"How are you here?" says Maricela.

"It will take too long to explain," says Juanita, "and I can already feel myself fading away."

"Where have you been? It must be . . . what? Fifty years now since the last time I saw you?"

Juanita's tears fall down her face. "Oh, Mari, I've been gone for a while. I passed."

Maricela's nods. "I know," she says. "I looked you up from time to time, and I found your obituary a decade ago."

"You looked me up?" says Juanita.

"Quite often. Just to see how you were."

"But I disappointed you," cries Juanita. "I let you down. I ruined your prom."

"Amor, you didn't ruin *anything*," says Maricela, laughing. "Yes, I was angry with you, but your date? Marcos? He told me your mom set the two of you up through church. He was *miserable* that night because he knew you didn't want to be there with him."

"Great!" says Juanita. "So I disappointed *two* people at that dance!"

"Nita, he was fine. You know he has a husband and two kids now? He's down in Carlsbad. Living his best life."

"But I *didn't* live my best life," says Juanita, sniffling. "At all. I regretted not going to the dance with you until I was gone, until it was too late to do anything."

"Juanita, stop it," says Maricela. "You helped me realize who I was. I never would have come out when I did without you. You were so . . . *yourself.* That's why I liked you!"

"But—"

"No, no buts allowed. That's my truth, mi amor."

Juanita smiles, but it looks so sad. "I wish I hadn't waited to tell you. I wish I had gone to the dance with you, Mari."

"So . . . why can't we do that now?" Maricela grabs her phone off the bed and scrolls through it. When she sets it down again, I hear a piano intro, then the harmonized backing vocals, and then I recognize the song. Sometimes I hear it on the oldies station on the radio in my dad's truck. The man asks an earth angel to be his, and Maricela grabs one of Juanita's hands.

"Dance with me, my angel," she says.

The two spin around, reluctantly at first, and I sit on the

edge of the bed, a huge smile on my face. Soon, though, the two of them fall into a rhythm, and I can't stop watching. They look *perfect* together.

When the song finishes, Maricela spins Juanita, and then embraces her again. "See?" she says. "We have all the time in the world."

I've never seen Juanita look so happy.

She gives Maricela a kiss. It's short, but it's a kiss that's been a long time coming. When Juanita pulls away from Maricela, there's a huge smile on *both* their faces.

Juanita hurries over to me on the bed. "This is it," she says. "I can feel it, David. Any moment now."

"What's going to happen?" I say.

"I'm done."

Her palm is open to me, and resting in it is her infinity charm.

It's sparkling a bright emerald green.

"Take this," she says. "To remember me. To remember what you *did* for me."

"Do you have to go?" I ask, and it feels like there's a stone in my throat.

She nods. "We all do at some point, and this is *my* time."

She stands up straight, and Maricela takes her hand. "Goodbye, Mari," says Juanita. "Thank you for giving me a little peace at the end."

"Thank you for showing me what I was capable of," says Mari, and then she wipes a tear off Juanita's face.

My friend steps away from Maricela and gazes at me.

"You only live once, David Bravo," she tells me. "I would say don't forget that, but you already know it deep in your heart. In your eleven years, you've lived a bigger life than most people."

And then Juanita—

Fea.

She's just gone, here one minute and then . . . not.

Maricela is clutching her hands to her chest. "Thank you, David," she says to the empty air where Juanita once stood. "Thank you for giving me closure."

I hold the infinity charm tight in my hand, and when I start crying, Maricela joins me on the bed, and then we hold each other tight.

I still feel safe.

"Come," says Maricela. "Let's rejoin the others."

She extends a hand, but I don't take it.

"There's something I need to know," I say. "About my birth parents."

Maricela's mouth closes, and she presses her lips together until they're a straight line. "Niño, I can tell you what I know, but I think *everyone* needs to hear it. ¿Entiendes?"

"Okay," I say.

Maricela takes my hand and guides me back to the living room. I can hear a loud, boisterous conversation echoing down the hallway, and when we get there, Yamira is in the middle of telling my parents and Antoine some story about Beto, who has his face buried in his hands.

"Mami, this is so *embarrassing*," he whines. "Do you *have* to tell them?"

Yamira looks up at us. "David! Mami!" she says. "Everything okay? Where did you go?"

Maricela speaks before I can say anything. "David here

just had some things to ask me about," she says. "And tell me. All is well."

She puts her hand on the small of my back, and it fills me with warmth.

I go sit next to Antoine, and he immediately takes my hand, which sends another flutter through my stomach. He tilts his head to the side. "Is she—?"

I nod. "She's gone."

It takes a moment for Antoine to process, but he finally nods his head.

I'm really glad he's here.

"So, Ms. Ramos told me she knows some stuff," I say, and I feel like my whole body is vibrating. "About my parents. Or . . . *our* parents," I add, glancing at Beto.

But as soon as say this, I see Yamira's shoulders droop. Beto looks away.

"What is it?" I say.

"I wish we could have been in your life for a million different reasons, David," says Yamira. "But now I'm realizing you could have known the truth the whole time."

"What truth?" I say. I turn to Beto. "Have you always known?"

He nods at me, his eyes glassy.

"David," says Yamira, "your birth parents passed away when they were taking you and Beto to the hospital after you were born."

I think, somehow, this is what I always expected to

hear, but the news is still hard to take. Tears prick my eyes. "They died?"

I can see tears in Yamira's eyes, too. "Yes. It was instant, and somehow, you two miraculously survived."

So, they're gone.

That's it. I'll never know them.

But . . . I also know that my other worry—that they gave me up because I was such a terrible, cursed child—is ridiculous. It always was. Why couldn't I see that before? Why did I let Tommy get under my skin?

I'm angry. I'm sad. I'm disappointed.

"I know it's a lot to take in, David," says Yamira. "And if you need more time, let me know. Whatever you're feeling, *all* of it is valid."

"Honey," says Mom, a bit of anxiety in her voice, "is this what I sound like with you?"

I can't help it; I let out a loud peal of laughter. "Yes, Mom," I say, wiping at my tears. "Wow, does this mean I now have *two* therapist moms?"

Everybody laughs this time, and it really does help break the tension. I wipe at my face again. "Wow," I say. "So . . . that's it."

"Actually, it's not," says Maricela. "I think I have an idea how you and Beto got separated."

"What?" I say.

"Abuela, tell us!" says Beto.

"Someone made a mistake," says Maricela. "Your mother

went into labor so quickly that she wasn't able to get to a hospital in time. She had you both at home. It was when she and your father were heading to the hospital that . . . the *accident* happened."

Maricela sighs. It's one of those mom sighs where you know she's annoyed at everyone on the planet. "You must have been separated in the hospital that took you in. Because of that, neither of you were labeled as a twin on your birth certificate, but . . . David, in your case, it was worse. Beto had his birth parents listed on his forms, and you . . . you had *no one*."

"Oh, no," says Mom. "Which means . . ."

Maricela nods. "David was considered an abandoned child. And even though Queen of Angels handled his adoption, we never put two and two together. David got adopted into your family, and aside from that moment in the hospital, Beto and David haven't been in the same room for over a decade."

"But now we are," says Beto, and when I look at him, he's so obviously overjoyed. "You're *here*."

"We simply didn't know you existed," says Yamira.

"Yasmín and Eduardo," says Beto, almost under his breath.

"Huh?" I say.

"Yasmín and Eduardo," he repeats. "Those were their names. Yasmín and Eduardo Lopez."

"You mean . . ." I glance over at Mom and Dad, my eyes welling with tears. "Those were my parents?"

"They were born in Los Angeles, but both of their parents were from different parts of Mexico," says Maricela. "We have photos, if you want to see them."

"I do!" I say. "Please?"

Maricela gets up to go get them, and I don't know how to deal with the million different emotions that are swirling inside me. I know the truth now. I know where I came from.

I guess that *does* make me . . . what?

"Beto," I say, "when someone asks you what you are, what do you say?"

"What do you mean?" he says.

I decide to tell the Ramos family about my presentation, which more or less set this whole thing in motion. By the end of it, Beto is nodding.

"I get what you mean," he says. "I mean . . . we're Latinx, that's for sure."

"There are so many terms you could use," says Yamira. "Mexican American, perhaps, though I don't know too many people who say that anymore. You could also do research on the term 'Chicano,' which could be a better fit for you."

"But basically, I tell people my birth parents were from Mexico," says Beto. "I find it easier to just be very, very open about it, because . . . well, people can be so *nosy*."

The relief I feel when he says that is so intense that I nearly break into laughter. "Yes!" I say. "They ask so many questions!"

Maricela returns to the room, and she hands me an old, wrinkled envelope. "That's all we've ever had," she says.

She hands it to me.

I let go of Antoine's hand and take the envelope like it will disintegrate in my hands if I'm not careful enough. I gently peel it open, and there are three photographs inside.

The first is . . .

Oh, wow.

There they are. Yasmín and Eduardo. They're the same height. It's clear that our wavy hair comes from our mother, but I can see our nose in Eduardo. The two of them are clutching each other tightly in an amusement park of some sort. There's a Ferris wheel in the background.

"Where was this taken?" I ask. "Does anyone know?"

"The Santa Monica Pier," says Yamira.

"We'll take you there," says Dad. "It's wonderful."

I look at the other photos. The second one is of some sort of formal event; Yasmín has on a golden dress, and Eduardo is wearing a black tux. The third has Eduardo posing behind Yasmín, her belly round. Beto points at it.

"That's us," he says.

Us. There's an *us* now.

But it's not just me and my . . . my brother. (Wow, that still feels weird!)

There's Antoine, holding my hand next to me, silently staring at all these images from a history we're just learning about.

There's la familia Ramos: Beto, Yamira, Maricela. It's

a new future, isn't it? I don't know what kind of family we will grow to be, but the idea . . . well, it's very, very exciting.

And then there's *us*. Me, Mom, and Dad. It almost seems silly now: How could I have *ever* thought I was cursed with them as my parents? I glance over at them, and Dad's clutching Mom, a wide smile on his face.

I was never cursed.

I just needed someone to help me see that.

MARCH
SIX MONTHS LATER . . . BUT NOT A MISTAKE, THIS TIME

On the far eastern end of Riverside, just before it starts turning into neighborhoods like Canyon Crest or Mission Grove with all their fancy, multilevel houses, there's a huge parking lot at the edge of a massive park. It's dark, just after sunset, and there are two cars parked together.

There's the Ramoses' small green sedan, the one that desperately needs a wash. Yamira and Maricela are sitting on the hood, and Gracie and Wunmi are having a little dance competition to the Selena song blaring out of the car.

We're next to them in the bed of Dad's pickup trick. Antoine is next to me, chowing down on some animal-style fries from In-N-Out. Beto is across from me with a vanilla milkshake in hand, and my parents have their backs to the cab of the truck, their hands interlocked.

I couldn't have imagined something like this when I started at Mira Monte Middle School. But I now have two more friends in Wunmi and Gracie, and I'm glad they were able to join us on a Friday night to watch the stars come out. I've been hanging out with Gracie a lot more since the truth of my origin came to light, and it's been really nice to have someone to talk to about all my adoption feelings. I don't feel like I have to hide who I am anymore.

Life with Beto has been amazing, too. We see each other all the time, and even then, it's like there isn't enough time for us to catch up on the eleven years we missed out. We're trying, though! He's a lot nerdier than I am, which has made it easy for him and Antoine to become friends, too. Even better, I decided to drop running from my schedule. I don't need to do a sport I don't even like in order to stay friends with Antoine, and he's been doing runs with Beto. I'm *very* glad I don't have to do that anymore.

Mostly, though, Beto and I are both adjusting to having a sibling for the first time.

It's . . . different. I think maybe there will always be a part of me that's sad not to have known my birth parents, but that doesn't mean I can't be happy that I now have Beto.

Wow. I have a twin brother.

I lean my head back and stare at the sky, waiting for the first twinkle of light. Dad squeezes my leg, and I glance at him.

"What's up?" I say.

"Just thinking," he says. "You know, when I was a kid, I used to do this all the time with my mom and my sister, Carmen."

"Do what?"

"Mom used to get takeout from this hole-in-the-wall Mexican place that put jalapeños in everything, then drive us out to the middle of the desert. We'd eat as the sun disappeared."

"That sounds nice," says Antoine.

"It was," he says. "I think because she worked so much— you know, it was just her taking care of us after Dad passed—that she wanted to make sure we had these special moments."

He doesn't say it out loud, but I think I know what he's hinting at.

This is one of those special moments.

Yamira turns off the radio and everyone gathers around the truck as Dad starts telling us stories about Texas. Like, how he and his sister discovered a den of coyotes on a hike. Or how they once watched a man evade a police chase in El Paso by hopping over the fence between Texas and Mexico, disappearing into the streets of Juárez. He's a very animated storyteller. He uses his hands and does all these voices for different people, too, so I don't even realize how much he's captured all of our attention until he points to the sky.

"First star of the evening," he says.

The single pinpoint of light shines brightly above us.

"I'd like to visit El Paso someday," I tell Dad. "To learn more about it."

He nods at me, his eyes shining. "I'd love that."

I fall into silence again. Without any hesitation, I reach

out and take Antoine's hand. He leans his head against my shoulder, and our friendship—which has changed since the start of the school year—feels full.

Full of possibility, too.

I think of Fea then as other stars appear in the sky. I hope she can still see me and that she knows how much she helped me out. I get why she kept repeating that catch-phrase of hers so often. I finally feel like I understand it.

I've only got one life.

And it's time for me to *live* it.

ACKNOWLEDGMENTS

Thank you to my agent, DongWon Song, who supported this book on its very strange and delayed journey to publication as well as encouraged me to expand into the middle grade space. I don't know what I'd do without you.

Thank you to the entire team at Harper Collins for your incredible support, not just for this book, but for my middle grade career. There were so very many people who made *You Only Live Once, David Bravo* a reality, and they must all be thanked. Shout out to my editor, Stephanie Stein, whose brilliance shaped this book's chaotic story and helped bring many of the smaller characters to life. Thank you to Stephanie's assistant extraordinaire, Sophie Schmidt, for all your kindness and brilliance, too! Thank you to the managing editorial team of Jon Howard and Gwen Morton.

The design of this book is stunning, so many thanks to the production team (Sean Cavanagh and Vanessa Nuttry), as well as the show-stopping design folks (Jessie Gang and Alison Klapthor). Helder Oliveira, I'm so thrilled you returned to illustrate the cover of this book, too. You brought David and Fea to life!

To my publicist at Harper, Jacquelynn Burke, thank you so much for your support and dedication to getting my books into as many hands as possible. And shout out to the entire marketing team, who are ALWAYS killing it! That means you, Emily Mannon and Robby Imfeld, as well as the entire school & library marketing team, who help my books find the kids who need them (Patty Rosati, Mimi Rankin, Katie Dutton, Christina Carpino, Josie Dallam).

Thank you to my eternal brainstormer and best friend, Sarah Gailey, who always encourages me to be more unhinged with each passing day. This book doesn't exist without you.

Thank you to all my author/publishing friends, but in particular, I want to thank the folks who did writing retreats with me, sat on Zoom calls to hold one another accountable, and who have helped me find my place in kid lit in these scary, uncertain times: Dhonielle Clayton, Zoraida Córdova, Justin A. Reynolds, Ashley Woodfolk, Tiffany Jackson, Kwame Mbalia, Jalissa Corrie, Saraciea Fennell, Patrice Caldwell, Adam Silvera, Arvin Ahmadi, Antwan Eady, Terry J. Benton-Walker, Julian Winters, Preeti Chhibber, Nic Stone, Angie Thomas, Claribel Ortega, Hugh D. Hunter, and I'm sure there are more. I appreciate you all.

And finally: thank you to all educators, librarians, reviewers, and readers of all ages for reading and promoting my books. I'm writing these acknowledgments as I continue to hear more and more about how frequently my books are being banned or challenged across the US, so it means the world to me that I have so many folks in my corner, rooting for me. Thank you. You make it easier for me to do what I do!